"...when the world ends, revenge begins."
---unknown

Praise for
LEAVE MY ASHES ON BLACKHEART MOUNTAIN

In Dave Matthes' enthralling narrative, the reader is never sure where it is all going, and the excitement grows with new discoveries as the protagonist follows an uncertain path in his quest. There is more thrill to the terrific descriptions than the breath of summer air. The plot is ingeniously written, with unsettling moments sprinkled throughout the story. The crisp writing is, in itself, a delectable treat, and it is hard to not get pulled in by the author's skillful handling of elements of the setting -- both geographical and cultural. _Leave My Ashes on Blackheart Mountain_ features relatable and genuinely flawed characters, strong plot points, and the overall writing is deft and balanced. A gorgeous read.
---David Reyes, _The Book Commentary_

Leave My Ashes on Blackheart Mountain starts on a gory note, showing Mahoney fending for himself in an unforgiving landscape. The world that Mahoney inhabits is a bleak, god-forsaken place with few pockets of civilization left. Matthes' raw writing and poetic prose not only brings out the bleakness of this world brilliantly but also effectively conveys the inner monologue of a loner like Mahoney. At one point, Matthes describes the bond between Mahoney and his horse so sweetly, you cannot help but believe he is capable of some good, despite the man himself denying so. The grittiness of the language is nicely offset by the dynamics between the multi-layered, complex characters. Set in a post-apocalyptic world in the far future, the novel brims with action. The illustrations at the beginning of each chapter are beautiful. The menacing plot builds to a high-octane climax, and the bittersweet ending provides a satisfying denouement.
--- Debjani Ghosh, _Reader's Favorite_

I was immediately taken with the setting of Matthes's book. This post-apocalyptic scene is striking in that it mimics the feel of the Old West in both character and setting. From the brief mentions by characters of modern times gone by to the hints of modern technology, readers are taken on quite a visual thrill ride as they try to piece together each scene. I am not a fan of westerns, but this particular book is so much more and carries readers on a captivating journey into the author's imagination.
--- _Literary Titan_

LEAVE MY ASHES ON BLACKHEART MOUNTAIN

THE TWO REVOLVERS SAGA
BOOK I

A NOVEL by
DAVE MATTHES

This book is a work of fiction.
None of it is to be taken in a literal sense or meant with offensive intentions unless otherwise specifically mentioned. Any resemblances to actual
events that occur in exactly the same fashion involving any persons, lo-
cales, or incidents is entirely coincidental. Any names of actual persons
that have been used within the contents of the story are used in a purely
fictional state to drive the motion of the story and its characters.

No part of this book may be reproduced for the reproducer's profit, except
for the use of quotation reference for the sake of reviews, without written
permission from the author, or without directly referencing the author and
the work of which the quote is taken from.

.

Independently published and printed in the United States by
AMAZON.
(C) All Rights Reserved 2020
All rights reserved by Dave Matthes.
Front and back cover design by Dave Matthes.

ISBN: 9781796223439

Also by Dave Matthes
available on Amazon

NOVELS
The Slut Always Rides Shotgun
The Passive Aggressors
In This House, We Lived, and We Died
Sleepeth Not, the Bastard
Bar Nights
Paradise City
Return to the Madlands
The Mire Man: *The Complete Trilogy*
Lockless Doors in the Land of Harsh Angels
The Sounds From the Hills Go Away When the Sun Goes Down
No Old Souls At Fury Tavern
MERCY
Leave My Ashes on Blackheart Mountain

POETRY AND SHORT STORIES
The Kaleidoscope Syndrome: *An Anthology*
Wanderlust and the Whiskey Bottle Parallel: *Poems and Stories*
Strange Rainfall on the Rooftops of People Watchers: *Poems and Stories*
EJACULATION: *New Poems and Stories*
An Anvil of Night, A Hammer for Dawn: Poetry and Stories
On the Verge of Burning Down the Church: Poetry and Stories
Black Hibiscus: New Poetry
The Whores of Alcatraz: Poems 2007-2019
A Scorched and Mystified Wilderness: And Other Stories

SERIAL NOVELS
Woodbury Tabernacle: Volume One

THE TWO REVOLVERS SAGA

THE YEARS OF WAR

BOOK I
LEAVE MY ASHES ON BLACKHEART MOUNTAIN
AVAILABLE NOW

BOOK II
LEGEND OF THE HORIZON VENGEANCE
COMING IN 2021

THE YEAR OF DEATH

BOOK III
MERCY
AVAILABLE NOW

BOOK IV
THE DEAD AND THE DYING
RELEASE DATE TO BE DETERMINED

THE YEARS OF REDEMPTION

BOOK V
THE CITY AND THE VEIL
RELEASE DATE TO BE DETERMINED

BOOK VI
ONE MORE GRAVE TO DIG
RELEASE DATE TO BE DETERMINED

CHAPTERS

LEAVE
MY
ASHES
ON
BLACKHEART
MOUNTAIN

Prologue

12 | DAVE MATTHES

After they'd clamped the chains around my little wrists, they waited for my mother and father to leave. They'd allowed for a good-enough distance to make work of itself, but that only lasted for so long. There were two more gunshots that morning, and after the air fell silent, I was told I no longer had to worry about mom and dad.

Some years long since transpired, a long, long time ago before I was ever a person, the last man who'd been alive during civilization's great collapse, laid down and died. And along with his death, the truth of how the world fell to pieces... how it all happened, died. Not long after that, it became less imperative knowing the truth of how it all went down, and more pertinent deciding how you were going to survive with the times that were given to you, whether they were years, weeks, or minutes. I was born into a world already accustomed to this change, so from the beginnin', I was taught a very specific way on how to survive and make the most of whatever came to befall me. Some might say I was lucky that way. Bein' I was the one livin' with those so-called lucky experiences, I'd say luck is only somethin' given to the people who died first.

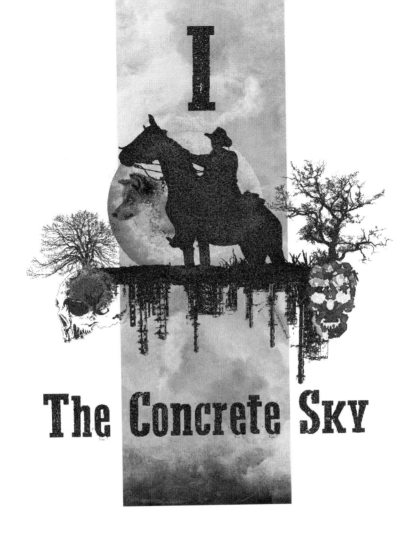

The Concrete Sky

I.
SYMPHONY of the WASTES

The world is an amalgamation of two things: the ground, and those who and what are still alive that walk upon it. The ground is the dirt piled over the sticks that used to be branches from once long-standing trees. It is the earthen muck and the mud and the lakes and the bones on the riverbeds, the thick, opaque green, dark forests where the air itself is too frightened to move. It is the desert, cold during the dark hours, and unkindly hot when the sun is seen at any point in the sky. It is the mountains, which I'm told back east are harsh and grey and covered with trees. Out west and northwest, they are covered in snow and rock and crowned by clouds. The ground is also the road, the cracked and fissured sections of concrete upon which people used to drive in gas-powered vehicles. The roads went everywhere in all kinds of directions like strands of webbing blowing in the wind. They formed bridges and overpasses, structures mostly collapsed due to a palpable lack of conservation. They cut through the thick, green, and during seasonally solstic times, dark, endless forests, whose grounds and dales dug deeper downward than the barriers of their bark reached. They stretched across the desert whether it happened to be a cold, moonlit night, or an afternoon in a blistering gulch Hell. They rolled over the mountains, along their ridges and in between their valleys. The roads were the true memorials to humanity's past. Statues and monuments fell long ago, while the roads remained. They let us know just how far we as a race wanted to go, or were willing to go. But for every mile of mapped out, recorded highway, with the fall of structured and politically-ruled civilization, there existed a hundred acres of unexplored, unsought-after, unremembered landscape.

And then there was us... people. There were still many of us left, just not in the same way as before. The older gents would say that history is always repeating itself, and every few hundred generations it goes as far as *correcting* itself. I'm not too sure what they mean by that, but for me the world has always looked the same, whereas the books that still could be found or were still possessed depicted the world in a much brighter fashion, anything and everything I came across on my travels, was anything but.

It'd been a few days since I'd seen any sign of water. Not many trees either. Just dirt, rock, and the fragments of broken up concrete highway I'd been following for the last month and a half; a span of time that was a broad estimate, it could have been more, or it could have been less. The wind was a murderous thief all on its own, tactless and futile both at the same time. The wind would sweep down from the northwest, from the tops of those brown hills carrying with it heaping masses of sand and dirt and other debris, sometimes molding it and forming it all into great swirling towers of twisting elemental force. At its least formidable, the wind came across the face as barely anything more than a breeze, the tiny dirt particles nothing more than harmless kisses bouncing off your skin. At its most menacing, the torna-dos came from the clouded heavens with the sole pur-pose of re-cultivating the land, and if you were lucky you only saw them from miles away. Currently, there were four of them I could make out, blowing through a distant valley. Their breezes could still be felt and their voices could still be heard as distant roars and grumbles. Mixed in somewhere with the vague moans and groans of the twisting dust devils, I heard something organic: the trickling of a nearby stream, shallow, perhaps ankle-deep with a rockbed of smooth, small, circular rocks.

The trickling stream-like sounds came from op-posite the distant rampaging dust devils. I ascended a rocky, yellow-grass hill and peaked over the top. Down below, where the hill slanted further off, there was in-deed a stream. At least eighty... maybe a hundred feet wide, dispersed with sandbars up and down its middle. Boulder formations corralled at its edges along either side, and down from the sky descended flocks of black birds, crows, or maybe ravens. Among the fowl populace there were pairs of what looked like swallows, or egrets, trudging slowly near the edges where the most abundant plant life grew.

I descended the hill, slowly, but excitedly. I was thirsty. Both canteens were empty, and had been empty for some time. I collapsed to my knees at the water's edge, bringing the water to my face with both hands, splashing its coolness against my cheeks, my forehead, and my chin and nose. The water trickled down my neck, down my shirt collar and soaked into my clothes. I smelled the water. It smelled clear. I touched the tip of my tongue to it. Nothing off, nothing sour or morose. I sipped a mouthful, swishing it around my mouth. I knew this was bad practice. I knew the proper techniques to purifying water but... I was just so thirsty. My lips felt like tree bark and my throat had been making a sound I could not define by any word or emotion. I drank. I took the ice-cold natural water down my throat and into my body. I kept on drinking and stopped only to breathe.

I didn't wipe my chin. I let the water stay and drip down my skin. I took in the cool air and exhaled, pleased for the first time in endless memory. I looked up and down the stream. The wildlife present were all behaving the same way. Drinking from the water. Swimming in it. The plant life growing at its edges were all tinged with varying shades of green...a good sign if I ever saw one. And across the stream, exactly opposite from where I knelt, there trotted, in a strangely pleasant fashion, a wolf. I stopped to watch. The wolf wore a fur of mostly grey, streaked with tufts of white, particularly around the neck. Around his eyes the fur changed to a darker grey and from his nose to his forehead there blended in a single streak of pure black. The creature slowed to a walk the closer he drew to the water's edge. He lowered his head, sniffing the ground, and he let out his big pink tongue to lap up water.

I removed my rifle from my shoulder. A wolf like that, someone in any town would pay a decent wage for the pelt. Hell, with the cold months coming, particularly around these parts, the demand for sources of warmth and protection was unlimited. And wolf meat, while not the greatest in taste, if one was fortunate enough to have preferences, was still meat. He looked skinny, a little worn by the world and his own travels, but there was always something that could be scraped from the bones whether it was protein or marrow. I raised a knee and rested my left elbow atop it, holding the rifle stiff but durably. Looking down the sights, I took a deep, heavy breath. The first breath.

The wolf was sitting now, lapping up the water heavier and with more enthusiasm. He was thirsty, just as I was. Maybe he'd been walking for as long as I'd been. He lifted his head, licking the sides of his mouth, scanning the horizon and watching the other animals. His attention turned to flocks of black birds and the pairs of egrets off to the side. The stream trickled over the rocks, the very edge of the water barely touching his toes, his paws. And he just sat there on the bank, his gaze eventually lining up in direct intersection with mine. He held his sight on me as I did on him. I noticed his eyes then and all I could think about was the wonder behind them. The drive, the instinct. What fueled him to keep goin' and goin'? He stayed there, sitting and watching me. There was no hostility that I could divulge, nothing in his posture that would mitigate a need to cause any harm, even to satisfy a hungry belly..

"Goddamnit," I said to myself.

I lowered the rifle.

The wolf remained, his gaze unflinching, his emotion unchanging.

"And you're not goin' to thank me, are ya," I said. The wolf remined, watching me, listening to me. "Listen beast," I called out, "my generosity has an expiration date! *I'm* still hungry! And your meat tastes better than any of these nasty birds around here! And your fur could put enough pay in my pocket to relieve a week's worth of stress and worry! Go on! Drink your water and get outta here!" But even then, I was already starting to walk away. I didn't hear any sign of the wolf moving. At the top of the hill, I stood and turned around. The wolf remained at the edge of the water, his eyes still locked on my movements. "Son of a bitch," I muttered.

I'd been so distraught over my decision to not

shoot the wolf that I'd forgotten to fill my canteens. But by the time I realized this, I was already five, six miles away from the river. I contemplated going back, but it was beginning to get dark. A little way's off there jutted out the sharp and crooked shoulders and rooftops of dark and broken-down houses, sitting along a stretch and a bend of a one-street neighborhood. Maybe in the morning I'd go back, but now I needed to find shelter for the coming night.

I stood outside the short street.

I watched the houses.

There were seven of them, all dark, no lights inside. Nothing to indicate anyone in the vicinity. Anyone, normal or less-than unhinged, anyway. There were over a hundred different types of hungry-minded-people, cannibals, various gangs who didn't give two shits about decency or morality, scums, ragglers, scavengers, tribesmen, diseased, cursed, skinless, toothless, the completely mindless and deranged, and even the blind mutes (although they usually stayed hidden in the mountains far to the west of this region entirely) that didn't need sources of light to keep warm or to cook their food. Their survival needs generally required only darkness to make any sense to them. So, the next step would be to listen. To listen for any creaks in the wooden structures. Any changes in the wind. And for the nocturnal wildlife, they would be coming out soon. The sounds and calls they made to one another was always a good way to know if they themselves detected any danger, assuming they weren't aware of your own presence. A midnight songbird (named for when they were most heard, but they were also known to come out around sunset), would sing a song long and mournful, similar to a mourning dove's tune, but the thing that made these birds special is that if they felt as though anything on the ground might endanger their landing for their hunting game, their song would be short little bursts of an almost chirping, like the sound a finch might make, or a robin. The trick was listening long enough to make sure the midnight songbird didn't change their tune before you decided to make your move.

I listened.

Nothing.

No chirps.

No songs either.

The sky was dipped a sad gloom of purple, pale and desperate towards the horizon where the sun still shone, but dark in the west, almost black, where the sky had started to greet the night. The night clouds were all but gone in the west, and only a few ridges of pink and orange drifted off toward the east. A small flock of black birds exploded from an underbrush and vanished into the distance. And then they came. The song of tranquility. The small street was safe, and so I made my way out of my stance and eventually decided the third house on the right would suit my shelter needs the best, as its walls appeared to be the most sturdy and the least broken-down.

The front door had been unhinged long ago and the brass hinges might as well have never been brass at all. The previous owners didn't seem to like carpets or rugs, so all the floors were hardwood, and judging from the hollow sound my footsteps made they had a basement. I moved from room to room. I sat on the couch in the living room area and a big plume of dust exploded as I sank down. The cushion was still soft, and comfortable, but the smell, I'm afraid would just be too much. I could handle a lot, and also a lot of smells of varying degrees of bad. I could handle a corpse. I could tolerate excrement, and old excrement. But something that had been on this couch whether recently or otherwise, it had decided to stick around for the long haul, and smelled... just... otherworldly. I got up, dusted myself off and looked towards the stairs. The sun had now left the sky completely and the purple and dark blue hues had all faded to a dark, pitch, endless black. The house was too dark to see, but I did have a crank lantern that still had a little bit of charge left. I moved the crank in the charging direction and the light sprang to life, lighting up the room around me with a vague, hazy luminescent glow. The walls and the ceiling and the floors ached and gave out a whine and a few splintering moans of disapproval to my being there. I took to the steps one at a time, listening for anything or anyone I might have missed during my initial taking of precautions. There was no sound to be heard but the building's dispirited discontent.

The first door upstairs, I pushed open with the end of my rifle. I let the light shine in. The room stood empty. Completely. No furniture. Nothing hanging from the walls except an almost colorless, peeling wallpaper patterned with shapes of trains and rocket ships and lassos ready to be loosened. There was fixed into the wall straight ahead one square window, the glass broken, the moonlight shining through with gentle, luminous shafts. I moved on down the hall and pushed open the second door with the end of my rifle. Inside there was a bed, a bedframe rather, with a single mattress on top. Laying on the mattress were two figures, corpses. Presumably lovers. But they were all if not mostly bone. Their clothes clinging to the decrepit, rotting curves of what remained of their bodies told me they were once a man and a woman. Next to the bed laying on the floor sat a knocked-over stack of books, the edges of the pages and the covers torn, bent, browned and dusty, and among those lay an old handgun, which even from here I could see was rusted beyond resurrection. Returning my examination to the bodies, I let the light of my lamp shine over their shapes, and there I saw the unmistakable, jagged-circular shape of a bullet's entry in the sides of each of their skulls.

Somewhere off in the distance, a growl of thunder gurgled up from the earth and rolled across the sky. A flash lit up the sky, followed ten seconds later by a crackle, and another rolling growl. And then arrived the tiny taps of raindrops touching down atop the roof.

I pushed the flesh and bones off the bed and slumped myself down onto the mattress. I could feel every single spring. Every fold. Every inconsistency. The rolling thunder was a lullaby, always had been. But something crossed my mind through my ears. A scratching. A scuttling. This house had vermin. Vermin meant food.

I sat up and listened.

My possessions in all my pockets settled until there was silence. And there it was again.

SCRATCH, SCRATCH!

.....pitter pitter pitter pitter patter patter pitter patter....

In the dark, there was very little chance to catch anything, unless you could literally see in the dark. I could smell most things, I could smell the shit smudged on the ass of a horse a mile away, and sometimes I could detect variances in the shadows; I knew the difference between the shadows of branches moving in the wind, and an arm with a long, rusted-edge knife being gripped in the hand at the end of it, and my sense of hearing was unmatched; if you were whispering to a loved one in the night, I could tell you where the man-eater was hiding, and in which closet, waiting for you both to fall asleep. However, I could not see the little seemingly invisible creatures haunting the crevices and nooks of this nearly-abandoned house.

I climbed out of bed, shining the light of my lamp over the pile of bones and skin and the old clothing they had been wearing during their last moments. I reached down into the pile and pulled out a still intact ribcage. With the other hand I snapped off the lower spinal cord still attached. I looked at the bone formation up and down, turning the ribcage over and under, shining the light onto it, checking to see if the bones had hollowed out too much. After a certain amount of time, bones became too frail to use for anything, even a toothpick. And the way you could easily tell this is by shining a light on the backside, letting the glow show through the bone. The more translucent the bone, the more likely it was to break prematurely. But these bones were still fairly young, young enough for what I needed them for.

I walked downstairs and from one of the windows tore a section from the mesh screen. I cut a tiny slit in it and placed it on a table. With my knife I cut small indentations in various spots on the back side of the ribcage, circularly around each rib bone. I then began snapping each rib until I held a near-perfectly-surgical half ribcage. Outside, puddles had begun to form in the dirt, changing the ground to mud. I was fortunate for the rain. A clump of hair and flesh had been clinging to part of the ribcage. With this I dipped into the nearest puddle outside to soften it until it was malleable. Placing the screen over the half ribcage, so that each gap between the ribs were covered, I then placed the moistened flesh and hair around the edges, pressing it around the screen so that it held in place.

One had to be crafty with catching these small vermin. And since they only fed on one thing, I had to give up a little of myself for the final piece.

I placed the ribcage trap in a corner of the room somewhat near the front door. With a lighter in my pocket, I ran the flame up and down the edge of the blade for a moment. I then cut a small slice into my arm and let the blood soak a small piece of cloth. I placed the bloodied cloth into the inside of the ribcage trap and made sure the tiny slit in the screen was accessible to whatever found interest.

Back upstairs I lay back down onto the mattress. The pile of bones next to the bed seemed of no consequence anymore. I reached down, check the gun just to be sure, but it was empty. As I closed my eyes, I hoped the morning would bring me something to eat.

Dawn arrived, and I awoke to discover that the storm had passed. The ground outside looked wet, and reflected a dull brightness under the overcast sunny horizons. When I woke, I woke to the sound of a tiny screeching. I stretched my bones and my arms and my legs, unsheathed my knife and made my way downstairs. In the trap I'd set, that one of the two people upstairs had been kind enough to contribute towards, were four large mice, so fat that they couldn't seem to press themselves back through the hole in the screen they'd each climbed into.

"Hey little fellas," I said, kneeling down. One by one, I stuck the knife in, catching their throats. After they were all dead, I removed a small bottle from my pocket and one by one squeezed the blood of each mouse into the bottle. The blood, as I was taught long ago, could be used to set traps just as the one I had just set. Also, it was useful in setting false trails if you found yourself being hunted. The blood would go bad of course, but it still looked crimson on rock surfaces, and if you were good enough at your craft, you could make an enemy think you were injured and fleeing in a totally different direction.

When all the blood had been drained, I wrapped each mouse up into a cloth and shoved them into a small bag, which then went into a larger pocket in my duster.

I stayed in that house for two days, stuffing my face with mouse after mouse after rat after rat. They were everywhere in the walls and let me know when it was time for me to eat by scratching their little scratches. The rowdier members of the family gave off little squeaks, like whispers to the others to let them know they had a problem: me, Rancid Mahoney, current curmudgeon of their short, little lives. They didn't know me by my name, of course. To them, I was simply a monster eating them all one by one. At first, they were easy to catch, but the thinner the family shrank, the more cunning they became. On the second day of my occupation, they stopped falling for the ribcage trap. One meaty bastard must have had large, sharp teeth, as I found evidence of something chewing *out* of the trap. Bastard could probably feed me for three days if I ever caught him, and I started to wonder if I had been imagining him at all. Something that big I think I would have been able to at least hear, or see on occasion. Unless he didn't live in the house at all and only used it as shelter, like myself.

One night, I decided to force myself to stay up all of the hours just to see if I could witness anything. Any creatures who might serve as a justification for my imagination. I sat perfectly still, covering myself in an old tarp and some blankets to keep warm. I slowed my breathing so that not even a fox could hear me. And I waited.

I gave myself a generous view of the front door, which I left open. Outside, the night sky turned a pale purple, no clouds, no fog, no mist. Just bright stars and a mostly full moon. A smell drifted into the house through the opening. Someone, somewhere had a campfire going. I could smell the burning wood. Maybe I should abandon my hunt of this massive night creature and instead head out into the world. I could track the camp, find its maker, kill him and take everything I needed. An easy kill that came gift-wrapped with plentiful rewards, that was always the best-case scenario.

I waited another hour, thinking on the options laid out before me, the freedom of choice and very little room for failure on the obvious election of the effortless path.

I took a breath and could almost taste the camp-fire smoke.

The glow of the fire came from the other side of a hill not too far away. I kept low, and stayed at a near tip-toe pace. The night insects scurried out of the way, some of them giving off angry little chirps and cackles. As I drew closer to the glow of the fire, I stopped so that I could listen. No change in sound. No movement or noises except the wood on the fire spitting and spatting. I breathed quietly, moving closer and began ascending the hill in a crawl. While on my knees and elbows, I peered over the crest.

Before my eyes could break the top of the hill, I heard the sound of something snapping, like a twig. It went *SNAP*, and then the air returned to nocturnal silence.

I peered over the top edge.

There was the fire, small and built quickly with nothing cooking overtop of it. I couldn't see inside the tent, but hanging from a nearby tree not three feet from the fire, hung the body of presumably whomever built the fire. He dangled from a noose tightly snug around his neck. I stayed there on my belly for a moment, about to head in, seeing as though he'd already taken care of the hard work for me... when from behind the flames I caught them. The eyes, and the exhaled breath of the creature they belonged to.

The wolf crept into the light from the darkness, one massive paw in front of the other, stopping just below the hanging man. He sniffed the bare toes, licking one with a quick flick of the tongue. He then hoisted himself up with his two hind legs, latching on to the man's chest with his two front paws, and with only the tiniest of efforts, tore the body down. The rope snapped all the way and the body fell to the ground with a slump, almost rolling into the fire. The wolf sniffed around, and decided first on the neck. He dug his teeth in, tearing the throat from flesh, twisting and yanking with a series of low growls and grumbles.

I thought maybe I could kill the wolf. Fate was telling me something. This was the second time seeing the beast. And now might be the best time to do it. But again, I couldn't even bother myself to reach for my rifle. The creature, even as he ate with ravenous method, was a beautiful thing to behold. He tore into the flesh of the dead man on the ground, and I couldn't feel bad for the self-lynched man. He was providing for this creature, this animal who only lived on instinct and could therefore never be evil, judgmental, or wrong.

When the wolf finished its meal, he lifted his head and licked his chops. The night was dark, of course, but in the firelight, I could see the stains around his mouth. He looked about to trot off, but instead he stayed behind. Because he heard it too. The sound of a baby waking up, stirring, letting out a little whimper of confusion... from inside the tent. The ears of the creature twitched and he started creeping toward the tent. I waited. This was still not my place to intervene. I couldn't intervene. No matter what this creature did, it couldn't be evil, judgmental, or wrong.

He crept forward, sticking his nose into the tent, and the baby let out one last little coo. The wolf dove in, suddenly eager for yet another meal, his ravenous, unforgiving appetite rejuvenated. The wolf growled and barked, crunching down easily on the undeveloped bones and flesh of the one inside the tent. The feeding lasted only a minute, as the wolf had found it no large task to scarf down the small form as opposed to its full-grown parent. When the feeding was over, the wolf peered out of the tent, listened for a minute further, both of his ears twitching intermittently, his nostrils expanding and contracting in short bursts of air-detection. He then dove out, returning to the darkness of the land away from the fire's glow.

I heard the sound of a shotgun being pumped. It sounded faint, but unambiguous. The calm of the camp in the wake of the wolf had been soothing until now.

"Minimum distance to achieve the desired effect of a shotgun is around fifty yards," I called out without turning around, "by the sound of it, you're just on the edge of that minimum. So, either you're real good with that thing, or you've got the blessedness of God on your side."

"Maybe I'm both," the man called out with a harsh voice, a throat gone too far without water or any sort of nourishment. "Maybe I'm a damn good shot. Maybe God is on my side."

"Have ya looked around lately," I laughed, turning to face him, "there ain't nothin' anywhere worth praisin'. That means you *better* be a damn good shot. I see ya now, too. Hidin' in the dark there. I can hear ya breathin', hard and tired all at the same time. Sounds like you're exhausted, sounds like you're gettin' close to the end of your *own* rope," I walked closer, barely able to make out the exact shape of the man. I couldn't see his face yet, but I could trace the outline of his weapon. A shotgun, of course, but with a short barrel, which meant even less of a chance for him to hit anything at the range he stood within.

"Don't move any closer," he called out. I stopped in my stride but only because I needn't go any further anyway. I could now make out the man's face. He bore a scar on his cheek and it looked as though he were missing some teeth. The hat resting on his head had seen better days, particularly around the brim.

"Now what is it ya want," I asked.

"Whatever ya got, mister," he said, a little unsure of himself. "Food, ammunition, your weapons. Anything."

"If you were to take all of those things from me, you'd be increasing the likelihood of my death out here. So why don't ya just shoot me and get it over with. Mercy killin', ain't no harm in one of those. This way no questions have to be asked. You can just take... anything I got, be on your way and hope to your God the cards continue to fall in your favor."

"I beg your pardon mister, but, I ain't really one for killin'. It's not what you would call a hobby of mine."

"Really? And here you are *threatening* to kill me.

All of a sudden it doesn't feel like much of a threat any-more," I took another two steps forward and he started to shake.

"I only kill if I have to, mister," he said, "and right now you're makin' it hard for me to be patient."

"Why don't ya put that gun down, you ain't gonna hit your mark with it anyway," I said, "and I'll see if I have somethin' I can spare. I'm sure I got somethin' I can give ya, somethin' in which we both come outta this valley alive."

He swallowed, his aim wavered ever so slightly. "Really," he asked, "you would just, give me some of your things?"

"Well, not a huge chunk but I'm sure I can find it in my heart to part ways with a few things. I've still gotta get home, after all."

"Well," he started to say, taking in long, heavy drafts of air into his lungs, "well, maybe," his aim began to lower, "how do I know you won't shoot me as soon as I put my gun down?"

"You don't," I chuckled, "that's the thing about trust, mister. It don't mean dick amongst strangers."

"Funny. My uh... my daddy used to say that uh, the only difference between strangers and friends is trust," he said, to which I only shrugged in reply.

The man thought it over in his head. He looked up into the dark sky and I saw the whites of his eyes. He must have made an agreement with himself or maybe he was sayin' a prayer to whom he truly did believe to be a god above his head.

"You know, I wasn't always like this. I wasn't al-ways pointin' guns at people," he said.

"Don't matter how ya were," I said, "*or* how ya got to who you are. This is who ya are *now*. Pointin' guns at people."

He hadn't noticed that I'd walked ever closer to him. I stood not even twenty feet from him when his eyes shifted and the grip he held on his shotgun stiffened.

"Relax," I said, "see this is a common problem you drifters seem to not realize ya have. Ya need to relax."

"Can't relax, mister. Maybe it's you who needs to take a look around," he said.

"Who was the last person you killed, and why did ya kill him?"

"What business is it of yours? Things like that are personal to a man."

"Well I don't know. You have your shotgun pointed at my face. Seems like you were the one to get personal first. I think I have at least a little right to know something about the man who may end up being my killer. Tell ya what, let's start off small. That scar there on your cheek, where'd ya get it?"

"A man with a knife gave it to me. And I killed him shortly after."

"Is he the last man you killed?"

"Maybe he is, maybe he isn't."

"Sounds like there's more to than just a man giving another man a scar and that man killin' him as payback."

"Maybe there is, maybe there isn't."

"Ya know, my camp is just over there. Why don't we go there, and we both can eat somethin', and you can tell me more about that scar? And then at the end of it, we can go our separate ways."

The man with the shotgun appeared to be calming his own nerves down. His shoulders didn't move so much while he breathed, and both of his legs had nearly completely stopped with the knee tremors.

"I gotta say," he started, "you're the most-polite gentleman I've ever met out here in the world."

"I get even more polite when everyone has their guns lowered, too. Some might dare to call it romantic."

He lowered his shotgun all the way, and took a less-defensive stance. He sighed with relief and took a calm step back to adjust himself.

"So, you're out here all alone, that's just brave or stupid or both," I said.

"Well," he said, "I wasn't always alone. Everyone else just died off little by little-like. I'm the, uh, the last one out of the original group. Never thought that would... never expected it to be me at the end."

"Well, ya don't haveta worry anymore," I said, shooting him in the stomach with one quick motion. He stumbled back, dropping his shotgun and almost falling completely to the ground. I shot him again in the chest and he fell the rest of the way down. He wore a face bursting with bloodshot surprise, but it was impossible to tell if that was due to the pain of the bullets, or my betrayal. He sputtered, probably trying to ask me why. I stood over him, picking up his shotgun. I checked the chamber. "You sad bastard," I said, "there ain't even any shells in this thing! You're gonna lay here and die over an empty shotgun?" He shook his head, pleading, but there was no need to plea. I put a third bullet in his skull right between the eyes. He stopped moving after that. I tossed aside the shotgun and checked his pockets. Again, nothing. Just a man with nothin' in his pockets at all.

I returned to the house, having found nothing of real use at the campsite. The man who elected the noose must have been out of supplies himself, influencing his final decision. The sound of the baby being eaten alive stayed with me, though, and so I forgot about the hunt of my own, and of the river I meant to return to. When the sun rose in the morning, I gathered up my things and left the house, heading further into the east.

II.

HONEST HEARTS
of NEW CANTERTON

I'd told the man with the empty shotgun that I still had a need to get home. Of the context of our short-lived relationship, that part was the most-true. During the twenty-five, twenty-six years I'd been breathin' and walkin', home had presented itself or existed in various forms along the spectrum of what everyday folks referred to as "acceptable housing", or simply, shelter. I did my time early on trying to figure out my likes and dislikes only to come to the conclusion that for someone like me, preference, not only was hardly ever readily available, it also just didn't matter. Home these days was to be found in New Canterton: a region of midwestern land consisting of Gunther P. Ostrander's mining facility, the quarry, its neighboring town, and the widely-proclaimed impregnable outer wall which protected it all.

The smoke stacks showed themselves first, sticking out from behind a sharp, rancorous ridge of mountaintops like a spine protruding from the hunched back of a dire bear; the billowing towers reached high with a melancholy anger toward the sky, an emotion no one who bore witness to them ever sought a truth for. In the guts of a valley of sand and dirt and multitudinous pale rock formations, the mining factory stood proudly like the castles of the past once did. Black and silently furious, it was held up by massive, steel posts and plating, only now just becoming corroded with the passing of time since the great collapse. Of the smoke stacks, there was one prominent concreate stack scratching the sky letting out curling and swirling plumes of black smoke, evaporating into the oncoming grey rainclouds and beside it, just out of view if looked upon at the right angle, a smaller, less-important stack, that to my knowledge no longer served any purpose, stood short and anxious, intimidated by its taller, wider permanent next door cousin. The sounds of people digging and hammering rocks and cutting into the earth emanated from the quarry three hundred yards to the north, only further emphasizing that the factory itself had no real voice of its own.

      The factory compound had this sign hanging up right outside of the main entrance reading "OSTRANDER and BOOTHE, Co." and underneath in smaller letters read: "of New Canterton". To the extent of my knowledge, back in the early days the place had been run synonymously by Gunther P. Ostrander, my current employer, and a Christopher Carl Boothe, sometimes known as C.C. Boothe, an older, much wiser man than most, given the current state of world affairs. Ostrander and Boothe walked everywhere like two friends who'd found a fortune, and who, much better and more impressively, found a way to share that fortune. Their pride and joy, being this mining compound which they eventually evolved into something grand that many people came to see, request work at, or even live within. Beside the main factory, there was the quarry where most of the work was done, but also not quite in sight had been built a small town where much of the workers lived with their families. I'd lived there for a time before Gunther approached me about enlisting into what he called "much more important work than simply going out into the world to procure history books or resources that could be used as consumable sustenance". By that time, Boothe had already passed on. He'd reached a pretty late age, and had fallen ill with pneumonia. Eventually it got so bad, the sickness went to his head, and one night wandered out passed the Out Wall, sneaking passed the guards and out into the wilderness. He was found some weeks later, his body hanging from a noose, beneath an ancient tree with long widespread branches. The lower half of his body had been torn to shreds by wildlife. Some believed he hung himself, knowing his own fate, while others speculated it could have been that he crossed unfortunate paths with the Crimson Collars, a band of degenerate monsters who had once been respectable men, if you could believe that such a thing even exists. Ostrander never, if not rarely, talked about Boothe's death, but the little he did say about it he said how it hit him hard and that he'd gone through his own personal hell for a time, a "spiritual renaissance", as he called it. It wasn't long after that he started doing business with a one Henry Kenroy, a man of questionable fortitude who walked with a wide birth That is to say while most men grew taller in height while growing up, he grew more outward, wider in the midriff. His neck was thick, and so you could no longer make out the features of his throat, to the extent of which when he was eating and he swallowed, no muscles in the neck contracted, no throat bounced. The food just went in and down into his gut. Whenever he walked into a room, he bore the look of a man who expected everyone to already know to give him more room to breathe, and if they weren't privy to that acorn of information then to at least respect the fact that they were now in the presence of a man who required that extra space. He was a man of entitlement, something I didn't know much about, but such a trait had been known to give any who wore it a certain stink that no nose could detect, and only a hard understanding of the world outside could provide any protection against.

In meeting Kenroy, I think it may have filled the void Boothe left behind, as much as it could, at least. Ostrander still had his quiet moments, though. And there were times he stood on his legs like a time-worn philosophy more than simply my employer who patted me on the back whenever he thought I'd done a good job. Through their relationship, Ostrander helped Kenroy found Vermouth, a town to the north, a town that Kenroy was now, and probably always would be, the mayor of.

The sign reading "OSTRANDER and BOOTHE, Co." still hung outside the mining facility. Gunther once said to me that Boothe had earned the nickname Two Seas, because he'd been one of the only men in the known country for having been to both coastlines, several times in fact, and living to tell about it. He said Boothe had a saying, that "on a map, or a globe, two oceans may appear to be separate, but once you've seen both, no one can tell you any different: that they are the same body of water".

These days, be they stormy or calm for literal reasons or otherwise, Gunther P. Ostrander sat on the throne of this fortress, overseeing the mining operations, making sure security stations all remained up to date and purposeful. Off the books, he also ran a small business on the side. A business I, according to him, was the only direct employee of, or rather, I was the only employee with the exact task that I had. Back in the beginning of our relationship, he once confided in me that I was the only man suitable for said position, that this occupation was one designed specifically for a man of my talents. Of course, that wasn't always true. There'd been a time in which I doubted his honesty in that claim, and eventually I discovered I had not been far off from being wrong. In short, Gunther Ostrander employed me to survey various stretches of land, clear out seemingly abandoned towns, and seek out evidence for a particular mineral no one with a full brain was convinced actually existed. Blackvein, he called it. Said it was the miracle cure to anything, any kind of trauma the human body couldn't otherwise withstand or recover from. Blackvein, when instrumented the right way, sped up the human body's ability to heal itself, no matter what the injury. Blackvein was the missing link to keeping the soul and the spirit alive while the body healed itself. Originally, Gunther Ostrander explained the importance of only having me privy to his quest for this mineral, until I killed five of his other prospectors. Had to. They too were under the impression they were the only ones on the hunt. We all ended up in this mostly abandoned town some ten or eleven miles outside of Ostrander's Mining Factory. Every bullet was shot that day, and only myself walked away from the ditches. I returned to Ostrander, put a gun to his head demanding answers. He said only unsmart men ever only plant one seed. He said it trickily, with not an ounce of begging for mercy in his voice. It was almost as if he'd expected this outcome. The only reason I didn't kill him then is because I needed the money, and he always paid up. He paid good too, better than anyone as far as I was concerned. And I had enough confidence in my abilities that if he did betray me again, I could handle whatever he threw at me.

His office was carved out of one of the upper levels of the factory with a large rectangular window giving an expansive view of the valley and the ranges of snow-capped mountains in the distance. He'd had a balcony built out there, a crude structure at first but over time perfected once he tracked down and hired an actual welder. From the balcony, you could see the quarry, and hear all the workers. You could see the dust rising up out of that bowl in the earth, and you could see for miles in either direction, across the dirt and the rocky plains, until they came to foothills and those foothills rose up into the feet of black, unmanageable mountains. Looking straight up, the massive arm of concrete that was the main smoke stack reached high up into the sky until the very top vanished into the clouds. The place had truly been a feat of engineering, back from when the world and civilization still had any meaning. Ostrander had said he hadn't been the first one to stake a claim on this land. He first had to win it over. People with rough skin and mean faces had moved in prior to his arrival, people with hopes of turning the factory into a palace of slaughter and torture. Ostrander never went into great detail about how he'd been victorious in the conflict, but he did say it had been around that time he first became aware of the existence of Blackvein. He would on occasion look closely at his hands as if he saw something there in those palms that only he could see. Memories, maybe, stains of memories. "Any man of the world these days has them," Ostrander would say, "They either find a way to live with them, or they don't."

On his desk lay the piece of paper with the heading in big, black bold lettering: "WESTWARD EXPLORATORY PROJECTION TREATY", an article of truth, law, and privilege assembled during a time long before I ever opened my eyes for the first time. I rarely saw this piece of paper, and whenever Gunther had it out it was usually because he was contemplating something he claimed to have a deep meaning, that "all men should look into if they want to better their own life". I didn't know much about the actual history of the world and the only people who claimed to were only purveyors of the truth, and not actual holders of history. To me, it seemed like a fool's errand to uncover the exact goings on of the past. But Gunther was something of an aficionado. He said knowing history, even a little bit, gave a man a strength to his roots that other more ignorant folk will never know.

He cleared his throat.

"When they said Rancid Mahoney was back, I thought I might have still been dreaming in my sleep and it was still the middle of last night," Gunther Ostrander walked into his office, his face having been freshly shaved, still glistening with the shine of an applied moistened towel. He walked in, straight and without any limps or struggles. The muscles in his forearm flexed as he shook my hand, and his cheek bones hardened upon the smile he exhibited when beholding me. "You took a long stretch, over a month this time."

"I went out there," I said, "but I didn't find no mountain," I said, "I mean sure, there's lots of mountains out there. But this one, this-"

"Blackheart Mountain," he finished for me.

"Yea, that one," I said, "I mean, despite *all* the outlandish claims to the contrary amongst the ever so-loving populace here, I'm startin' to think you might really *be* losin' it. There ain't a damn rock or pebble out there with the description you gave me, which was not much to go by anyway."

"Now, now," he gave out a light chuckle, patting my back, "you just haven't looked long enough, my friend. It's out there. I've seen it, from a distance. But it's been years and I know for a fact it's not just a storybook place. And under this mountain is where it's all at, Mahon."

"A mineral capable of saving the human race. If you say so," I said.

"It's not if I say so, Mahon," he said, "it *is* whether I *say* it is or not, it's *truth*. It's not a truth I'm trying to sell to you, for you to buy, like some of those greedy nutjobs out there. Truth, real truth, is not a commodity, Mahon. It's intangible and priceless. Am I not paying you enough? Gentlemen of your particular malleability are getting to be harder and harder to come by, it's even harder to keep one on your payroll long enough to establish a report, and harder still to maintain that trust once it's been established," his cheek muscles tightened around the jawbones again, "I'm losing trustworthy people by the week, Mr. Mahoney. I'm starting to think I may not have the wallet weight to meet their wallet space."

"The money doesn't have anything to do with it, Gunth'. The money fills my pockets fine, hell I don't even need all ya give me. I'm just sayin' this place that you say is out there, may not really be out there. It's not an uncommon fact to catch wind of somethin' that sounds too good to be anythin' other than fresh bullshit. And no one would fault ya for fallin' prey. It's like a virus, sometimes ya just get it. And it is true, like ya said, trust is a hard thing to come by."

"You just need to keep lookin'," he said, as confident as ever, "keep lookin' and keepin' the faith while you're lookin'."

I walked out onto the balcony and he followed. We both leaned against the rail and it just felt right, standin' there. But it also felt wrong. This whole quest of his, the search, his mind may still be in its place but maybe the place had changed. I'd seen people go just a little bit crazy, all the way to being absolutely nuts, six bullets shy of a full chamber. Sanity out in the world was not a common thing to find, at least not fully. And any that could be found, usually didn't last once someone on the opposite end of the spectrum caught wind of their existence.

"It's been too long to recall an exact number of days since people have... lived with civility, civilization. And I know there ain't no goin' back to that sort of life, only a fool would believe it so. I just, I want to *try* to. The people of the country, and of the world I'm sure, have been burning enough. I have an eye for the future, Mahon. I want to be able to share that view, and not just with the right people, but with everyone. But in order to get there, a series of choices will have to be made. As with any foundation that must be built, ground must also be broken," he always said these sorts of things with a serious but hopeful ring in his voice, a hopeful melody, almost bent entirely on the assumption that I understood his need and his purpose. Gunther Ostrander was far and wide a man of speeches, and most times even when he wasn't givin' one, he just sounded like someone you could believe in, even if you knew it deep down to be bullshit. Like Blackheart Mountain... I can't obviously speak with absolute certainty on the matter, but I'd spent quite a fair amount of time out there in the world lookin' for it. The idea of Blackheart Mountain was startin' to really feel more like a bad joke made by some poor fool long ago who told it to someone who in turn didn't find it funny.

"I don't doubt it," I said, "maybe you're right. Maybe I just need to keep lookin'. But I'm getting' tired of being left emptyhanded, honestly. I'm not an easily discouraged man, but this is roundin' that corner pretty fast."

"I hear ya, Mahon, I hear ya. I know it can't be easy out there, I want you to know that I recognize your sacrifice with the utmost appreciation. It's why I think so highly of you," he replied. From the direction of the quarry, there suddenly came a crash and a burst of smoke and dust. Ostrander groaned, slapping the top of the railing, "Goddamnit," he said, "I keep tellin' em to grease the gears and they won't have any problems. Minin', I tell ya, Mahon. It's not as glamorous as it sounds in all those stories of yore. Maybe I ought to bring back whips for crackin'. I'll be back. You just rest up for a while, whatever ya need. Head back out soon though, the problem with searching for somethin' that can cure the world is that no matter how mythical you may think it is, there is always someone *else* out there doin' the same thing you are, even if you haven't run into em yet."

And with that, he left the office.

I stayed out on the balcony, it was rare to find this kind of undisturbed respite. About a mile, maybe less, in just about every direction, Ostrander had had a concrete and steel-reinforced wall built with only one gate, the gate that was opened for me whether I was re-turnin' or leavin'. At the gate there were a dozen armed guards at any given time, on constant switch outs so as to maintain a dependable level of strength, attitude, and efficiency amongst the ranks, and even more of these specially-trained and assigned men patrolled the ram-parts of the wall all the way around. So up here on the balcony overlooking the valley and the quarry, one had no need to worry. Not about interlopers. Not about food or drink. Not about a damn thing. As far as I was con-cerned, and anyone else residing within the encircling concrete barrier, this place was the safest place on earth.

Just as I was to leave the office, the door opened inward, and in she stepped. She had her hair tied back, it had been more brown the last time I saw her, but she still looked pretty as ever.

"Oh," I said, stepping out of her way, "I'm sorry."

"You always say that," she said with a smile, "you don't have to say those things to me."

Cassandra Ostrander was Gunther's wife, married since before he and I met. There isn't much to tell about her, at least not worth retelling in a less than romantic way. I've known her for as long as I've known her husband, and that might be the most tragic thing of all.

She stood there, closing the door behind her. We looked at each other waiting for the other to say something. Something like "it's good to see you again" or "How've ya been?" Instead, we kissed. She pulled me in nearly knocking the hat off my head. I felt her small hands grasp either side of my face, her lips pressing hard against mine. When finally we decided we'd had enough of the embrace, we pulled away from one another with the quick exchange of a smile.

"It's good to see ya again," I said.

"How've ya been?" she asked.

"Oh just," I removed the hat from my head, running the other hand through my hair, "the usual business, I guess."

She smiled, nodding slowly. Cassandra never asked about her husband's work, at least the work he assigned to me. She knew what kind of man I was, Hell, she might have been the only woman in the world who knew what kind of man I was, and still loved me for it.

"I, uh, found something you might like," I said, reaching into the inside pocket of my coat. I removed the flower, a white pretty little thing with a yellow center, the green stem still mostly intact. "Found it a little way's west from here. Took me by surprise when I saw it, almost thought it wasn't real. It wasn't the only one though, so I picked the prettiest one."

She took it and smirked.

"You mean you picked the one that *you* thought was prettiest, not the one *I* may have thought was prettiest, why not pick them all and let me decide," she said this seriously at first, but then smirked. "Shouldn't have done that," she said, "if it was the prettiest one, you should've let it be. You could have brought me out there and just showed it to me, and you would've conveyed the same emotion you are now."

"You're right," I said, trying to hide the guilt in my voice. But she smiled still.

"Still," she said, "it's a pretty thing to look at. I have something for you too, thought it's not exactly a flower. I have some news that came to me while you were away."

"Oh really?"

"The doctor said she's healthy," Cassandra said, a slow smile of a different sort beginning to spread across her face.

"She?"

"Yea," Cassandra said.

I moved in closer, putting a cautious hand to her stomach.

"We're going to have a daughter?"

"Seems that way. The doc said the tests aren't as accurate as the old days, but it does seem that way," a tear welled up and fell from Cassandra's left eye. A happy tear, something no one sees much of anywhere these days.

"We're having a daughter," I said again. Cassandra had not yet begun to show physical signs of the pregnancy, but already her husband had been correct in his assumption as to her condition. Of course, he had no idea as to the truth behind such a thing. Cassandra and I had been careful, with an almost horrifying precision. She and I could never be what we wanted to be, not now. I brought it up to her once, that we could sit down with Gunther and explain things, but even I didn't believe that. Gunther was not the sort of man to let something like this be simply "talked about". Cassandra was absolutely right in saying that he would destroy both of us if the truth were ever revealed to him. He wouldn't simply have us killed. He'd feed us to his pet beasts alive. We would feel every bite, every tooth and claw as they ate us. He'd done this sort of thing to anyone who betrayed him. And I'd always been there, forced to watch. Gunther said he needed me strong, being the highest in both rank and respect employed on his payroll. He needed me to see every ounce of horrific punishment. He said one day I would be trapped in unforeseeably horrible situations with these memories to look back on, to hold on to, a rope to pull myself out of the dark and high up to a safe place. And even as terrifying as those executions had been, I felt as though Gunther would do far worse to myself and Cassandra if he ever found out. The "commodity" of truth, as he put it, was priceless, though it was not without consequence.

"Are you going to the feast tonight?"

"The feast," I said vacantly.

"You remember, don't you? Gunther is having a festival of sorts. To honor the day he earned this place."

"Oh, you meant to say, a whole festival to brag about the memory of his victory in taking this place over from its last occupants," I laughed, "how humble of him.

I still don't know how you can stand him. I can't imagine what he must've done to get you to love him."

"Not everyone starts out being an intolerable creature, Mahon," she said, almost sternly, defensively, "I'm sure even you were prince-like one day long ago."

"Never, ever," I said. "I don't think festivals are really what I'm about, anyway, lady. Besides, I have to head out early tomorrow. I think I might have a few drinks and for the first time in some weeks, go to bed early, and comfortably."

"I see," she said. "So, you don't have time for a dance with me? With me and your daughter to be?"

"You and I both know that's not a good idea."

"He'd never suspect a thing," she said, "he has his mind on other matters, as you know. To him, right now, I'm just someone to help keep him warm at night, the nights he does actually come to bed. And this," she motioned to her belly, "for all he's concerned about, is *his* child, and that's all he needs to know."

"I'm already pretty tired," I said.

"You'll be there," she said, a little too confidently, "you always do this *big strong man* thing, and then you show up anyway. I know you too well, Mahon. You may be out there in world where everyone sees the worst parts of you, the parts you need to survive, but I know all the rest of you. The parts that matter, that one day our daughter will be taught about. When she grows up, she'll know that her father, was... a good man."

She left quietly.

She was right, as she usually was. Cassandra had a way with letting me know that I was going to do the things I said I wouldn't do. She said it with her words, but with a strength most of today's women only dream of having. Maybe that's where it began for me, the love I had for her.

It was as dependable a thing as any rock in the world rolling down a hillside to keep right on rollin' until it stops, to find the cart on wheels in my room waitin' for me. Ostrander knew my tastes, which weren't hard to surmise after bein' around me for a while, and by extension knew that money had always been the primary incentive for taking his jobs. A cart on wheels topped with bottles of whiskey, bourbon, vodka, and a jug of dark beer always waited for me in my room on the first night of my arrival after coming back from the world. It was a heavy thing, carrying the weight of a failed task, something that sounds as simple as finding a mountain, of all things. Although, locatin' one particular mountain in a world of mountains would never be as easy as drinking one of these bottles in a single pullback.

I grabbed the bottle of whiskey first and popped off the cork. I smelled the contents inside and instantly forgot about my woes, the bright red letter text inside my head that screamed "DEAD", because hell, if my eyes couldn't find a mountain out there, I might as well be dead.

My room had its own balcony, and from here I could see the quarry where the workers spent their days mining and digging and whatever else Ostrander required. Night had fallen, so in every direction there was pitch blackness. Had the skies been clear, I'd see mountain ranges stretching every which way. I'd see the great barrier wall and its gate. I'd see trees upon trees and the cracked earth. I'd see the far-off ruins of fallen cities, their skyscrapers hollow, lifeless husks now a blink away from collapsing to the ground amongst the others that'd since fallen in the days gone by. I'd see the stars, something I quite enjoyed during the summer months. The stars and the moon, and all the planets far out of reach. I'd see all these things if it weren't for the winter clouds always overhead, always taking away the light of the universe.

From the balcony, I drank the whiskey and let some of the liquid roll over my lips and down my chin. The liquid burned away the chappedness, the burn stung and I may have winced against it had I been focusing less on something else. Cassandra. The more I drank, the more the image of her form became skewed and fogged, much like the winter clouds' hatred for the stars above them, a vendetta of obscurity. Except I did not want her image to be obscured. It was simply the other edge on the other side of the sword, the simplification of boundaries. At least with the whiskey, I did not have to grapple with the feelings which come when it came time for her to blend into the rest of the nothingness. I could just keep on drinking. I could finish the bottle, and cradle the next. And so that's what I did. I drank, and the took a hold of the woman in my mind, Cassandra, we danced until I believed to be true, the sound the sheets on the bed made when the weight of our bodies pressed against them, a sound that only skin on cloth can make.

III.
And STILL
a DANCE YET to be HAD

For a world that had burned nearly entirely to ground so long ago, there were tiny pockets of civilization that could still be found in which the people existed with a sense of calmness, and gratitude for life itself. Gunther Ostrander's mining factory, and the quarry beside it, the townsfolk living in the hip-side town, New Canterton, was such one of those places. During the day, the factory moved as any other factory does, spewing spoke into the air as the mining processes processed. And to the north, the quarry came alive with workers as they did Gunther's bidding, sweating and bleeding, sometimes to their own deaths. But at night, such as this one very night, when Gunther held these memorial festivals to immortalize his own past, the people whom he held under this thumb came alive in a different way. This was the side of them that appreciated the strictness of his rule. All of the violence he could, and sometimes did, inflict upon them to get the work done, was suddenly forgiven. It was as though they had all been led to believe that there was no other way of life, no other way to successfully survive the cruelty of the wasteland outside their borders. It was embedded into their minds, and played out fantastically in their dreams while they slept. To venture out beyond the concrete wall, was to accept not only death, but carnage. I didn't agree with every strategy Gunther used to oversee his people. Their fears about what the world outside their own was capable of were not all that far off from the truth, but on nights like tonight, that all went to bed. And these festivals were, in a way, Gunther's kinder side giving back to the people.

The festival always took place in this clearing behind the factory, that somewhat fell between the factory and the town. There were strings of lanterns hung up that gave off a warm, golden glow. Music played from a quartet of men Gunther had assembled from the talents he'd discovered in them years ago, talents he discovered as he put it by mistake while listening to some of the workers sing while they worked. He was able to procure and restore several instruments from nearby settlements that had once been sprawling cities and in no time, he had his own band playing whenever he felt like it, saving the best songs to be played during his festival. I wasn't the biggest fan of these sorts of gatherings. I didn't feel truthful to myself whenever I stepped out onto the dance clearing, even if I filled that time with dances in Cassandra's arms. Gunther never seemed to care, despite my insecurities. He was never one for dancing either, though he demonstrated a stronger hate for it, and in his eyes exhibited his love for Cassandra by allowing her to dance with anyone whom she wanted because he knew how much she liked to do it. And it always just happened to be me she chose to dance with. Tonight was no different.

As soon as I walked out onto the wooden clearing, she spotted me, and grabbed a hold of my free hand, pulling me the rest of the way toward the center of the dance floor. The music was slow, but relaxing, the players playing strings along the beat of a light drum. Cassandra positioned one of my hands on her hip and took the other in her own hand.

"Jesus, Mahon," she laughed, "no matter how

many times we do this it's like you can never remember the proper placement."

"Well, I'm a fool for a myriad of reasons," I said, trying my best to follow her feet, trying even harder to stay in step. "It keeps me up at night, trying to figure out how you could have found yourself a much better dance partner by now, but remain reluctant. It's frustrating, lady. You're frustrating."

"Yes but," and she drew close so as to whisper in my right ear, "nobody else steps on my feet quite like you do."

We danced two dances, and then retired to the bar, where I had me a glass of brown whiskey from one of the finite bottles Gunther had tracked down and acquired. And Cassandra drank a warm beer, despite there being the option of having a cold one. The world had ended, of course, but one of the few remaining conveniences left over from the generations passed, was that of refrigeration. It was easily maintained with the technology left over, but of course, only those in high places still had access to said technology. People like Gunther Ostrander. Cassandra said drinking a warm beer comforted her in a way a cold beer only cheapened her disposition, whatever the hell that meant.

Sometime during my second glass of brown whiskey, the music began to slow, and I suppose that excited something in Cassandra. She grabbed my hand again and took me to the dance floor. Once we arrived where she wanted to be, she told me to put both of my hands on her hips and to pull her close. I told her no, because, hell, Gunther might be alright with us doing a jig here and there, but what she wanted now was the deep, slow, romantic kind of dance. Gunther would not be a fan of that.

"I don't give a rat's ass about that man," she

said, "I'm here with you now. You're here with me. And he's planning his next big endeavor. You're mine now, and any time I get with you I'm not likely to just slip away. Now dance with me the way a man and woman are meant to dance."

I sighed, because it was all I could do. And then I did as she told me. I held her close. I felt her head rest against my chest. I felt the tips of her fingers gently caress the back of my neck where the hair grew thin. As the music played, I couldn't help but feel the littlest bit of sadness.

Cassandra moved on from our dance to see to other guests, her friends, I suppose. I took to the bar again and found a stool so comfortable, I thought I might sit there until the sun came up. I ordered my usual, the nicest glass of whiskey my credit as one of Ostrander's employees could buy, and spun around to watch the crowd. It wasn't until then that I noticed the figure standin' next to me was someone I had been familiar with in the past, but had not seen in too long a time.

Ever since I first met Frank Delmont, he'd been a guiding light in the darkest of my travels. You could say he taught me most everything I knew today, minus the experiences he didn't have a personal hand in. He worked for Ostrander just as I did, though the last I recall he handled the "lower spectrum" on the list of important matters, simply because he'd earned his right to work in a relaxed state. He didn't sit in the stool beside me, but rather stood, leaning forward with both elbows atop the wooden slab. He smelled like he'd been drinking since breakfast, and really, a man like him deserved to. And there were times I saw a little bit of my future self in his present-day boots.

"Delmont," I said, "well ho-lee shit."

He turned his head just enough so that his sideview included my person, and when he saw that it was me, a faint grin creased his half-shaven cheek. He drank from his glass and licked his lips.

"That you, *Ran-cid* Mahoney," he asked, shaking his head, "never did understand the meanin' of that name."

"Legend says my parents were two very fucked up individuals. I wouldn't know the extent of that," I said, "I'm surprised to see ya. You never struck me as the kinda guy to attend these sorts of gatherings."

"I'm not. I like to think of tonight as a sort of retirement party, just nobody knows it but me, and now you," he drank more.

"Retirement?"

"I'm done with it all, Mahon. I told Gunther when I got back from this last job, I was done. And so I'm back, and so I'm done."

"Why's that?"

"It's just my time, old buddy," he said, "I've done the rounds. I've earned enough. I've risked enough. I've survived enough. It's time I take some time for myself, before my mind goes to mush." He turned around in his stance, facing out into the crowd, nodding as if he were conversing with only himself, more than agreeing, wholeheartedly accepting. "You know... it doesn't matter how skilled a man is, his survival, I'm sayin'. All those abilities to fend for himself. His will to survive, eating bone marrow from an ill-fed rat just to keep himself goin' one more mile. How to sleep, make one's self invisible long enough for the wrong eyes to go away. Eventually a man's ability to live ceases to be. Not his will, but his ability. It happens to everyone. I want to... do something for myself, for a change, before that happens to

62 | DAVE MATTHES

me."

"You're the toughest guy I know."

He shook his head with a sympathetic smile.

"That's not what I'm talkin' about, Mahon. Anyone can be tough. You listen to me, Mahon. And listen good. The only way I survived this long is by abiding by a set of principles, just a list of ideals that made the killin' and the darker stuff easier, and in many cases, seem more logical. I learned from experience, by seein' other guys fall prey to it, they let themselves forget that it was business, and they couldn't differentiate from when it was pure survival. And that neglect, that complete and utter abandonment happened just at the right time needed for them to lose their heads. I promise ya, Mahon, it'll happen to you. It didn't happen to me because I didn't let it. But that's also why I'm done. I got this feelin' the other night that if I kept goin' with that mindset for much longer, it would make me into a man that is no longer a man. We've already done so many things in the name of currency, but that's just the world, and we've accepted it. There has to be some law each individual man keeps to, that he... that he keeps sacred."

Delmont seemed to forget I was there for a moment, and in that moment he finished his glass and placed it on the bartop behind him, waving off the barkeep when he offered another drink. Delmont adjusted his stance, leaning now with one elbow back on the bartop.

"We can't let the world get us while we're still alive," he said.

"So then," I started, "where ya headed off to?"

"Now if I told anyone, wouldn't that defeat the purpose of leavin' this place behind?" But he smiled at it, regardless of the logic he once instilled in me to never,

ever let anyone who might consider you a loose end aware of where you might be. "A long time ago I told myself if I ever did retire, I'd head east. So that's where I'm gonna go." He stood all the way up and patted me on the back, adjusting his hat. "I'm tellin' ya that because you're the only one I trust with that sort of information. And maybe, if you're up to it one day, you can come find me, and we'll just be two old farts. Retired, and having only to *wait* to die, instead of fightin' to prevent it."

Frank Delmont walked away, his walk coming with a barely noticeable unhinged quality that could be attributed to however many glasses of booze he'd consumed. Or perhaps he'd simply sustained enough injury or absorbed enough personal horror to have permanently cursed his temperament. But even with the limp, his stride was dark and obvious against the lively and jovial crowd, and as he blended in with the people, slowly growing more and more imperceptible to sight, Frank Delmont become a featureless stranger. He didn't look at anyone around him, and if they looked his way all they'd see is a man with only one thing left to do.

"That man right there, is a legend," the man's voice came from the one, and the only Douglass Flood, another of Gunther's guns for hire. He wasn't exactly the smartest man chosen to untangle a spiderweb from a thornbush, but Gunther had a purpose and a reason for hiring everyone. Douglass and I did a few jobs together until I told Gunther I was walkin' unless he stopped puttin' him with me. Douglass Flood was a man with an idiot face and an idiot voice, and whoever worked with him who wasn't careful, they'd eventually find themselves deader than dead because of his idiot-level stupidity. I didn't like him, but because he also worked for Gunther P. Ostrander, killin' him was just outta the question.

"Yea," I said.

"Ya think maybe one day, we'll walk away from a joint like this, with hair the same color, and with a stride just like that?" Douglass Flood drank tequila from a small glass, and he sweat from his temples all the way down his neck into his undershirt. The man smelled lie shit pie, and on his breath danced a ballet of shattered childhood hopes.

"I dunno about any of that," I said, disinterested, trying to let him know I didn't feel like talkin' without having to put in the work of actually having to tell him so.

"Aspirations are a good thing, Mahon," he said to me, drinking his drink, "aspirations give a man a sense of purpose. It outlines their shape, ya know, their... physical shape. Changes him in the end, too. That Frank Delmont, phew, whew boy... he's got a shadow behind him."

"Listen, Doug, I'm not terribly excited about the idea of conversing with anyone right now. So, if ya don't mind, I'd just like to enjoy my drink, alone," I said.

"And then there's you," his tone deepened, and I knew it was the drink talkin' because any time he happened to be completely sober, he would never have taken that tone with me. He learned that bare-knuckle lesson a long time ago. "A grump on a stump. Just takin' jobs and gettin' paid for em."

"Seems alright to me," I said, "suits me just fine. Better than subcontracting unfortunate folks to do the dirty work for me. How many unsuspecting brutes you got in your little posse these days?"

"I'm not sure a man like you is full of the kinda trust that gives weight to his steps," Douglass said. I turned to look at him, and told him with my eyes to calm it down, to take it down a level. He was already drenched in his own sweat and he looked as though one more drink might end his night and start his day with a sledgehammer headache.

"Finish your drink, Doug," I said to him, "then go to bed. I promise ya can do any job Gunth' gives ya with a full mouth of teeth, maybe even a half-full mouth, but ya won't be able to impregnate his horses if you inspire me to break your arms."

Douglass took the hint and downed his drink, patting me on the shoulder.

"You're right, Mahon. You. You're always right," he said, stepping away, "That's your damn talent right there. You're always right."

I turned back to the barkeep and he already knew what I was goin' to ask for.

The following morning, just before the sky would start to change from early-morning grey to mid-morning-grey, I'd saddled up my horse, a large breed whom Gunther had affectionately referred to as Gunpowder. Through my experience with her, I'd decided that Gunpowder was not at all a good name for such a beast. When something, a horse, a dog, or anything really, is given a name like "Gunpowder", one might assume that said creature has a spark about them, something fierce and formidable. A beast named "Gunpowder" trampled the world with each step. Gunther's Gunpowder was anything but that. She was sweet, and I don't mean to say that as an insult. She was unusually sweet, even to someone like me, near the beginning where we sniff each other's breaths just to get a better idea of one another. She never bucked, never tossed me. Gunpowder was more of a friend to me than my old man, and I won't even try to explain that one further.

She was quiet when the road demanded it so. By the fire each night, she stood as a guard stands, except I doubted she'd have it in her to put anyone down if it ever came to such a thing. As such, I renamed her. I started calling her Eleanor, after a name I'd seen on a gravestone that hadn't been completely rubbed away. She seemed to like it, but I can't really explain how I knew that. Whenever we made eye contact, she knew something about me even I never knew. I suppose that's about as strong as a bond between horse and man can get.

Eleanor had been sick from a colony of intestinal leeches having made home inside of her digestive track for the last few months, which was why I was just seein' her now for the first time in what felt like ages. I rested the brow of my head against hers and we both recognized each other. It was our way of tellin' each other the sweet things.

"So they got ya fixed up, did they," I said to her, "well, that's good, girl. I dunno about anyone else in your life, but I've sure missed ya."

We bumped heads again and her shiny eyes glinted with a mutual feeling. It was just us again.

And so, just as I climbed up into the saddle and patted her oak brown, muscular neck, Gunther walked up toward us with an eager expression on his face. He looked like he hadn't slept a wink in a week. Dark circles hung beneath his eyes, giving him an almost-dead look.

"Hey hold up there a sec, Mahon," he said. I already knew what he was going to say just by reading his smile. He wore the same smile every damn time.

"I'm already in the middle of the last assignment you bestowed upon me, Gunth'," I said to him. "Takin' on extra work can complicate things, like payment."

"I know," he said, "I know. But you're headed to

Vermouth, right?"

"That's sometimes my first stop when I ride north," I said back.

"I got a favor to ask of you. It's not something I'd typically give to you because you're unquestionably worth more than that. I'd just as soon have one of my regulars take care of it except none of my regulars are around, killed maybe, or just deserting. Like I said, I'm losing men by the week."

"Out with it."

"Well, I'm in a bit of a picklepit, Mahon. See one of my workers down in the quarry, unbeknownst to me apparently, is a criminal. Killed a man or two, or three, whatever, just outside of Vermouth. Turns out one of those men was the mayor of Vermouth's brother. You remember Henry Kenroy, civilized man. Word evidently got around that the man who killed his brother is stayin' here, workin' the quarry. And the mayor of Vermouth, whom I am in very good standing with as you know, has requested that he be sent to Vermouth so that he can be seen by the proper... authorities. I figure, since you're headed that way anyway, you could just bring him along with ya."

"Not a chance in Hell," I shook my head, giving Eleanor a little kick to get going.

"Mahon, come on now," he pleaded, grabbing a hold of one of Eleanor's reigns. I look him dead in the face.

"Hands off my horse, Ostrander."

He took a moment to realize what he'd done, and complied, letting his hand fall back to his side.

"This is important, Mahon," he said.

"Not a chance. I'm not that sort of hire. I'm better'n that sorta work and you know it."

"I'll pay ya double if he gets there dead or alive,"

Gunther said, "triple if he's alive."

"Babysittin' some poor sucker all the way to Vermouth will only slow me up. And then, I'll have to track down the damn smelly-ss, cactus rat mayor, which will only slow me up more. I don't ever stay for longer than a few drinks in that town, if any at all. It's best to just pass right on through. That whole area up there is Crimson Collar territory, you know that."

"Yes, but," he said, "you're a smart guy. You know how to handle yourself. That's part of why I hired ya. You know how to improvise better than the best."

"Every man gets killed one way or another, Gunth'. Every man. He can't escape it. And the way I live, I'd like that day to be later than sooner."

"Do you want to know a secret, Mahon? I've never had to fire a gun once, not once, in my entire life. It's not that I'm a coward, I've just... through various failures and successes alike, found that it pays more to always know someone who *will* fire a gun. Ya know I, uh," Gunther seemed anxious, a tone of voice under his breath unfamiliar to me.

"You're bein' a little unlike yourself, boss," I said.

He stood with his hands on his waist and he kicked a small pebble. "I just found out that uh, that I'm havin' a girl. That we... Cassandra and I. We're havin' a little girl."

I didn't say anything back.

"I'd like to be there for her while she's growin' up, as long as I can. If I don't get this guy back up north, it'll cause an unnecessary rift between Vermouth and New Canterton, and by extension, Mayor Henry Kenroy and myself. I'm goin' to be a father, Mahon. I can't be takin' those kinds of risks anymore."

I didn't say anything back.

I sat in the saddle with Eleanor motionless. I turned to face Gunther, a signature of mine that let him know I was in agreeance. Reluctant agreeance, but agreeance nonetheless. His expression began to heighten, and he nodded.

"Wait right here," he said, "I won't be more than a few minutes getting' him."

"I bet you're gettin' as tired of this shit as I am, aren't ya girl," I said to Eleanor. Her tail swished, which could only mean she agreed with me. "I've gotta learn to just say no, ya know? Maybe we ought to leave, make our way east like old Delmont. I hear the people out there are different. A little less... ambitious. Maybe that's what we need, girl."

A little wait later, Gunther was walking another horse out with a man riding in the saddle. His hands were bound in leather, and his hair dirty, unwashed, like the other workers in the quarry. And he wore something over his face, something metal that seemed to be purposed for inhibiting his ability to speak, as mostly the lower half of his face was covered. Gunther stopped just beside Eleanor and attached a metal chain from my saddle, to the other rider's.

"This here is Til Drange," Gunther said, "he's worked in a quarry for a few years. Good worker, or so I've heard. I don't, uh... before today, believe I've... ever actually met him face to... *face*, heh. So, I hate to be losing him to the hangman. But the law is the law, or that's what they say."

"What's with the... thing on his face," I asked.

"Oh that? Oh, don't mind that. That's just so he can't bother ya with his talk. See, he's a good worker, but he's kind of an asshole too, according to the quarry masters. I've heard some reports about him that label Drange as being rather mouthy when he gets the chance.

I know it's a few days ride north, so only take it off to let him eat."

I let a grunt out to let Gunther know I was perturbed, as little as it mattered.

"You get to Vermouth," Gunther started, "ask for Mayor Henry Kenroy as soon as ya do. He's especially eager to receive Mr. Drange here. I would imagine a death sentence at the end of a noose is not far out of the question, but for a crime as personal as he committed, I doubt it'll be a quick death," he patted Til Drange's thigh encouragingly. "Anyway, get on out of here. It's a long road like ya said. And it feels like winter is comin' on a little sooner than it did last year." There was indeed a brisk wind coming down from the mountains. Already I could smell the snowfall coming. It would only get worse the farther north we rode.

"If it gets too cold and I can't find any wood, I'm using Mr. Drange's body, here," I said to Gunther. "I ain't freezin' to death for no man who's takin' his last ride anyway."

"I know you're joking," Gunther said, "but in the event you aren't, if he doesn't get to Vermouth alive, don't come back around here. Not even if you find Blackheart."

"Interesting to hear you make that kind of threat," I said, nodding to the wind, "I'll keep that in mind. You ready, Mr. Drange?" I looked the man in the face, into his eyes where I could still make out what kind of a man he was even with the hunk of metal covering the rest of his expression. He didn't say anything, of course. But then again, he didn't do much of anything. He looked me in the eye as I did to him, but there wasn't much I could make out. "Well, now. I guess that makes me the fool in expectin' anything out of ya. You know where you're goin'. I'm sorry that I have to be the one to take ya. I'm not much company on long rides. And I don't much like strangers either. Although, I suppose every person I ever grew to care for was at one time or another a stranger to me."

We rode out along the path toward the gate in Gunther's concrete barrier wall. As we approached, the guards nodded, acknowledging me, and the doors opened, contraption after contraption operating to release its hold. The doors slowly swung open in an outward direction, and before us, the world stretched out and away, waiting. At the exact moment the doors shut behind us, the first tiny flakes of snow began to tumble down from the sky.

The road north, which eventually led to the settlement of Vermouth, was not an actual road, nor had it been one of the concrete highways of the past. The "road" was a slight indenture in the land formed by years of habitual travel, bends in the grasses from too many boots, horses, or wagon wheels. This "road" dug into the dirt and the fields of the land and through a rocky terrain not all that hard to traverse, even to the uninitiated. At first, the ground lay level, an assemblage of small hills capped with sun-bleached grasses and flora that seemed to bloom whether it was winter or spring. Without my tow, I could reach the town in a day, maybe a day and a half if I didn't run into trouble. But with this load... this "Til Drange", we travelled at a slower pace. It's never smart to ride full speed when you're escorting someone of so-called importance who absolutely must get to his destination.

"Ever been to Vermouth," I asked Drange, not at all expecting him to respond, "no? Word on the street says ya have, or around those parts at the least. Well, my opinion it's not a very exciting town. They call it the Last Warm Town because of the snows. The northwestern road out of town leads right into the harshest mountain road in the region, where even durin' the summer months the white fluffy stuff can fall from the sky. I've been there, to the town. But I make it a point to drop in for as few visits as possible, and whenever I do find myself there it's never for very long. Ya ever heard of the Crimson Collars? Sure ya have," I said, "guns for hire, like me I suppose. Actually they really aren't like me at all. I work alone. And these Crimson Collar folk, they're pretty organized. And when a gang is organized they get shit done a lot more efficiently, but don't take that as a regard of respect. I'd kill every single one of em on sight out here," I looked at Drange. His head hung heavily against the weight of the metal device attached to his head. His ears were exposed so I knew he could hear me. He made no effort to let me know he was listening, however. "Ever hear of a man named Mancino Rolandraz? Woo, nasty fellah. He's the head of the Crimson Collars. Doesn't make many public appearances, if he can muster it. He does all his dealings in private, and through vicarious stand-ins. Keeps him safe, I guess. This is all, just, rumors, of course. I could be spittin' complete lies or half-truths. People like their street talk and their gossip, gives em a sense of security, I think. I can tell you're bored, so I'll shut up," I said.

On the first night, after I got the fire going, I helped him down from his saddle, leading him over to a log upon which he could sit on.

"Now," I started, "I suppose I should take that thing off of your face so you can eat something. I do have that as a permission."

His eyes met mine as if waiting for me to start

disassembling the thing.

"Trouble is, I'm sorry to say, is that I really have no idea how to get this thing off of ya," I laughed to myself, "I guess I should've asked the old boss to fill me in on all that. You wouldn't happen to know how to get out of it, would ya?"

He nodded his head slowly, motioning with his head toward his hands that were still bound, telling me that he could get it off but only if his hands were free. I laughed at that, probably a little too hard.

"Wow," I said, "you must really think I'm a special kind of stupid to do that. Maybe I just, not let you eat tonight. A man can live a scarily long time without ingesting food, I know. But, I'm not what you'd say... a cruel man. And personally, taking you on this trip is less of a pain in the ass than most things I've done for Gunther," I unsheathed my knife, and cut his bindings, "you take that thing off, and maybe I'll have someone to talk to for a while. Or maybe I don't like the sound of your voice and accidentally kill you with this knife. Slice your throat so that you never say another word."

Drange did something to the back of the metal head piece, pressed something and switched something else. I couldn't be sure really. He did it so fast that when he lifted it off his head, he tossed it to the ground and yawned, licking his lips and cracking his jaw.

"Thank you," were his first words to me.

"Eh, not such an annoying voice, not yet anyway."

He didn't say much at first. I cooked up some sausages and gave him half of what I made. He scarfed the food down like he hadn't eaten in a month. He finished his plate before I finished my first bite. I felt bad for him. Pity, I guess it was called. I slowly offered him my own plate. He looked at me like I was crazy.

"But then you won't eat," he said.

"I'll make more," I said.

"I'm assuming you've rationed your food. Won't making more this early on our little voyage upset that design?"

"I hunt better than I cook, if you can't already tell by the blandness of these sausages," I said, "anything I need is out here amongst the dirt and the trees. I'll be just fine." He took the plate from me and ate my portion faster than his own. "They don't feed you workers in the quarry?"

"Ha," Drange laughed, "that's a good one."

"I say somethin' funny?"

"Yea, ya did," Drange said while I threw another sausage on the iron skillet, "the part about us being fed, I mean, we're fed, but it ain't no delectable sausage link cooked over a fire out in the wilderness. And the part about us being *workers*. Workers, wow. That second part was particularly funny."

"That's what you are, unless I'm missing something."

"*You* work for Ostrander. You do a job. You come back. You get paid. What? Did ya think I was just some shmuck from town who needed work so I asked the bastard for it? I'm from out here... way out here. I come from the *land*. I've got earth in my fuckin' blood, pal. Earth. Not a single one of those poor *workers* asked to be there. How long ya work for Gunther?"

"It's been a while," I said after a moment of contemplation, as to whether or not I should put the metal thing back on this guy's face, "few years maybe more, maybe less."

"But a decent amount of time, you'd say. Long enough to have seen how his business really makes its wealth. Or, long enough to be blind to the man's real business," Drange snatched the half-cooked sausage off the skillet with his bare hand, taking a bite into it before I could take it back. He chewed, swallowed and bit off another piece. "That man is a bad, bad man, let me tell you," he laughed, finishing the meat.

"The man has a questionable set of morals, I'd say, but I wouldn't go as far as saying he's a bad man," I said. "I've met worse, and I've killed worse."

"You only say that because he pays you," Drange said, "he pays everyone that he needs, and that's the whole rub of the coyote. Pays everyone, except the *workers* in the quarry."

We sat around the fire for a while in silence. I didn't much care to hear the man speak any more than what I'd already heard. He could have been telling the truth, but he also knew where I was taking him. A man in that position will say just about anything to get out of certain death, if that is what he feared most. He stayed on his side of the fire, willingly allowing me to chain his ankle to the ankle of his own horse. Eleanor stayed still next to that horse, I imagined the two of them sharing war stories, having some kind of conversation havin' something to do with flies or how horses used to live way back in the day before the world-ending war. Til Drange spent most of this time listening, and looking up into the night sky. He bundled up against the cold, but didn't appear uncomfortable. More noticeably, he didn't wear the mannerisms of a man who was patiently waiting for his transporter to fall asleep. He showed no nervousness, no alertness to what I was doing on the other side of the fire.

It wasn't until his eyes started to flutter with sleepiness that I took my own noticing of something else in the night. The flames glowed lowly, but still against the night sky, and even darker darkness carved its way toward us. One figure at first, followed closely by three others. They were all dressed in similar clothing, leather wraps around their bodies, their skin tanned and darkened even under the moonlight. The one standing out ahead of the others, presumably the leader of the group, bore markings of some kind of paint across his brow and upon his cheeks. Drange sat up from where he lay, startled but not afraid. He looked around as if to grab for a rifle for protection. But I had all the weapons, and my rifle had already been drawn, aimed for the main with the painted face.

"Who are you," the man with the painted face started. His voice came out low in volume, subtle, but the man commanded it with a force that could uproot an entire forest.

"About to ask you the same thing, chief," I said.

"I am not the Chief. And you are on Tuskatawa land," the man said.

"Tuskatawa," I said, "you know what? I've heard of you people. Very little, though. I do believe I've seen some of you from afar, but never up this close. So please do excuse the fact that I have my rifle aimed for you head. This is somewhat of a new experience for me- coming into contact with... Tuskatawa... not aiming a rifle for someone's head."

"We are not a people that makes ourselves known, often."

"I know," I said, "you're people one with nature, that metaphysical stuff. You keep to the mountains."

"I ask again," he said, raising his voice a little higher, and I thought the ground might shake because of it, "who *are* you?"

"Well, this here fellah with the chain around his

ankle is Til Drange; prisoner, and son of a bitch. And I'm Rancid Mahoney, just a guy with a job to do. We're headed up the road, which I know for a fact is not on *Tuskatawa* land, up to to Vermouth, a settlement that is also *not* on Tuskatawa land. See this here prisoner of mine apparently has some swingin' to do at the rude end of a rope. So, now that I have answered your question, maybe you can answer mine. Why do you think we're on *Tuskatawa* land?"

The man with the painted face, from behind the firelight stood firm and unmoved by my proclamation. But I knew I was right. This was not Tuskatawa land. The Tuskatawa were just a tribe of people, supposedly assembled a long time ago at the time civilization fell to its knees. Anything I've heard of them was of course pure rumor, speculation, myth, legend. They were a quiet people, at least as long as I'd been on this earth. The most popular rumor regarding them told tale of a long-ago and far away era, around the time the world first fell. At the time there'd only been a small group of them; men and women who claimed to have native blood running through their veins. They founded the tribe, taking civilization's collapse as a sign from their gods whom even they themselves had grown to forget about. As I mentioned to this man with the painted face a moment ago, I'd never crossed paths with one up close, and I never ever expected to. It was honestly, a little alarming.

"Something has begun," Til Dange suddenly spoke up.

"Come again," I asked, while the man with the painted face and his three companions stood still.

"You see, Mr. Mahoney, while you're doing the work of the madman Gunther Ostrander, the work you're doing is... well, obviously you haven't caught on yet. The Tuskatawa have been sighted more and more, word of the sightings got back to us in the quarry from the runaways who were caught by Ostrander's other men... before they were killed. Most of us thought they were just talkin' crazy. But I guess it's true."

"*What's* true?"

Drange took a little bit of pleasure saying what he said next. He enjoyed it, he agreed with it, and moreover anything else, he seemed to have a want to be apart of it. When he talked, it didn't feel as though he were talking to me, but rather that he was exchanging words with the painted-face Tuskatawa. Their eyes met and lingered for a time. There was something between them I wasn't privy to, and it frustrated the hell outta me.

"Mr. Mahoney," he said, "we *are* on their land. That's what happens when there's revolution in the air."

Drange's gaze left the Tuskatawa. He and I locked eyes for the last minute while he spoke, but when we turned back to see what the four intruders were doing, they had already gone, vanishing completely into the night, for no disclosed reason other than they were done with the conversation.

The night sat still, and the fire began to die down further. I threw on another log and a handful of twigs. The wood began to spit and spatter, sending swirls of orange fireflies into the night sky. Drange sipped some hot coffee in a tin can, his eyes never leaving the darkness that surrounded our camp.

IV.
The COURIER
and the DOOMED MAN

I awoke later than I intended, to the sound of crackling, dying flames. Drange was already up and moving around. What surprised me more is that he didn't make an attempt at escaping, and if he did, he either failed or actually did escape, and was trying to make a fool out of me. Captives had a habit of doing that sort of thing, the smarter ones. They would free themselves in the night, and pretend to still be restricted to their environment. And when they saw that you weren't lookin', they either made a run for the mountains, or went for your throat. I'd just met this Til Drange, so to assume anything about him would of course be unwise. Except he was still wearing the chain around his ankle. I'd fastened them tightly, more tightly an any normal man would consider to be comfortably secure. I fastened it so that when I did remove the iron, there would be bruising left behind to remind him; something I learned how to do a number of years ago.

"You're still here," I said, sitting up, climbing out of my sleeping bag. I rubbed my wrists each with the opposite hank, feeling the bones beneath the skin. I leaned over, taking each boot off one at a time to rub my ankles in the same way. I did this most mornings to help in the waking-up process. Drange watched me as I moved from one ankle to the other. "Why the hell are you still here?"

"You think I'm the sort of fellah to make a run for it," he asked, "maybe I would have been, if not for our visitors last night."

"You afraid of four itty bitty tribals? I see," putting my boots back on and getting the coffee tin ready for brewin'.

"Afraid? No. Not afraid. But I ain't stupid, either. They're still here," Drange said to me, nodding towards the hills a little farther off west, "up there in those hill-buffs. I caught a glimpse of one just a little before ya woke up. They don't seem like the type likely to kill real fast, unless they have to, but it's obvious they don't trust ya."

"And they trust you," I laughed.

"No way of knowin' for absolute sure. But I've got charm workin' for me. You, you're just an ugly golem of a man. I've got it on good authority that my looks make me more... approachable. It's been proven in all societies of humankind, the people who are trusted first are always the more physically attractive ones. I was born with boyish features, but, I started lookin' like a real man before all the other kids. I've had it goin' for me all my life."

"Startin' to... understand why Gunth' put that thing on your face," I muttered, "speakin' of which, what's the deal with that there metal contraption old Gunther had fastened to your head? There somethin' I should be aware of about you that he hasn't filled me in on? You an unruly biter? Some sort of human snake? Are you a snake, you *cute* son of a bitch?"

He laughed, accepting the tin cup of coffee I handed him.

"I'd been a *worker* in his quarry for a long time, it feels like. And a while further before that I did a bit of work for the mayor of Vermouth, the same mayor you're takin' me to so he can hang me. While workin' for Mr.

Kenroy, I found out a few things his kin was getting' into. His brother, Caleb, got in real deep with the Crimson Collars. You're right what ya said earlier about 'em, of what sort of folk they are. Just a few slit throats shy of losing their humanity completely. And anyone who gets tangled up with them loses somethin' they aren't ever getting' back."

"I know the gang," I said, "not personally, but I crossed paths, in a way, with their leader, Mancino, once. He was gettin' on a train and I was getting' off. We didn't make eye contact. We never met face to face. But I knew who he was. Later that week, found out everyone on board that train was slaughtered, even after they handed over their goods. He's a real tough son of a bitch."

"Yea, well," Drange continued, "I killed a bunch of his men, including the Mayor's brother. Found out young Caleb was gettin' into their ranks. I tried tellin' Mr. Kenroy, but he wouldn't have any of it. It's real hard to get anyone to believe anything like that, I'm sure, especially when your own blood is on the line. Well, his brother Caleb was ordered to take out the bank in Vermouth. He and the group of men he was sent with weren't no trouble at all to dispatch, but the mayor still didn't believe a word of it. I got outta town as fast as I could, knowin' he'd be sending the lynch mob with a price on my head so high whoever caught me and brought me could rebuild the entire free world. About that time is when I fell in with your employer, Mr. Ostrander. Who I promise you, is not the man you think he is. And when I say I fell in with him, I don't mean that he offered me to work for him outta the kindness of his heart."

"Yea about that," I drank my coffee, swished it around my teeth, and swallowed, "you got somethin' to

84 | DAVE MATTHES

back those words up with? I'm not a very trustin' guy myself, and I'd be a liar if I said I admired the man, but you seem dead set on upturning my entire opinion of him. Sounds to me like you're just tryin' to escape the long way around."

"I could kill ya right now," Drange said. I took note of the chain still linking him to his horse. He wasn't bound at the wrists anymore, but it would still take the man a decent amount of effort to make any sort of move toward my killin' spots. "Hell, thought about how I'd do it last night. Wouldn't be hard. Came oh so close. Just to see if I could do it."

"I'd like you to just try somethin' like that, man," I said with a smirk. Admittingly, I didn't think much of this Til Drange. He seemed skinny, too skinny, especially in the neck to really worry about. I'd caught wind of a few fellah's with his appearance. They all seemed to have the same mindset. They all had strategies, reasons to believe they could take down mighty giants and kill any man who's been killin' most of his life. And they all snapped like twigs once I got my hands on 'em.

"You don't think I could take you down?"

"I *know* you couldn't take me down."

"What makes you so confident?"

"It's logic, really," I said, pouring another cup of coffee for myself. When he reached out his tin can for a refill, I swatted it away. The empty can clanged against a rock and rolled to a stop in the dirt next to the horses. Right beside a midnight pile of their shit. "I've no doubt you have some ability to be proud of somewhere, most men do. But killin' ain't one of em. So, you killed a handful of Crimson Collar dupes. You got lucky. You killed the mayor's brother. I happen to have it on high authority that Caleb was a little bitch, a priss. Any random roll of the dice more and he'd been born with a cunt and two tits."

"On high authority? And whose might that be?"

"The only one that matters: my own," I grunted, drinking my coffee, "Caleb was always lookin' for validation with the wrong crowd, it's no surprise he fell in with the Collars. They take almost anyone willin' to carry a gun in their name."

"Stand up," Drange stood up, the chain on his ankle jingling as he did so. "Stand up and show me."

"I ain't fightin' you. I ain't fightin' for no sport neither. I've got nothin' to prove."

"You do have somethin' to prove though. Because *I* have it on high authority that *you're* a priss. Why, if you'd been conceived a day earlier, you mighta been born with a cunt and two saggy tits. And I'd be havin' this conversation today with an ugly, old, woman."

Ostrander was right. This Drange fella was an asshole.

"Look, you can even keep the chain on me," he said to me.

"Like I'd take it off anyhow," I laughed, standing up. I removed my long coat, and cracked every knuckle in both hands. "What are ya tryin' to get outta this, anyway? I ain't gonna free ya, even if you put me on my ass."

"I'm not doin' this for freedom, pal," Drange said, cracking his back and his neck. He worked on his stance for a moment, looking down at the ground with both eyes. When he was satisfied, he beckoned me to swing first. I couldn't help but stand there on the opposite side of the dying fire and just watch him. He was truly a man of pathetic existential nonsense. I moved forward, slowly around the pile of embers. He kept both eyes trained on me. Not my fists or my feet, but on my eyes.

"I feel horrible about this," I said to Drange, "I feel like I should chain my own ankle up. Make things fair. But even that wouldn't tip the scales in a favorable way for ya."

"I don't need ya to do that sort of thing on my account. Come on. I can't wait for you to feel these hammers."

"Heh, ya gotta work on your shit-talkin', man. That's one thing for sure," I said.

Drange lunged forward, swinging a fist with an outward swing. I admit, he swung fast, and if it had succeeded in hitting me, he might have sent me back a foot or two. But he missed. I barely had to flinch out of the way. He swung again, and missed again.

"So far you're impressin' me," I said, "tell ya what, you land one good hit, chin, nose, earlobe, wherever, and I won't put that metal mechanical behemoth of a gag back on your ugly, undeveloped face."

Drange swung again, and again. Each time I only needed to move out of the way a few inches. It didn't feel like I was sparring with a man who was even trying. I felt bad, almost.

"You have to be pullin' my leg with this attitude of yours," I said, "you learn how to fight in a pit of quicksand? No, wait. It was your daddy who taught ya how to fight, that's it."

"Why the hell haven't you swung back at all," he asked, lowering his fists, exhausted with impatience. At exactly this moment, I took my own swing. He didn't have time to block or contemplate a counter move. My right fist caught him in the chin so hard he fell backwards on his ass. Rubbing his chin, he looked up angrily, like he'd been cheated. "You cheated," he grunted.

"Ain't no such thing as cheatin'," I said, kicking him in the thigh with the toe of my boot, "but I'll tell ya what, I'm not gonna put that metal piece of junk back on your head."

"Why not?"

"You're too goddamn entertaining," I said.

On the second day we took the dirt road further north with an emphasis on a westward lean. If we leaned east, we'd hit the border of what used to be Nebraska, and we needed to stay tight with Colorado until we reached the border of Old Wyoming. Vermouth lay just south of the border, south of what used to be Cheyenne, if the maps of the old years were anything to go by. The snow fell harder now, but it was not yet cold enough for the flakes to stick to the ground anymore than an inch or so. At dusk, we made camp. Drange kept his eyes to the west. When I followed his gaze, I saw what he was seeing. The quartet of tribesmen sitting on their own horseback high up on a ridge just under the failing sunlight.

"When do you think they'll make their move," I asked Drange. He licked his lip where I'd split it with my fist.

"I don't believe they're going to, to be honest. I think they're just watchin'. Scouts. We are heading away from their land, at least where it used to be last I remember."

"You said there was revolution in the air," I said, "with that in mind, the borders of their so-called land could be anywhere at this point."

Drange looked away, mulling everything over in his head. "The little I do know about these people, they do have their own rules as a tribe when it comes to killin'. That bein' said, they do have their exceptions."

"Then we better sleep with one eye open tonight, each of us, right? Tomorrow we'll be in Crimson Collar territory, so we'll have them to contend with as well if we aren't as lucky as we've been. But you can relax, I'll protect ya, with *these hammers*," I laughed, getting the fire set for the skillet. "Besides, you fought so good earlier this mornin', I'm gonna let you do the cookin' tonight."

"What?"

"Sausages are in the satchel on the left side of Eleanor's saddle," I said, patting Eleanor's neck, "make em delicious enough and I might even remove that chain of yours."

Drange looked at me like I'd been shot in the face with a double-barrel shotgun.

"Hah, of course I'm kiddin' about that. Chain looks good on ya, anyway. Sovereignty ain't in your future in any way, shape, or form, buddy."

We ate. We slept. Not a disturbance to wake us all night. The tribesmen never came to camp. They stayed up in their hills. In the morning, we saw the smoke from their own camp. They knew we knew they were there so there was no point in pretending otherwise, I'm sure. As we took to the road once more, they stayed behind, just as Drange assumed they would do. If they were planning on a sort of revolution, they must still be in the beginning phases of such a thing. A successful revolution, if one is to survive the course of planned events, must be thought out with more than one strategy, as anyone of the land knows. And since there hadn't been an actual full-blown war in years and years, even before I came into this world, it would be interesting to see how they planned on breaking the world's back just to bend in their favor.

Before we wound a bend that would take us into a descent down a hill straight for the valley in which Vermouth was set, I turned to face our pursuers. The four Tuskatawa sat atop their horses, the man with the painted face distinguishable by the way his shoulders were that much broader than his companions, an intentional visual demonstration of superior strength maybe. They stayed up on that hill, looking down at us, not saying a word, not giving a call, totally motionless. Seeing them up there, I felt a sort of... solitude within, a solitude that maybe had always been there, sitting beside the aloneness I had already allowed myself to succumb to. That aloneness which enabled me to survive out on my own while in the world. The aloneness, I was at peace with, as it allowed my muscles the strength to move forward with all of the harshness of decisions I'd have to make. The aloneness calmed my heart, kept it from exploding from the chest. It allowed me to know that the nature of what I was doing, no matter what depths I'd otherwise have to sink to, was being done with the highest level of morality at my disposal. Because if I survived, if I came out alive at the end, how could whatever I'd decided to do, be the wrong choice? This new solitude I felt when gazing upon the four watchers... it didn't mix well with me, despite the calmness it evoked. This solitude was not at all in congruence with my kind of aloneness.

"We goin'?" Drange called out, waking me from my trance.

"Yea, we're goin'."

"Good. I wanna get this hangin' over with. Hell is waiting, ya know."

"I'm sure if it's waited this long, it can wait a little longer," I said. We started off on down the hill into the valley, upon which the snow had now begun to stick faster and with more commitment. The horses, Eleanor in particular, didn't approve. I promised Eleanor I'd find her a nice warm barn she could stay in while I took care of my business. We rode on as the sun crossed above our heads, touching the middle-most point in the sky, and at the time, we caught first sight of Vermouth.

Vermouth was not a settlement as developed or even protected in the same fashion as Ostrander's New Canterton. There were no barrier walls and the buildings were all constructed out of wood, sticks, and sometimes you might find metal slating for the walls and the roof-tops. Everything was well put-together, so much that even the harder rainstorms and the windstorms from the east had a hard time knocking things down. There were several large homes where the more penny-starved folk lived. Beside these were a half dozen or so tenement structures stacked together like pancakes on a shit plat-ter where the rest of Vermouth's denizens lived. In the center of town, three main dirt roads came to a point where a singular building stood: the most well-put-to-gether structure in the whole damn place, where the mayor Henry Kenroy, made his stay. I'd seen the man on a number of occasions but only briefly exchanged words with him. And each time I'd crossed paths with the man he seemed to have gained at least ten pounds around the midriff. He was fed well, he ate well, and his voice de-manded that he always eat well. Not exactly a tyrant of a man, he did command a wealth of respect from a certain amount of the denizens in town. But he was a strange sort of man in that he never seemed too bothered by the existence of the Crimson Collars. I just think the idea of putting in any sort of effort that didn't have anything to do with eating or lounging around put a thistle in his panties. He hated them, of course, and whenever he could, he'd hang a captured member publicly. He was always speaking with a reassuring tone that the "Crimson Collar Threat" was being addressed daily, and would very soon be gone for good.

We rode into town, and things just, fell quiet-like. Folk sitting on their porches and striding along the wooden walkways outside of storefronts all looked with a silent curiosity towards the two newcomers to town, one riding at the front and the other tied to his horse. I'd been here on my way up north and a few other times in between, but I never stayed long enough for much anyone to recognize me. The mayor, however, knew my face almost better than his own brother. He once told me he'd never forget my face as long as I kept on doin' the dirty work no one else was willing to do.

Snow covered the rooftops of the old wooden buildings, and they all seemed to lean forward from this, like old men tired from standing up all these years. Every now and then a slight gust of wind would push a heap of snow from the canopy's, plopping down to the ground with that softness snow makes when it falls from tree branches. Folk watched, some lighting their pipes, some spittin' their stuff into the white snow at their feet. It was all an eerie feel, as though we were expected, and everyone goin' about their business outside had been instructed to welcome us in a certain way designed to evoke an uneasy dread.

"So, this is the town where I'm gonna die," Drange muttered. Having decided to not return the metal helmet to his head, I'd started to feel like Drange was just another guy I was sharing a job with, the rare type work requiring more than one set of hands. I had to be careful feelin' this way, as it could very well take me out of my level-headed way of keepin' spacially aware. But also, I may be rude from time to time, and yes, I do get a heathy amount of pleasure in making assholes uncomfortable... which I suppose makes me an asshole just the same, but I wasn't so cruel as to deny a man the right to speak during his final hours, not unless he deserved it. "Ya sure you can't just take me out into the valley and shoot me in the chest? I wouldn't tell anyone. You could say that asshole Mancino Rola-whatever did it and got away."

"Sorry, man," I said, "this isn't personal. It rarely is. Besides, the boss wouldn't believe me on account he knows I never, ever, let anyone *get away*."

"Whatever ya say," Drange said.

I hitched both Eleanor and the horse Drange rode in on right out front of the mayor's abode. The good Mr. Henry Kenroy had already climbed out of the confines of his warm home and stood out on the porch at the very top of the steps, his hands resting on his hips and his belly sticking out like an infected growth. He looked pleased, and I don't think it would be a stretch to say that he groomed his bushy, grey mustache just for this very occasion.

"Now I know, when I last heard word I'd be receiving such an honorable guest to face his well-deserved justice, he'd be wearing my favorite speech-inhibiting device. Hell, it's only the cornerstone of the dealings I have with Mr. Ostrander. Every transfer I've ever had the pleasure of making, or having, has worn it," mayor Henry Kenroy didn't sound genuinely upset, he seemed to be reciting the beginning of a well-rehearsed joke, "I can't imagine the sewage this person has assaulted you with from his mouth. I should sew it shut before letting him swing. He'd look like a ragdoll embroidered by a five-year old."

"He wasn't any trouble," I said, "a weak little

man, actually." I shoved him toward the mayor. "Well, that's all for me. Mr. Drange, happy swingin'." I tipped my hat to him.

"Right," he replied.

"Now, now wait just a minute there, Mr. Mahoney," the mayor waddled on down his steps. Two of his men grabbed a hold of Drange and dragged him off inside the house where, I presumed, he would await the time of hanging. "I want you to know something, and it's not an easy thing for a man like me, to say, to a ...a man like you. See, uh, you and I are both on quite a different track in life. I'm a... uh... someone the *people* can look up to for... guidance, and maybe a little security. And you're a... uh.... well you're a man someone like me is grateful for to have when rocks really fall from the sky, ya know? I'm sure our mutual acquaintance Mr. Ostrander feels the same in his own way, since you've been working for him more directly. He and I were, well... we had a much more active friendship in the past than what we have now, it's a bit depressing really. These are difficult, difficult times to decipher, Mr. Mahoney. There's no one real true way a person can make it through without getting themselves dirty. I can see you're a man who has made peace with that. So, to show ya how grateful I am, and the people of Vermouth are surely grateful to have a ruthless murderer like Til Drange off the streets, the saloon is yours for the evening. Anything and everything. Whiskey, beer, women, a hot meal, whatever you'd like. It's yours."

"I don't know about all that, as gracious an offer as that is," I said, "I've got myself a flask and I'm fine eatin' what I got in Eleanor's saddlebags. And to be honest with ya, I've got myself a woman and she's a pretty one, so I think I'll sleep alone tonight."

"You, a woman? How on earth did someone like

you bag yourself a woman? By woman, I assume you mean someone who'd just as soon marry ya? You make it sound like a serious thing, is all I mean. Like poetry. And you, my riddlesome man, are not a poet."

"Now how do you go about makin' assumptions like that? How do *you* know I'm not a goddamn poet? Why if I had a pencil, I might even write you a goddamn poem."

"It takes a certain finesse, Mr. Mahoney. A certain mysterious quality. And yes, while you have your mysterious side, I'm sure, it's not of the same... consistency. The difference between the viscosity of a poet and yourself is quite opaque, I'm afraid, not to dilute your overall character of course."

"Mhmm, well, maybe I will have that drink," I said, "a plate of hot food might be nice too. That saloon of yours still up a ways there?"

"Off to the left, yessir," Henry Kenroy slapped me on the back joyfully, the dull midmorning glow from the sun hanging behind snow clouds giving his blue eyes a curiously peculiar gleam. "They'll take care of you there. I already told em you might stop in today. Word of caution, though, and this is purely cosmetic, but if you find that you don't quite enjoy the food, don't speak the truth of those feelings. The cook is a bit handsy with his emotions these days on account of a recent, um... a rather unfortunate death in the family. I almost had to have a noose made up just for him the other day," he said with a light chuckle, "which of course then I wouldn't have a cook and, well, angry mobs and all. Who needs that? Am I rambling? I'm rambling."

I shook my head but told the man he had nothin' to worry about.

"When's the hangin' gonna be, anyway?

Drange's I mean. I wouldn't mind seein' that. Spent a little time with the man. I feel like I owe him that much. A sendoff, more or less," I asked as I started making my way down the snow-smeared dirt road.

"Tomorrow morning, Mr. Mahoney. I like to do my hangings as soon as the first winkings of sunrise begin to shine over the horizon. If it snows tonight, with the way the wind feels at present, it'll sure be a beautiful morning for a lynching!" And with that he returned into the protective arms of his fat, obtrusive home.

V.
"The CRIMSON COLLARS MUST DIE!"

To the right of the saloon entrance, a sheet of parchment was nailed to the wood with a series of corroded nails all bent at the heads. On the paper was stamped in thick black letters: *"THE CRIMSON COLLARS MUST DIE!"* And in smaller lettering near the bottom it read: *"Any members of the Crimson Collar Gang turned into the Mayor will be promptly hung in the town square. Anyone who turns in information leading to the apprehension of gang members will receive one thousand clips for purchase of spirits in the saloon, and five hundred krits for meal credit. Anyone who turns in information leading to the apprehension of, or captures and turns in the leader himself, Mancino Rolandraz, will receive all of the following, but not limited to: full pardons for any and all crimes committed, a sum of currency to be determined by the Mayor Henry Kenroy, a stake of land within the boundaries of the county of Vermouth, as well as permanent guaranteed employment in the town of Vermouth, and a special mention of contribution in the town's records forever to be memorialized in the forthcoming holiday which celebrates the death of Mancino Rolandraz. Alternatively, anyone caught aiding and conspiring with the Crimson Collar Gang will be executed, along with any and all members of their family. Their family history, if any exists, will be erased from the town's records. Please keep the scourge that is Mancino Rolandraz in your constant vigilant thoughts, and remember: THE CRIMSON*

COLLARS MUST DIE!"

Between the large printed words at the top of the parchment and the smaller body of text below, there was drawn a rather crude image of presumably Mancino Rolandraz's face. In the image, the man was drawn with a grin, showing rotten, animal-like teeth. He was meant to be thought of as a monster, and perhaps he was right to be. All the good towns had them, beasts, that is. Old Dakota had Mad Hawk Manny, who'd been wanted for a stretch of not less than two years for puttin' his fingers and the rest of hisself where he don't belong when it came to several of the town's daughters. Last I heard he was still out there grabbin' women and laughin' about his exploits over campfires, but the frequency of incidents had since lessened and so people just seemed to not care as much anymore. Longmurk Dale, a basin to the far southwest notorious for the potency of its locally-brewed mirewasp wine, was home to the Killthorn Brothers, Jack and Davy, who had since been apprehended and put to death. They were a special duo, though, and weren't on the run for long. They came back to Longmurk on the pretense of having decided they'd torn out the throats of enough children and only turned themselves in because they were bored of doing so, and because now nothing they could think of tickled their demented lusts for strange adventure. And way out west where I'd never been but heard plenty about from the barflies at New Canterton, there was rumored to live in a nice little town called Bethlehem Peak, a man whose true identity was not known, but the stories went about callin' him 'The Night Louse'. In Bethlehem Peak, every so often a body would turn up with much of its skin removed and any skin that had been left behind appeared dried up, as though the blood had been sucked dry. Apparently, someone was goin' around at night makin' unsavory meals of the populace, that is, savory to him, but unsavory to everyone else. As far as I knew this 'Night Louse' fella was still at large. I know I for one had no intentions of ever payin' a visit to his town.

I'd never met Mancino Rolandraz, but I'd heard enough to know he was not someone I wanted to have any dealin's with. If anything, I'd sooner put a bullet in him before listenin' to what he thought about the local politics. If Old Dakota, Longmurk Dale, and Bethlehem Peak found a way to survive while their monsters existed, I'm sure sweet, sweet Vermouth could do that very same thing.

The beast of the saloon was loud and attacked the ears far out into the street. The beast's talons reached the streets fairly early in this town, which wasn't surprising giving the overall temperament of the populace. Most of whom, based on what I knew and everything I'd witnessed since the first time I'd set foot here, were disgruntled, dissatisfied heathen who had probably once been somewhat civil with one another, perhaps before Henry Kenroy took over as mayor. It wasn't hard to sympathize. His house was at the very center of town for all to see. I wasn't privy to his bookkeepings, but something was absolutely askew with the way the rest of the town looked. Since the saloon was always open, day, night, and every hour in between, the angry people of Vermouth were supplied with an endless array of outlets through which to release their inner strife.

I pushed open the saloon doors and instantly my nostrils were overwhelmed with the scent of body fermentation, sweat, and a mix of urine, shit, both human and animal, and all manner of booze and alcohol that somehow was always in stock. Upstairs, the whores with their prettied-up faces and cavernous cunts waited for the arrival of their next prey. As I walked in, their eyes were the first I felt, like knives with the power to hypnotize.

"I was told you'd be stoppin' by," the barkeep said. The man smelled from here. Nothing to bathe in, I'm sure, but there were streams out in the valley in which to dunk one's self in, no matter how cold it was. I recognized him from the last time I was here, several months ago. But something was different about him this time. As I took a seat at the bar and adjusted my longcoat to hang down behind the barstool, I focused on what might have been different about his appearance.

"Been a long time, Mahon," he said, placing a whiskey glass in front of me, filling it up with the stuff that he knew I liked, the kind that always warms, and gets hotter once it's in your belly.

"A month and a half, at least, maybe more," I said, "didn't you have *two* eyes back then?"

"Oh, you mean this," He lifted the leather eyepatch from his left eye, and sure enough where an eyeball should have been there now remained an empty, fleshy socket. "You're right. Lost it to a hock snake about three weeks ago. Bastard snuck up on me while I was sleepin'. Woke up with the shits, as always, and as you know when that happens I wake up much faster than normal folk do. Spooked the damn rattler and before I knew it, damn thing sank its venomous fangs right into my fuckin' eye. Buddy of mine I was with had no choice but to cut my whole eyeball out."

"Ouch."

"Ya damn right, ouch," he laughed, "it's fine though, I'm still alive and slingin' drinks, as you can see. Want anything to eat? Chef back there has got some mean gopher stew on the heater. Should be done any-time now. No clips or krits required, as usual."

"Yea, why not," I said. "It's not on my dime, so, sure."

"Alright then," the one-eyed barkeep jeered.

I took my time with the first glass. I decided it was a good thing to sit and just relax. It was a rare thing when I was afforded the opportunity while out on the road in the name of Ostrander. I hadn't really meant what I said about enjoying seein' Drange hang, either. I never liked lynchings, seemed like a crime to do that to a man, even the vilest. Being Drange was being hung for something that I myself might've done, well... to watch him die and enjoy it just seemed too harsh a thing.

I figured I'd have myself a few drinks, eat up, and head out on the road again. To the west of here were more mountains in which I hadn't fully explored. Maybe I'd run into more of them tribesmen and they could point me in the right direction. Or maybe they'd kill me for trespassin'. I was bound for an arms-open greetin' from the dangerous end of a gun one day anyhow.

I spent my time there on the barstool as I did any other time. Drinking down the brown whiskey and let-ting it warm me up. Around me, an endless flutter of un-civilized conversation roused with the passing of every quarter hour. High-pitched cackling that was supposed to be laughter flooded my ear canals like a flood of mol-ten hot sewage straight from Hell's asshole itself. I never took part in the conversation, I avoided it whenever pos-sible. And usually anyone who attempted to engage me in said artform I simply ignored, which most of the time I was successful at, or I'd have to flash them the eyes. The eyes that said without sayin'. They knew the look because regardless of their short, useless existence, they'd seen it before, and they knew what would happen if they continued on down the path they started.

The whores tried their best. Sometime after lunch hour they always came down from their roosts. At half-passed noon, the ones without a cock already inside of them descended the stairs ready to flash whomever crossed their paths first. Today, a blonde with bruises splotched all along the surface of her upper breasts, tipped her pretty little eyes at me. She took the stool to my left and undid her blouse from the top. I didn't have to turn my head at all, her breasts were so large. Pale and bruised, but impressive nonetheless.

"You been sittin' here all day, man, with no company, no nothin'. How does a man get on with no company for so long a time," she said with a tiny voice. With her left hand she rubbed her left nipple, and I watched it grow hard. "Some of the girls have been placin' a bet of their own. You like men or somethin'? Darlene, up there, the brunette with the Adam's apple, she's got this wild idea that you don't like people at all. You one of them livestock fuckers."

"No," I said, "I've got a woman, and even if I didn't I wouldn't risk losin' the hardware between my legs for the likes of one measly hour with you, or *Darlene.*"

"Excuse me, sir, but I happen to be one of the disease-free items up for grabs, which is good because that allows me to charge a little extra," she said proudly.

"You're really winning me over with that charm," I said, raising my glass to the barkeep, letting him know I needed a refill. He poured my glass and let out a chuckle, knowing full well this blonde bitch beside me had no chance with me.

"So is that a no," she asked, reaching down

between my legs. I felt her tiny hand feel around for the shape of my cock. I was a man, of course, and so I did feel the hardware stiffen up a bit. But my heart wasn't all the way in it. And so it wouldn't matter what tricks she tried. "Ah, there ya are," she smiled, "there's your little man. Somethin's tellin' me you really ain't got a woman. You just think you're better than the gents in this place. Well, you might be. You very well might be just from the way your cock feels."

"Lady," I turned and faced her, reached down with a free hand and latched on to her wrist, pulling it away from my hardware, "I meant what I said, and I only ever mean what I say. You're pretty, I'll give ya that. Your bruises tell me you could be a half-wild time. But your voice sounds like a defective train whistle, and I ain't leavin' this town by rail or by carriage. You'd best put your effort into someone more willing, someone who smells like shit and don't care where they stick it. Namely, anyone else in this place but me."

"Well," she slid off the stool, frowning, buttoning up her blouse, "no one's ever talked to me that way before."

"And I bet no one's ever made love to ya either, now get lost, go on, beat it," I muttered, returning to my drink.

The one-eyed barkeep returned with a glass in one hand and a cloth in the other. He leaned in my direction with one elbow on the bartop.

"Nicely handled," he chuckled, "I've gotta say, I honestly have never seen anyone resist their advances with such flawlessness. You sir, are a hollow-tip bullet in a world chock-full of cottonweed."

"Maybe," I said, drinking down my fourth glass. "Jesus, is it after noon already?"

"Yessir," the barkeep said.

But something compelled me to stay, maybe it was the whiskey. Maybe it was just the idea of not having to do anything at all as long as I stayed here. I needed the reprieve, I told myself. And maybe *that* was the whiskey talkin'. My vision had begun to blur a little, and that wasn't a good thing. Luckily, I knew how to counter such an attack: more whiskey.

"You got any rooms to rent upstairs," I asked, "I might need a place to crash."

"Nothing would surprise me more if ya didn't," the barkeep laughed, "and yes, I do, but don't worry about the cost. Mr. Kenroy was almost scarily confident that you'd need a bed tonight."

"What a guy," I said, "what a guy."

The blur of boozefodder shifted as the hours passed by. The tide of blurriness pulled me out to sea, and soon I arrived at dinner hour, just before the time changed over to six-ish. I sat at the same stool, drinking from the same glass, only I knew gravity had gotten stronger because I had begun to slump lower to the bartop. I started thinking about Cassandra. And the daughter who would never truly be mine. Through my whiskey mind, I imagined killing Gunther, and I could do it too. I could probably get away with it, with enough planning. Instead of sitting alone at a place like this, Cassandra and I could make away from the mine, from the quarry, from New Canterton altogether. Through my whiskey mind, I saw us riding away. East, most likely. Eastward, from what I've heard, the people were different. There were the few religious cults, but the settlements out there were better protected by more people who would be less likely to take advantage of you. Those were just rumors, of course. Could also be worse out there than out here. I'd never been out east. I'd never had the chance to dig that way. Cassandra would come with me. I knew she would. She once told me she "truly did at one time love Gunther, and a part of her always would, because that's what a heart does when there's nothing else it knows how to do. And when ya start somewhere so strongly, something about that beginning always sticks with ya. They... they become part of ya, and before ya know it, you forget what life was ever like without them". But immediately after that, was when she confessed her love for me, and for the same reason.

The sky outside fell all the way to black. Little lamps inside the saloon were lit, painting everything a hazy shade of gold. I couldn't stomach any more of the brown whiskey, so I asked the barkeep to hand over the key to a room upstairs. At the same exact moment the key was placed on the bartop, the saloon doors swung open, and inward a man stepped, behind him followed closely five more men, all of them wearing a deep, maroon-red scarf around their necks. The man in the middle, however, was much larger than the others. He bore a familiarity I couldn't yet recall, but I, like many others, heard of him before. At the very least, I'd seen him out in the world, but I'd never heard him speak up close. He stood taller, his arms were like tree trunks, and his black beard was greased straight down to the top-most button on his shirt. He wore his hat tipped low, so that his eyebrows couldn't be seen. And when he took his steps, the glasses on everyone's tables trembled like frightened sprites.

In his hands he held before his face the parchment that'd been nailed to the side of the entrance out front. He wore a bemused expression as he read the words out loud, especially emphasizing on the parts that said "THE CRIMSON COLLARS MUST DIE," he growled, laughing, "THE CRIMSON COLLARS MUST DIE ...*anyone who turns in information leading to the apprehension of, or captures and turns in the leader himself, Mancino Rolandraz, will receive all of the following, but not limited to: full pardons for any and all crimes committed, a sum of currency to be determined by the Mayor Henry Kenroy, a stake of land within the boundaries of the county of Vermouth, as well as permanent guaranteed employment in the town of Vermouth, and a special mention of contribution in the town's records forever to be memorialized in the... the,*" he narrowed his eyes and for a moment the grin on his face while reading dissipated, "*...in the forthcoming holiday which celebrates... the death of Mancino Rolandraz,*" he laughed and laughed, crinkling the paper into a small ball and letting it fall to the ground at his feet, "dear me, even the artist's rendition of my face got it all wrong."

The saloon fell silent, except for one of the more unruly gentlemen who'd probably been the only one in the place drinking longer today than I had. He giggled at something, and the sound emitting from his wide-open mouth must have been taken in offense, because the largest man of the six who'd just walked in, turned towards him and with a knife as long as his own forearm, stuck the pointy end all the way through the rowdy drunk's chest, turning it and twisting it until the laughs stopped. He removed the knife, and wiped it clean on the shirt of the man he just killed, then sheathed it.

"For those of you who don't recognize me, which wouldn't be your fault if all ya had to go by was that piss poor portrait nailed to the outside of this establishment, my name is Mancino Rolandraz," he said. "It has come to my attention, that a particular man... a murderer, has come to this town. Now, anyone who offers *information* that leads to the *apprehension* of this individual, will be paid graciously," he chuckled, using the words like toys he'd found layin' out on the street. With his boot, he lightly kicked the crinkled-up piece of paper with his face on it in the direction of his stride. He walked around the place slowly, like a lion, looking deep into everyone's eyes. With his next step, he stomped a foot onto the balled-up parchment, flattening it.

The drunks were too drunk to help, though. And anyone else not drunk enough were still frozen from what just happened. "His name, is Til Drange. And he killed four of my men. Four," he drew closer and closer to the bar, his men with him spreading out amongst the others, some of them taking the whores by their waist, licking their chest all the way up their neck and across their face. They growled heinously, thrusting their mid-sections against the whores', insinuating fornication. But even the whores wanted nothing of them. Even for them, these creatures were more animal than man.

The barkeep was nowhere to be found. He'd run away and hid just as soon as Mancino and his men arrived through the doors. Smart man, that one-eyed barkeep.

Mancino approached the bar, leaning his back up against it not more than two feet away to my left. He turned his head toward me, giving a sniff of the air.

"Have you and I crossed paths before," he asked. Now I don't know if it was whiskey, but I paid him no mind. I didn't even twitch an ear towards him. "Hey, you," he slapped my arm with the top of a hand, "I asked you a question."

"I'm tryin' to drink here," I muttered, still lookin' down at my glass, "it's a sacred thing, ya know, to some people. The bond between a man and his glass of whiskey."

"I never really heard of that before," Mancino said, "wanna tell me about it?"

"Not particularly," I said.

"It's just that you seem familiar, that's all. And I don't mean that I've seen you before, I know we've never actually met. But I'd be a damned liar if I was to say I never heard of the one... Rancid Mahoney. And I'd be even more damned to presume you were any other man."

"What gave me away," I asked, drinkin' from my glass.

"Well it wasn't the stench, I can tell ya that. You're from uh... what's that place called... New somethin'."

"New Canterton."

"Yea, New Canterton. What a place. What a monument of... ignorance. Silly to think that the people who live there think they're safe, or somethin'."

"Safer than they would be much anywhere else, out here, amongst the real animals," I said.

"Do *you* know who *I* am?"

"I heard of ya, read about ya, don't know too much other than that."

"Amongst a plethora of *other* things, it's my job to know or at least be aware of certain individuals and their goings-on. I know you're a tough guy. You wander. And you get paid for it, interesting arrangement," he swiped the bottle of whiskey in front of me and reached over the bar, grabbing a glass for himself. Mancino poured almost a full glass and lifted it to his lips, taking a sip. "And look at us, you've heard of me and I've head of you. Ain't that cute."

He drank his glass all the way until it was empty,

slamming it down on the bartop.

"Now, I know not all of you knows who I'm talking about," Mancino turned away from me and continued on with his presentation, taking the same blonde, busty whore with the bruised tits who approached me, by the waist and pulled her in close. He smelled her neck, grinning in satisfaction, licking his lips. He smelled inside her ear and with the very tip of his tongue, licked the earlobe. She shuttered, and for a moment I believed she turned her attention to me, begging me for help. Mancino smelled her neck again, and moved his nose to her lips, the lower of which he took between his teeth. He gave a slight bite and released her when she gasped in disgust. "A woman like you is a rare breed," he said. Mancino then returned his attention to the rest of the saloon. "I'll tell ya'll what. I'm gonna go upstairs with this here beauty and fuck her brains out. You all have until I'm finished with her to tell me where I can find this... Til Drange." He started moving her toward the stairs, pushing her, shoving her. He growled like a tiger, advancing with tightened, bulging muscles. Every time she resisted even a little, he grabbed a hold of her with less reserve. At the top of the stairs, she finally had it, and slapped him across the face, spitting on his cheek to drive it all home. "Well now," Mancino laughed, wiping the saliva from his cheek with one hand, "I guess I'll just have to play this differently." He grabbed her by the throat with one hand and began to squeeze, kicking her legs out from under her. "Instead of fuckin' her, I'm gonna strangle the life outta this here whore," he growled, "you all have until she's dead to tell me what I want to know."

Not a soul in the saloon moved. The drunks didn't know what do to. The other whores were terrified, not having an inkling about how to fight back a man of this terrible presence.

Mancino squeezed harder and held her down with a heavier force. He let out a grunt every time he tightened his hold.

"She's dyin' quicker now," he said with a grin, "this whore has a small neck. Not a whole lot of time to think about your options."

"Alright, alright," I said, putting my glass down impatiently, "I've seen enough, hell we've all seen enough of this." I stood up, adjusting my long coat. The men who came in with Mancino eyed me, each of their eyes turning into drills. "I can tell ya where this Til Drange is, no problem. But ya gotta let the whore go."

Mancino didn't loosen his grip. By the whitening of his knuckles, he only tightened it. The blonde whore let out little wisps of desperation, her choking nothing more now than sputters and whimpers.

"Where is he," Mancino asked calmly, holding the whore down to the floor. Her feet kicked behind him, pounding the wooden planks.

"I'm the one who brought him into town. Took him to the mayor's place. He wants him hung in the morning, I guess. Apparently one of the men he killed, one of *your* men, was the mayor's brother. Now let the whore go!"

Mancino kept right on squeezing. He squeezed so tight, the next sound that could be heard throughout the saloon was the sound of her throat being completely crushed. It sounded like pieces of glass being stepped on. Her legs stopped kicking. Her entire body lay motionless as Mancino rose to a standing position. One of his toadies grunted happily, having enjoyed the show.

"Seems to me that a lot of people really want this man dead," Mancino laughed, beginning to descend the stairs, "so you knew this, but allowed two people to be killed here tonight. You didn't even flinch. You didn't blink when I stabbed that laughing hyena by the door. You didn't even sound all that urgent when you told me to let the whore go."

"I'm a man of calm disposition during scenarios in which most generally piss themselves. It's a curse, I guess," I muttered.

Mancino reached ground level, his heavy feet falling like thunder. Even from here, I could see that he stood a good half-foot taller than myself. He cast a shadow behind him and in front him, day or night, I'd imagine. As he drew closer, I adjusted my stance appropriately.

"In this entire world we live in, *how* have we never met?"

"We're meeting right now," I replied, "and already we're discovering so much about each other."

"Do you know anything about the Crimson Collars? Do you really know who I am? I mean, yes, I've already announced my name. And I asked it kind of threateningly before," he let out a light laugh, "but there is a lot of difference between knowing a man's name and knowing who he is, wouldn't you say?"

"Yea," I said, "I can get behind that sort of philosophy. I've heard a lot of things about your people, heard even less about you personally. The most popular horror story back home amongst the kids being your parents were eaten by a pack of wolves when you were still just a little squirt. Now, they all are brought up to believe it's just a fairy tale. Something to keep em inside at night. But I know it's... less of a fairy tale, and a lot more like the truth. A terrible truth. Must've scarred you for life. So, to answer your question, I do know who you are, though I've made it a top priority to avoid all matters that might involve crossing paths with the Crimson Collars. Not because I'm afraid of you. But because even the most hideous of insects with the smallest minds, the most dried-up aptitudes for life and the respect for others deserve to be left alone to their own devices. I have had and still don't have any intention of getting on your bad side, but because to do so would come with threatening consequence."

"Oh, you don't," Mancino said, "you don't want to... fall on my bad side. Just throwin' this out there, sort of a fancy of mine from time to time. Do you have any proclivity for... joining the cause?"

"The cause?"

"The Crimson Collars? The cause of my design. You see these five other men here with me... that's close to how we started out. But we are not merely a gang anymore. The stories telling of how we are, are in truth merely how we used to be. We have more purpose than when we first started out. A cause. We have... a cause."

I looked back towards the door to the saloon, to the man with a bleeding hole in his chest from Mancino's knife. I looked upstairs to where the whore's lifeless hand hung over the edge of the second-floor balcony. If things went on as Mancino intended, I'd probably be looking down at the corpse of Til Drange soon enough.

"I dunno," I said genuinely, but of course I already knew my answer. I turned around to the bar and reached back for the bottle of brown whiskey, pouring myself another glass. "As a man who is already employed by, quite a high payer, and one with his own cause, a cause that, no offense, comes with a hell of a lot more tangible believability, I can't believe I'm saying that, I will have to let you know some other time. Perhaps in the morning, when my head has cleared and I can make a more... responsible decision. As you can probably tell, I've had a few drinks." I was of course being entirely sarcastic. I had no intention of joining up with the demented Crimson Collars. And Mancino knew this without having to think about it.

He smiled warmly, nodding his head.

I lifted the glass of brown whiskey to my lips, but before I could taste any of it there came a loud explosion, like a gunshot. I let the whiskey fall from my lips and saw that Mancino had drawn his sidearm, and had aimed it straight ahead at me. From the barrel, smoke rose, swirling into the air above our heads. I lowered my eyes a little more, and down at my midsection, a little left of my stomach, a new hole had appeared. Already I was bleeding out of it. And yet, I couldn't feel a thing.

"You probably don't even feel that, do you," Mancino said joyfully. He tucked his sidearm back into its holster and moved closer to me. I fell back into the barstool, but ended up sliding down to the floor between it and another. The blood seeped out more, soaking my shirt.

"Actually," I said, "I can feel it now," I wasn't lying. And I was no longer drunk. I felt the bullet inside, the lump, the new addition that weighed heavier than all of my organs put together, it seemed. I held a hand against the hole, trying to keep myself from bleeding out, but I had to admit, the pain was more than I expected. Mancino pulled my hand away, holding it down.

"No, no," he said with a soothing voice, "you're doing it all wrong. That's not how you're supposed to die, that'll only slow the process. It'll be easier if you just let yourself bleed out. It'll be okay. Don't be one of those fools that fights back when there's not a chance or shred of luck in their favor. You know, that story about my parents that all those kids back in your New Canterton tell each other, well... you're right. It's true. And let me tell ya somethin': when a wolf tears out the throat of its prey, he does it to make the death happen sooner, so there is less fight, less resistance. It's better for the wolf and the creature he's killing if the one bleeding out lets the blood bleed all the way out."

"Yea? I take it you know that from firsthand experience."

"My father, as the wolves ate him alive. He resisted. He thought he might live. But no matter what, when the wolves draw in, if they're hungry, they will eat you. Whatever you thought you had going for yourself in life, all of a sudden you don't have to worry about anymore. I've heard that the realization can sometimes come as a relief, but others... it can make a man cry."

The pain started to go away, and it was at that moment I truly thought I was going to die. Right there in Mayor Henry Kenroy's fucking saloon, at the hands of this disgusting excuse of a human being.

"Is that you in there, Mancino Randingo?" There came a voice from outside, and even through my haze of slow, bleeding death, I recognized it. It was Til Drange... but it couldn't be. He was at the mayor's place, incarcerated like a caged animal. There's no way the man outside of the saloon...

Suddenly there erupted from outside a dozen gunshots, and two of Mancino's men fell to the floor of the saloon, one missing half of their skull and the other their throat run through with a trio of brightly-feathered arrows.

"Anyone not an inbred sack of horsehit in there associated with the Crimson Collar sons of bitches, get down to the floor and stay there till the guns stop shootin' and the arrows stop flyin'!" I heard Drange call out. More gunshots rang through, blasting holes in walls and bottles and glasses. One more of Mancino's men went down dead with two arrows in his chest. Mancino seemed to forget about me and leapt over the top of the bar, taking cover behind it. His two remaining men took cover of their own, shooting out towards the door of the saloon. Somewhere between all the gunshots, a noise like a chunk of wood landing on solid winter dirt from high up sounded. I peered through my haze, and saw that another one of Mancino's men feel, this one with a thick wooden arrow shot right into his left eye, the arrowhead sticking out the back of his skull. There came another cry, a warcry pitched high and fierce. Four tribesmen dressed in furs and leathers crashed through the front door of the saloon, all of them wielding tomahawks and daggers. They took the last of Mancino's men with their daggers and tomahawks, the man's screams only lasting a moment, taken over swiftly by the sound of steel cutting through flesh.

Mancino patted me on the head, I felt his hand.

"Have fun bleedin' out, pal," he said. I could only assume he fled, finding some window somewhere and crashing through it in his escape.

A moment passed, the dust from the gunfight dying down. The tribesmen looked to me with curious, but still so furious eyes. And in walked Til Drange, his rifle aimed outward as if expecting Mancino to come out of hiding just long enough for him to get a shot off.

"What," I muttered, tasting the blood on my tongue. I was bleeding out faster now, I could feel it. All of the feeling starting to leave me from the waist down.

"Quiet," Drange said, kneeling down, "shit, he really got ya good. Don't worry though, we've got ya covered, don't worry."

"How did you-"

But Drange chuckled, looking up to the tribesmen. "We have to be fast," he said, "he won't last much longer."

"It's okay," one of the tribesmen said, and I recognized him. The man with the painted face. "We have plenty of time."

"Plenty of time for....what...?"

My head felt heavy, my eyelids began to feel nonexistent.

"It's okay if you pass out, man," Drange said, putting a supportive hand behind my neck, "we ain't gonna letcha die. Ya hear that? Ya ain't gonna die. Not today."

But by the time his words reached my ears, being the last I heard, I was already caught in a net of darkness, being dragged deeper and deeper into the blinding depths of nothingness.

II

The Glass Floor

VI.
RESURRECTION

The wolf looked back at me from across a narrow stream that was little more than a trickling run-off. He stood up on all four paws, the fur on his back calm and relaxed but his sight immovable, trained, and stationary. From his lower jaw, droplets of water fell back into the stream from whence he drank, the water was calm, the surface immovable, calm, preserved, like new glass, clean glass. As he breathed, puffs of cloud emitted from his mouth. And then he ran off out of sight.

When a sound of thunder made the ground shake, I came to the understanding that I was not dreaming the wolf. I was laying down on my side on a makeshift cot with a distant pain in my stomach.

The thunder came to a rolling halt, as several tribesmen on horseback moved into view. They spoke amongst each other, one of them with a painted face pointed towards the horizon, speaking in some language I was not familiar with. He spoke sternly and with unbridled confidence, commanding those who listened, and those who listened, listened intently, as though no other voice in the world, not of this earth or from the heavens mattered. The other riders took off in the directions in which the man with the painted face commanded, their leader staying behind. When the man with the painted face dismounted, he turned his attention toward me.

"You're awake," he said without emotion. I remembered who he was; the memory of him arrived within two blinks of his arrival. He was the man whom Drange and I ran into just before reaching Vermouth. He'd been accompanied by three others then. Another flash appeared; I think I may have seen him in that saloon... was he the one with the tomahawk? Nothing made sense as of the moment. There were too many jagged edges with which one could hope to piece together.

"Depends on what you mean by being awake," I grumbled with a dry throat. I tried to move, but the previously dull pain in my stomach rose to greet me, wrenching my guts in the same way one might wring out a wet piece of clothing. The sensation prevented me from doing much more than wincing, and so all I could do was accept it. "Aw, hell."

"You're still healing. We only gave you a small dose," the man with the painted face said.

"A small dose of what?"

"Blackvein," he said with the seriousness of death on his tongue. "We mine, process, and administer it here."

"Blackvein," I mumbled. Yes, that was... that was what old Ostrander wanted, wasn't it? The so-called... *miracle* mineral. Was it true then? Was it a real thing? I supposed in some way it would have to be, unless I actually was dreaming. Or maybe I was dead, and this place was... my heaven, or hell.

I lifted up my shirt, the blood from being shot had turned to a shade of maroon copper. On my belly, I saw where the bullet had gone in. I don't remember having felt it going out the back. The point of entry appeared as any year-old scar does, a lighter color of skin healed over. Except this scar bore a darker shade, almost black, unless my eyes were tricking me. A black mark on the side of my stomach, with several small traces of black lines branching out from it, like black... veins.

"It took a little while to remove the bullet," the man with the painted face said, "but our... surgeons are quite efficient. That mark you see now is a sign that you are healing. You will live with that mark for the rest of your life." He started to move as though he were getting ready to leave.

"Wait, I have questions," I said. If I sounded grumpy to him, it's probably because I truthfully wasn't in the best of moods.

"They can wait, I'm not sure I'm the best person to be answering them."

"Why did you do this?"

"*I* didn't do anything to you. It was the Chief's final decision to save your life. Your friend, Mr. Drange assured us you were worth the expenditure. For his sake and your own, you better be. Blackvein is finite, and we don't implement it unless absolutely necessary."

"My friend," I coughed, almost laughing, "my friend. Tell me then, where is my *friend*?"

"He should be coming back soon, by eveningfall. He is out with a hunting party."

"And... where are we, exactly?"

"Blackheart Mountain," the man with the painted face said to me, "when you are better, and you can get up to walk, we can acquaint you better with our people."

"When I'm better," I growled, but it sounded more like a grumble more than actual words, like a stomach that's hungry, "I *am* better."

"We gave you a smaller dose than what we give our own people. For that, you'll need to make up for it with rest. And when I say you must rest, it's the kind of rest of which you don't move. You lay as still as possible, other than breathing and eating. Let the minerals do the work. Depending on your biology's strength, the pain will lesson in about a day." The man with the painted face walked off out of sight, leaving me to my cot in what appeared now to be a tent... or a half-pitched teepee, which was cubicle in shape. There was no front flap, it was just open, and because of this I felt a constant breeze of freezing, brisk winter air. But there was a small fire going nearby, and the warmth it gave was enough for now.

I took in the sounds, waiting for Drange, my *friend*. My view was not all that informative. I saw snow and a slope going down steeply straight head, but also to the right a slop beginning to incline upwards, and I imagined the foot of this Blackheart Mountain being every bit as impressive as Ostrander claimed it to be. Ostrander had told me stories about what it may look like, according to the stories he'd heard. The top reached up to the sky so high, that it was said to break through the atmosphere, the summit an immeasurable block of ice. Another story told of its origins as a volcano, that once erupted so powerfully it devastated the area around it for miles, leveling towns and entire cities, and that when all the death had passed and the volcanic ash-filled sky had cleared, the volcano died and froze in time, existing in its current state since. The tale of this... Blackvein, which the existence of the mineral itself was at least true, had been obscured through various storytellers' lusts and wishful thinkings throughout the years. Ostrander would frequently refer to the idea that like any myth written by man, its origins could be traced far back before the world tore itself to pieces. He went on to say most of what had been proclaimed about the mineral must have simply been embellishments written by those who never actually believed in Blackvein but had a love for the attention gained when talking about it. "Fame," Gunther Ostrander once said, "fame is a cancer, Mahon, and no way a man should die, though I suppose sometimes it is something unavoidable no matter how unintentional. That's how you can tell the difference between the sincerest of people, and those who have no real meaningful drive in life."

Ostrander first sent me to find Blackvein with the promise that if found, and if even half of the stories were true, the mineral could turn the tide on bringing civilization back to a place of firm foothold and one day maybe even surpass what we once were. "Mahon," Ostrander said to me, "this is more than just employer," he motioned towards himself and then motioned towards me with both hands, "employing his employee. A man must, constantly see everything that he can, he must anticipate any and all possible outcomes. I realize that if this mineral is discovered, with that discovery comes with it a certain responsibility to use it accordingly, you realize. If you find it, you mustn't tell anyone, except myself. If word got out that such a thing really does exist, my friend, we could put into motion something truly devastating. The idea, the hope, that civilization can be reconstructed may be the ultimate victim of that discovery, should the power to wield it fall into the wrong hands. Whoever possesses this mineral, it could mean the different between the evolution of that hope, and the death of it."

And yet, as noble as Ostrander doubtlessly intended to sound, even then I knew there was fault in his words. There existed in his stance a fissure, an absence where something pertinent to understanding the sanctity of humanity might have existed as part of an otherwise... wiser man. I didn't fully know it then, however.

Because I was a man in need of money. I remembered what Drange had said about the man. And it could be that there was some truth to that.

The dull, morose winter light cascading down through the occasional cloudbreak brought with it a gust of snowflake-filled air. I pulled the bear fur covers closer to my chin, and for the first time since I could remember, I felt a shiver that I couldn't control. One of the tribesmen threw a few more logs onto the fire outside my tent, giving more life to the orange flames. There came with the flames a glow that reflected off the inside of my tent, making it a bit troublesome to tell exactly what time it was. If I had to guess though, it was indeed close to or exactly evening, or as the man with the painted face put it, "eveningfall". I tried to roll over to my other side, but the pain in my stomach returned, reminding me to lay still while the mineral did its work.

"You better listen to Owl Wing's instructions, man," it was Til Drange, standing just outside the tent, wearing a grin like a kid on his birthday. "That stuff ain't gonna heal all by itself unless you give it a still body to work with."

"Owl...Wing?"

"The Tuskatawa with the painted face, Chief Tenskatawa's son," he said, as if I should already know, "Although I just call him Owl."

" Tenska...Tenskuh-what...? Owl....?"

"Tenskatawa and Owl Wing. Of the Tuskatawa Tribe," Drange must've known I had no clue what he was talking about or at the very least had no idea why he thought I should know more than I did. But it came to him, and his expression let me know that he remembered something important about this current exchange, "that's right. I've, uh… well, I've got a little bit of explaining to do, as I'm sure you're a bit in the dark."

"In the dark," I asked, "last thing I remember clearly is handin' you over to the head honcho over at Vermouth to be hanged. Next thing that I can only recall in pieces, is hearin' your hollerin' outside of the saloon, and then in comes blazin' a bunch of these… Tuskatawa folk. Yea, I'd say you've got some explainin' to do."

Drange pulled up a wooden stool that looked like it'd been made with a kid's ass in mind, but he sat on it all the same. He removed his hat to scratch the top of his head and ran a hand through the chestnut brown strands. "Well," he started, "without going into excruciatin' detail, you were the only one not in on it."

"In on what?"

"Mancino Rolandraz," he continued, "the Crimson Collar leader. Ya see, the old mayor of Vermouth and your employer, Ostrander, came up with this idea. It'd been made highly known by Rolandraz himself, that he wanted me dead for killin' those men of his. He tore the countryside apart lookin' for me, just… slaughterin' everyone. The death toll was getting' staggerin'. So, me, a slave workin' in Ostrander's quarry," he stopped, seeing the narrowness of my eyes when he referred to himself as a slave, "yea, a slave, Mahon. But we'll get to all that. Your boss came to me, knowin' who I was, with a plan that could result in either the capture of Mancino Rolandraz, or end in his death. Either way was acceptable. Plan was to have me transferred to Vermouth to," he kinda got a little giddy with his words, "face my crimes for killin' the mayor's brother, which of course, he doesn't actually have a brother. It was all a falsehood created to give my transfer purpose. With Mancino's many eyes watchin' the roads and the land, it was almost a sure thing he'd hear about me bein' moved to

Vermouth."

"I'm pretty sure I know where you're goin' with this," I said, sitting up against the pain in my stomach, "I ain't layin' down while you tell me I was an instrument in the bullshit. So, you all, the three of ya, used me to get ya to Vermouth so this Mancino Rolandraz fellah could be caught or killed. Well, a lotta good that did seein' as he got the hell away."

"We had to have a fourth party who had no idea what was goin' on," Drange said, "those Crimson Collar people, they may be crazy heads, but they're sharp too. If you'd known about it all, chances are they'd be able to tell just by your body language no matter how good an actor you may be. That was a chance we couldn't afford to take."

"Tell ya the truth though, I'm actually a pretty terrible actor," I said, nodding my head, "if I ain't givin' it straight it just doesn't feel right."

"Exactly, and yes, while that's a good trait to have," he replied, "it's not something we could risk. Unfortunately, as you know, he did get away."

"So you and old Gunth' are in cahoots with one another," I said, wincing against the mineral's work, "how can that be, you bein' a slave and all?"

"He said to me that if I helped in the endeavor, I'd earn my freedom," he said.

"So now you're all buddy buddy, the three of ya, I find that hard to believe," I said to Drange, though he seemed to find humor in my assumption.

"I, uh, I didn't volunteer to help out your boss and his compatriot because I wanted to be friends with 'em. Ostrander is still someone who needs to be dealt with the right way. He sent you out here to find Blackvein. A man like Gunther Ostrander is the absolute last person who deserves to be in control of such a thing. Keeping its existence secret has been the Tuskatawa way of life since they discovered it. And as long as the Tuskatawa and myself are alive to continue that tradition, Ostrander and those like him will suffer before they get their hands on it."

"So now what, big man," I growled, holding my stomach, "you're just gonna go back and kill him? Can't do it. Can't be done, I'm afraid. I'm sure at least part of you knows that, bein' you were there and all. I know I'm new here, but unless you've got an army of a few-hundred thousand painted skins willin' to die, you don't have a fly's fart chance of takin' him down. And with Kenroy on his side, you have even less a chance. Actually... Kenroy is a sillyheart, a real bitch of a man. Even his own people are set on believin' he sucked at his momma's teet until he was thirty-five, but only because she died, otherwise her titmilk would still be his main source of nourishment. He may not be a threat so much himself. But he has connections. And Ostrander, Ostrander alone is a master tactician. I hate to throw salt on your pecker, but like I said... I've gotta give it to ya straight. And that's what you're gettin'. You go against that man in battle, you'll die an even bigger idiot than the poor sucker who fathered ya."

"Well," Drange looked down to the wintered ground, reaching down with a hand and cradling a few clumps of hardened dirt, "these people, here, the Tuskatawa, may not be brilliant tacticians of war, and if it's one thing they've taught me, it's to be patient. I've been lucky-enough to have been in their good graces for many years, Mahon. I've got a history with these people; I've learned a lot from them. They are well aware of what sort of threat Gunther Ostrander is. If they weren't, I'm sure they'd have attempted an assault on him already, and most definitely failed." He let the hardened dirt fall back to the ground by the toes of his boots, clapping his hands of the stuff left behind. "You better get back to your rest."

"I'm fine," I said, shifting my weight in an attempt to get out of the cot. But the sharp pings and healing flesh where my recent wound lay had something else to say about that.

"Give it another day or two, you'll be fine," he said.

"Another day or two?"

Drange stood up, looking outward from the tent I lay in. He sniffed the air, found something he liked about it, and smiled a little at whatever it was he admired.

"Hey, where's my horse?" I admit, remembering Eleanor had only just come back to me. I remembered hitchin' her upon arrival in Vermouth. But then there was the saloon and that nasty business. And here I was. "Where's Eleanor?"

"She's fine," Drange said, "she's over with the others gettin' fed now. Don't worry. Tuskatawa treat their horses better than they do anything or anyone else." He left, walking on down a path winding out of view. I let my head fall back onto the pillow, and the sharp ache in my belly slowly waned to a mere discomfort. A day or two, laying here in this cot while this stuff healed me? The way Ostrander made it sound, Blackvein was supposed to be this great thing... but then I remembered what Owl Wing had said about them only administering a small amount, just enough to keep me goin'. If they'd given me a regular dose, I'm sure I'd be on my feet in a more desirable timeframe. Then I could get back to Ostrander, let him know that I'd found the mountain, and more importantly, Blackvein itself. I understood that Drange had an affinity with these people, the... Tuskatawa. But I had a job to do. I had given Ostrander my word, and no, I wasn't upset about the setup for Rolandraz. I was entirely sympathetic towards the idea of secrecy and strategy when it came to getting a hold of someone you wanted dead. And now that I'd become acquainted with Rolandraz, and with his style of getting what *he* wanted, should the time come we cross paths again, putting a bullet in his head would be a far easier thing to manage.

No surprises next time, nothing to stop me but my own sense of timing and adjustment to atmosphere, two things I'd already mastered, and mastered further every day I managed to survive.

VII.
A TRIBE of TRIBES

When it came time to feed me, a woman with bronzed skin and hints of dark paint beneath her eyes walked into the tent with a tray of meat strips and raw vegetables. The meat was dry and the vegetables had no flavor, but none of those detriments ever bothered me. The woman with dots and lines beneath her eyes didn't say anything, and didn't wear an expression that would allow me to determine her mood. She stood until I finished eating and promptly removed the tray from my cot. In the same motion, she vacated the tent.

When night fell, I detected the flickering glow of several fires throughout the camp. Through the sheet of the tent closest to my cot, I watched the shadows of many Tuskatawa, short and tall, men and women, some of them merely walking here and there, some of them breaking the stride of a normal stroll and falling into brief interjections of dance and play. And just outside my tent, a half dozen set of tiny eyes peered in from behind the flap. Kids, children, with tanned faces and dark hair. I could only see the top half of their faces but I could tell by their raised cheekbones that something about the presence of an outsider, me, grabbed their curiosity. I laid on my back, looking at them with my own eyes and they just stared back like a pile of spying raccoons. I laughed to myself. I laughed at their strange innocence.

"I'm not gonna put on a show, if that's what you're waitin' for. I'm the only clown in existence who don't do tricks."

The little ones stayed focused on me, some of them grabbing a hold of the tent flap with their little fingers. Suddenly a woman came by, shooing them away with waving arms. I noticed it was the woman who brought me my food. The little dots of paint beneath her eyes looked as though they had worn off somewhat throughout the course of the day. When she succeeded in shooing away the last child, she stopped to look back into the tent. Probably to see if I was awake or asleep, or if the kids had disturbed me at all. For a moment, I thought that she might have actually cared about my wellbeing. But when I flashed her a toothy grin, her face remained unchanged in a way most women appear when they want to convey a feeling of indifference. She didn't care about me. To her, I was a burden when she could most definitely be spending her time in a more worthwhile way. She left and I relaxed back into my original position of mixed, uneven slumber.

It must have been hours, maybe less. Maybe my mind was just not used to this type of existing. The voices outside died down as did the flames, but the woman with the paint under her eyes came back.

"I can tuck myself in, thanks," I muttered, not entirely sure she understood me, and only because she hadn't said a single word. She maintained that position, handing me a porcelain cup half-full of some kind of liquid. I smelled it, and immediately almost dropped the cup. The smell reminded me of some kind of low-grade, dehydrated urine. I assumed she meant for me to drink it, an idea I was not too keen on. "What the hell is this?"

The woman stood back by the tent flap, waiting for me to drink the cup. She had her back turned to me.

"Hey, Painted Eyes," I called out, "what is this

stuff?" She turned her head toward me, her left ear having listened to my words. She breathed in deeply, as though contemplating her next move. "Look, I uh, I get the feelin' for some reason you don't like me, or approve of me bein' here. And that's fine, I get it. Most people have those types of feelings toward me, especially the ones who know me. But," I said, "I'd just really like to know what this stuff is before I drink it."

"Tea," she said, her voice was small, but only because she made it so, "to help you sleep."

"There, now was that so hard?" I looked back into the cup, smelling it again. "Never smelled tea that smelled quite like this."

She turned all the way around.

"It's not supposed to smell good," she said, as if I was supposed to know that already, as though I, me, were a man well-versed in the ways of tea and other Tuskatawa confections, "we, give it to those who have been given the Blackvein. We've found that sleep can be troublesome when the initial healing processes are taking place. This tea will relax you so that you can find rest."

"Do I have to drink the whole cup," I asked.
"Yes."

I took a deep breath and then downed the whole thing in one gulp. Surprisingly, the tea didn't taste as bad as it smelled. Though I wouldn't exactly ride all the way to Vermouth if they were pourin' it straight from a fountain. I handed her back the cup and she took it.

"Good," she said.

"And your name," I said, licking my lips, trying to figure out exactly what the tea tasted like, "what's your name? I assume I'm going to be seein' you a whole lot during these.... healin' days."

"Sanuye," she said, "my name is Sanuye."

"Sanuya," I said.

"Yes, now, rest, go to sleep," she said, and she was gone.

"How's my horse," I mumbled, already my speech beginning to slur.

"She's content," I heard the woman say.

I swallowed the last tiny dribbles of "tea" I'd licked off my lips and... she was right. I felt the sleep come on to me like a dust storm gusting in from the north. My head felt as though I were leaning back, though I knew I couldn't have been. The tips of my fingers numbed and the sensation climbed up to my shoulders. My toes followed suit, and with the dying flickering light of the campfires outside the tent, my sight went to black.

It could have been only a moment later. A minute, if not thirty seconds. But I was awake once more; a bleak, winter morning sunlight poured into the tent. I awoke to the sounds of wood being chopped, animals eager to be fed, and children far-off, laughing and playing. My head did not waver, nor did it feel heavy, and I found that I could sit up all the way, swinging my legs around the cot and resting my feet onto the ground. For the first time, I was able to take a look at my surroundings comfortably. The cot I'd been marooned on only took up a small part of the inside. Adjacent to the foot of the cot, sat a trunk with my long coat and other clothes piled atop. Up against the trunk leaned my rifle, and my belt holster with my two revolvers nestled inside. On top of my pile of clothing sat my hat. As I looked at it, I suddenly felt naked, and it became clear to me that of all things waiting for me to get better, my hat may have been the most eager. I reached out and grabbed it, dusting the brim and looking it over. The hat looked fine, a little worn, but then again it had always looked that way. I placed it on my head, letting it hold down my hair. There, even half naked in my undergarments, I felt that much better. It was then I noticed something different about my long coat. Something... added. I picked it up and let the length of it unfurl. On the inside, there had been some new cloth sewn in. It was thicker now, and even as I felt it, holding on to the coat, I could feel its increased weight.

My undergarments felt loose against my skin though, and as I lifted my shirt to see how the healing wound was fairing, I thought that I must have lost some weight, or at least it appeared that way. My stomach seemed smaller, and my skin just a weed-frill's tighter. Where the bullet had gone in, the wound was completely gone. No scar, no trace of anything having shot through me, except for the veins. While healing, they had looked darker, and currently they could still be seen, but so vaguely that unless someone told you about them, you'd never know they were there. I saw them, and I ran a gentle finger over the spot where the bullet had gone through. The skin felt smooth and new, where the rest of me looked and felt like a man who'd exposed himself to the elements of the world.

Drange walked in, the toe of his right boot kicking up a little dust while tripping over a small rock.

"You're up," he said.

"Someone's tampered with my clothing. My coat, most specifically."

"Sanuye, the woman who's been feeding you, felt as though you might appreciate an extra layer of protection against the mountain weather. It can get pretty cold up here sometimes."

"Oh?"

"Hence the inlay. It's fashioned from a variety of the wildlife indigenous to the area, believe me, you'll be glad you had it when the wind really starts to blow. You'll feel like you're wearin' ten extra layers of skin." He let out a chuckle and nodded as if agreeing with his own explanation, and then he sighed, focusing in on my belly, "anyway, you... you're a fast healer, you remarkable bastard."

"I've always been," I said as if it were actually true, "Hell, between that mineral and that... tea I drank last night, who wouldn't completely heal from an otherwise deadly gunshot wound overnight?"

"Nuwati," Drange said with a quirk in his voice.

"Nu...what?"

"Nuwati. It's the tea. Well, it's a bit of a... departure from what Nuwati truly is. The Tuskatawa added some of their own ingredients to enhance the original properties."

"Is that where the smell comes from?"

"Yes," he titled his head sympathetically.

"I see. Sanuye is a pretty one, though. So at least I've got that goin' for me."

"Oh, you mean my wife? Yea, she's a pretty one, huh," Drange waited for me to look at him. I think he knew that I didn't know, and at the same time never expected to find that out about him.

"Your *wife*?!"

"Married her five years ago, this year," he said. "Hell of a woman. I've known her for the entirety of my life thus far, though. Sanuye was just a girl when I was found, and we weren't exactly friends at first. But you know how time can change people."

"Married," I laughed, "funny."

"She didn't give you any trouble, I imagine."

"Trouble? Hell, she barely said much to me at all. Started to feel like she didn't like me much!"

"She doesn't," Drange laughed a hard chuckle at that, "she's actually disgusted by you."

"Why the hell for?!"

"Somethin' about your face, honestly. Yea. Thinks your ugly. And not so much in a forgivable way that less mentally-fortunate folk can be."

"Ugly?"

"I was only comin' in to check on ya but it looks like you might be ready."

"Ready for what?"

"The chief wants to meet you," he said, "wants to size ya up. I am, after all, the only reason why they took ya in. The Blackvein. The nice tent. You can thank me later."

"Why do I get the feelin' I'm being ransacked into somethin' I wouldn't normally have anything to do with?"

"I don't suppose you know another word for 'ransacked' that has a lesser-intensive definition of the meanin'."

"No. It's ransacked, or it's ransacked. There is no in-between this or that."

"The chief might have a few questions in regards to your boss, Ostrander. Just a few. You know, a couple… fill in the blank-type queries. Nothing you can't handle."

I looked over at my pile of stuff on top of the trunk, most particularly my sidearms. I didn't need to reach far to grab em, but I'd have to be quick. I sat there on the edge of the cot eying them. Drange took note, nodding as a doctor does who wants his patient to think he understands their pain.

"You aren't being held captive, Mahon," he said, "you can leave whenever you want. Your horse is right out there. I can take ya to her now, even."

"I know what being held captive feels like," I said, "conversely, I know what being able to leave whenever I feel like really means. I ain't stupid, Drange. The second I leave here, I've got a target painted right in the center of my back. You know why I was employed by Ostrander. You know what I was sent out to find."

"Yea, but they don't," Drange kept his voice down, "I never told 'em."

"Why the hell not?"

"Because you never know who you're gonna need on your side these days," he said, his voice a raspy whisper, "hell, you could answer all the chief's questions with lies if ya wanted to."

"You say you care about these people, your damn wife is among 'em. And you're tellin' me you're gonna let me go when you know full well what is comin' back this way once I report to Ostrander. Explain that logic to me."

"Honestly," Drange took a breath, gazing out of the tent, "a little part of me is hopin' to turn your allegiances. Never really expected to be able to, and still don't. I figured you're here for a little while. Maybe I could change your mind. Because yes, I do know what lettin' ya go means. And you're right, there would be a target painted on your back. And Mahon, you should probably know, I never miss."

Silence took over the inside of the tent. Drange's amusement in my emotional squalor changed to that of a serious man's endeavor when he was ready to do the killin' thing. His brow arched, and firmed up. He didn't stand with clenched teeth, as a greenhorn might. He stood with one hand at his hip, and on that hip was holstered a sidearm of particular, exact, and solitary purpose.

"I see," I said.

"You aren't an enemy of these people, yet, Mahon," he said, "you still have that choice to make."

He let his hand fall from its roost atop the holster and moved to leave the tent, stopping just outside the flap.

"I'll tell the chief you're well, and I'll be back in a little to come get ya," he said. His words still took on the recent seriousness, but in a way, there was a certain apologetic quality to them. The crunch of his footfalls faded away as he sauntered off down the path. I stood up, stretching, letting my muscles scream impatiently while the tendons and the ligaments and the bones all did their best to catch up to the rest of me. My fingers, my elbows, anywhere there was a joint or a meeting of two bones where a nice cushion of cartilage should be, there was a pain that lingered, leftover from my time in the cot. I wasn't typically a man of rest, and while I enjoyed sleep and respite when it was afforded to me, I rarely spent much time on them. Even the time I'd spent with Cassandra, those moments we'd been lucky enough to have... laying in bed beside her, well... perhaps those moments I allowed to last, only because they were so unusually peaceful, so tranquil. My existence had not been introduced to those kinds of feelings, which sometimes required stillness to fully absorb and to be absorbed by. I admit I was still learning; I still had a long way to go when it came to fully understanding the importance of having a woman to love, and not just to love, but to enjoy... a lasting breath that exhales farther than a prairie-blown wind. I slipped into my slacks and adjusted the belt accordingly, thinking about the way Cassandra would undo that belt. Her fingers were of the delicate sort, looking strange and foreign whenever they touched any part of me. I suppose it was something she felt she had to do, something she couldn't fight against, as I felt about her. Even in this dirt-covered world, the life we all lived and tried to live, she was a figurine of faultlessness. Every day, I tried to come up with a reason why not only she knew of my existence, but more so, why she chose to abide by whatever gave fuel to her emotional needs bent in my direction. Every day, I wondered what I had done during my life, the long timeline riddled with self-indulgent occupation to deserve her favor.

Sanuye brought me another tray of food just as I was slipping toes into my boots. She wore the same face as yesterday, and beneath her eyes was painted fresh dots and a few decorative lines.

I smirked as she placed the tray on my cot. Our eyes had met for a second. She caught sight of my smirk, which added a little hurriedness to her step. When she returned to her post at the flap of my tent, I bent over and took a look at the food she'd brought me. Dried meat strips and a piece of bread. There was also a porcelain mug with clear-ish water inside. I sniffed the liquid and was pleased to find that there was none of the tea from last night to be smelled.

"Thank you," I said, "Sanuye Drange."

I waited for her to say something, but I think it frazzled her britches just a little too much to contemplate at the moment, if that was part of her attire. She'd been caught off guard, and I took enjoyment in that.

"So," I said, "how'd you come to marry such a guy?"

"I don't believe it's any of your business, Mr. Mahoney," she said quickly, unaffected.

"It's just a question," I said, taking a bite of the

dry meat, "From what I know of him, if it's all to be believed, he was a boy when he came to your people... he did say that's when he met you. And at one point or another, he was thrown in with the... so-called slaves under the eyes of a one Gunther Ostrander. I'm just tryin' to fill in some blanks, that's all."

She stood firm in her resistance, but I gathered from the passing of the moment's time, and how her breathing began to sound a little more relaxed, a little more... subdued, she felt as though divulging a little info wouldn't be outside the realm of inappropriate. Sanuye turned around and faced me.

"He wasn't just... caught, and tossed in with the rest of the slaves," she started, "he let himself get captured, so that he could find a way to save me. I'd already been digging in that quarry for a year. He'd been the only one of our people to believe there was a way, at that time, to get anyone out. His defiance tainted the trust the chief had in him. I guess you could say he's been trying to fully earn that trust back ever since."

"I take it he found a way to get you out," I said.

"He did, after a while. But at the cost of remaining behind himself. He stayed back so that I could get away. Ostrander's quarry-runners don't keep a face-count as much as they do a head count. And even then, it wasn't hard to deceive them. We tried to get away together, and we could have, until the very moment we needed in order for that to happen... he was seen. And allowed himself to be taken so that I could get away. That was... a long time ago."

"He got you out, and no one came back for him," I asked. Sanuye shook her head slowly.

"At the time, our people were not prepared to make such a risk for one person. Even him."

"Part of me suddenly feels bad for pryin' so

hard," I said, "I didn't think that was the story behind ya, you two. I'm sorry if I upset ya."

"You didn't. It's been a long-enough time that most of those wounds have healed," she brushed back her hair from the side of her face, but I wagered it was done so that I could see the scar: a deep-crevice from behind her ear down the rear-side of her neck. "And Til has returned. He told me that you helped make that possible."

"Well, it's a little more complicated than just that."

"So it is, I don't need to know," she said, "finish your food. I need to get on with my day." I grabbed the food off the tray and tossed it to my cot, where a piece of the dried meat bounced onto the floor and the piece of bread rolled into a space between the trunk and the cot-leg. I drained the warm water and handed her to the tray. "Thanks," she took it and was gone.

So, Drange risked his trust with the chief of these folk to save the life of the woman he loved. He stayed behind and took all that punishment, all that enslavement, his body being broken every day and rebuilt another, and then broken again the next. Ostrander, my boss, the one with all the promises and aspirations... I was starting to shift the fitted shapes of my ideas of the man. Could he be as cruel as the Tuskatawa saw him to be? And if he was that sort of man, why hadn't I been able to see such a thing? I'd spent my life adapting to the land and its remaining, surviving, desperate inhabitants. I fancied myself a smart traveler, there was hardly a situation I didn't get out of unscathed, but I always managed to find a way, most of the time by my own making, to make it to the next sunrise. Perhaps I'd grown arrogant in my stride. Someone like Gunther Ostrander, whom I was working for, would have to depend on that arrogance, in order to continue employing me. He'd be well-aware of it too, encouraging its presence as long as he could. He depended on my arrogance, my ignorance of his true impetus, so that when I returned to him with news of my discovery of Blackheart Mountain, there would be no harm done to the relationship we had with one another. I, Rancid Mahoney, was no stranger to betrayal, or short-handling of the truth. That didn't change the sharpness of its teeth every time it bit down.

Not long after Sanuye deprived me of her company, her other half showed up just on down the path a ways. I'd taken a stance outside my tent to get a good look at this Blackheart Mountain my employer was so dead-set on finding. When I'd stepped out of the tent, I found myself to be in what appeared to be a village, full with tribesman and tribeswomen walking here and there going about their day, the children running in stampedes. The village sat in the middle, the bottom-most part of a valley surrounded by wintry mountains, the largest of those resting to the northwest. Its sides were the darkest of all other mountains around it, so I presumed that it was the, up until now, mythical Blackheart Mountain. The mountain was so large, I wondered how I'd missed it during all my other travels. It could have been that I'd simply not traveled this far, that while making my way through the rest of these other mountains, whatever position I'd situated myself in, Blackheart Mountain simply had not been in view.

From its base, a wide trail wound across the valley floor, cutting through the snow with the tramplings of tribesmen walking into the mouth of a cave cut into its side, delving deep into the heart chambers. It was in there, I imagined, where the mineral Blackvein was mined and gathered and processed into whatever form they needed it to be in order to fuse it when human DNA.

Drange stood with his hands on his hips.

"Waitin' for me?" I called down.

"You're fully dressed," he said, "I can only assume that means your ready. Unless you plan on leavin'."

The conscience is a goddamn funny thing. When I looked at the children of the tribe running amongst the adults, their faces exploding with enjoyment for no particular reason other than running after one another... I saw my own child. I saw my daughter, and what she might one day become, if she didn't succumb to the horrors of the all-but-dead world. I saw the smile in her face, the childlike wonder. It didn't matter how terrible an environment was; there were always going to be moments when a child felt the inspiration to smile at something. It could be anything. A change in rainfall, the sound of splash a puddle makes when you step into it, embracing a new color, tasting food they never tasted before, waking up and seeing that it's snowing. She would find a reason to. But she was not yet born. And all these children here were already living their lives. They were finding reasons to smile, and taking those smiles further into laughter. If I went back to Gunther, I'd no doubt every single one of these people... men, women, and child, would be killed. Murdered by Ostrander's motivations of sovereignty. Then again... if I stuck around here long enough, I would certainly have to find a way to get back to Ostrander's factory. Cassandra was still there, as was our unborn daughter.

"I'll stick around for a little while. I'll meet the chief," I said, "not promisin' anything. I'll listen to his questions and if I feel like it, I'll answer em."

Drange seemed relieved, but not in the sense that I'd be inconveniencing him if the time came in which he'd have to put a bullet in me. As the saying goes: it's always easier to talk than it is to pull a trigger, or maybe, now that I think of the saying, it was the other way around. I wasn't sold a hundred percent either way. But he was thankful I'd decided to stay regardless. I joined him at his side and nodded toward him in acknowledgment.

"You're armed," he took note.

"A smart man knows to never leave his sidearms back in the tent," I said, thumbing the butt of one of the revolvers, "I'd have slept with them if your people hadn't stripped em from me." Slipping my arms through the sleeves of my long coat, I could finally feel the difference Sanuye's inlay made. The chill inside the tent was completely gone, and even as I stepped outside into the air of the village, when the wind blew, my shoulders only felt the force of the gust, and not its teeth. Drange noticed me feeling the long coat and I nodded to him, letting him know I officially approved of the upgrade.

I followed Drange through the village and down a dirt road toward the shores of a small lake, most of which had frozen over with thin sheets of ice. My position back at the tent had led me to believe that the great field of the valley itself was the only thing between the village and the mountain, but in fact the lake was part of that route as well. From on the shore, there was a dock in which several canoes tied to post, floating in the cold, black water. Crossing in a jagged line across the surface of the lake, ice had been carved out so that boats could be oared back and forth between this dock and the Mountain dock. I counted three canoes out on the water, two headed toward the opposite shore where Blackheart Mountain sat, and one on its way back to this dock. We did not get into a canoe to cross over into the shadow of the Mountain, however. I followed Drange further along the edge of the frozen water around a hilly, snow-covered bend. Around this we turned, coming to a fairly large hut, built strong that resisted the weight of the snow on its roof. Outside, a man with a painted face waited.

"Owl Wing," I said to myself, though it was loud enough so that Drange could hear.

"That's him," he said, "still doesn't like you much, so, take care of your words. Don't be an asshole."

"Doesn't seem like many of your people have a half-likin' towards me. Almost as if they know something about me they probably shouldn't," I meant this to be taken directly as an assault on Drange. And he responded accordingly.

"I told you, I didn't say to anyone why you were lookin' for this place. But don't take them for bein' stupid, Mahon. Especially Chief Tenskatawa. It could very well be said that the reason someone like him is still alive is that he has eyes and ears on every mountain, in every valley and forest from here to who knows where. I know I said earlier you could lie when answering his questions. I hope you were able to figure out I was only bein' sarcastic."

"Sure," I said, "no lies, then."

As we trudged up the muddied clearing toward the hut, Owl Wing approached the two of us, with a facial emphasis of hatred and disdain toward me.

"Owl," Drange said. Owl Wing nodded to him, but moved his eyes back to me.

"The chief, my father will see you now, but must hand over your weapons while speaking with him," Owl Wing proclaimed.

"You must not have thought those words all the way through, kid," I couldn't help but sneer a little. Did this... Owl Wing... think that I would be so easy? "I just got done talkin' to this here Drange, about these here revolvers. They're with me, at all times. Trust me, if what I wanted to do was kill your old man, I'd have gone in guns blazin' by now."

Owl Wing was not a fan of my reasoning.

"Mahon," Drange started, "I'll hold em, you don't have anything to worry about." He held out his hands, most likely in an attempt to receive the revolvers.

"You've been drinkin' some of that tea on your downtime, haven't ya?"

"That's the ticket into the hut. You can't blame us for worryin', but it really has nothing to do with *you*. It's just how we do it here." I could see there was no other option. There was an option, though. Go in guns blazin'.

I handed Drange my revolvers and he held on to them. He told me I'd get them back good as new after I was finished speaking with the chief. Giving Owl Wing the same nasty look he'd been giving me since my arrival, I walked past him and gently pushed my way through the hut's doorway.

Inside the hut he waited, Chief Tenskatawa. The man sat on a log with his knees raised. His head was half-shaven, the rest of his black hair styled to the side and flowing down to his shoulder. Before him a small fire surrounded by stones kept the inside of the hut warm.

"Your friend assured me you were a man of strong resolve," he began, his voice was deep and made only deeper by the confined acoustics of the hut, "you look to me like a man whose only destiny is to grow old, one who is already exhausted, not spent completely, but one whose expenditure is diminishing rapidly. You're already a tired man at such a young age, Mr. Ran....cid.... Mahoney."

"Friend, what is it about that man that makes you people think he's my *friend*?"

"Before you woke," Tenskatawa said, eyes still on the fire, "he spoke about you in a way conveying presumed friendship, a bond, had taken place."

"There ain't nothin' about that man I'd find interestin' enough to call him my friend," I said, and then I lowered my voice, dropping it down to a more indoor volume, "though, I guess, he did in a way, save my life."

"He *did* save your life," Tenskatawa said, nodding. I took a seat on a log opposite him, the small fire now exactly between us. I didn't say anything for a time, and neither did he. We both felt the air, taking in the currents and analyzing each other's company. He was a strong man, I could see. Even sitting, Tenskatawa commanded a strong presence. His bare chest showed a massive, muscular frame, the crevices of his collar bone deep and showing off the sculpture-like quality of his shoulders. He bore many scars, some of them small, probably from tiny daggers or brief brushes with large-thorned flora. He looked back at me for what felt to be a long time, and it soon made me worry, being I couldn't decide if I was growing more inquisitive about him, or less patient and therefore angry that we'd done nothing but sit here with nothing but a fire and little to no words between us.

Finally, it was Tenskatawa who killed the quiet.

"We are a people who've held the belief that to kill another man, is not as simple an act as ending one's life would mean to another, but rather it is to take his soul. Each life we end with our hands, we inherit the burdens of that life, the guilts, the pains, the worries, the woe brought on by anything unfinished. You might say that in a way, each life we voluntarily end, we lessen the quality of our own," he began, looking into the fire still, "The Tuskatawa are not a tribe of soul thieves. We do not kill unless we absolutely have to. The reason for such an act must be truly compelling. We realize the state of the world may demand otherwise, but it is how we keep ourselves free of the burdens. So, instead of simply killing our enemies, we would rather take from them something apart of their livelihood which would make the rest of their life a true hell, something that nothing, not even the mineral in our Mountain could remedy. However, to illustrate just how important it is that you understand what's at stake, in the case of your employer, Gunther Ostrander, I would have my tribesmen kill a thousand men just to get to him. In the case of Mancino Rolandraz, the man terrorizing this part of the world with his Crimson Collars, I would have my men kill a thousand men just so that I could cut out his eyes myself. There are certain men so horrible, that the acquirement of such aforementioned burdens is necessary. It is Law."

"My *friend* said to me that you had some questions about Ostrander. My *friend* said to me that you aren't quite all the way enlightened when it comes to my being here, lookin' for that out-there mountain. I get the vibe that was just a stretched truth."

"What is it you think?"

"I think you know exactly why I was lookin' for that mountain, which makes me wonder why it is I'm still alive. But the other part of me, the silent part which has an eerie tendency to get louder when it starts to feel the itch, has a ghost of a guess, and honestly, I think it's a pretty good guess. Maybe even spot on."

"Mr. Mahoney," he said, standing up. He took a

deep breath as though he were on the precipice of falling into a deep meditation; Tenskatawa already sufficiently projected the towering stance of someone more ancient on the inside than he might let on, someone who was fooled by no lie no matter how believable or delectable, but now he gave off the luster of a man who might really be a god, or someone who might one day have a statue erected in his image, "I don't need you to help strategize an assault on the factory. I don't need you to help us free the rest of those slaves still under the asphyxiation of your employer. There are other... tribes, groups we have... dealt with in the past, currently on their way here to aid in militaristic stratagem. Our intentions are not to destroy your New Canterton so much as it is to liberate it. What I want to know is why you'd continue to work for a man such as him, knowing well what sort of man he is at heart. You are a man of opportunity, no? Surely you must by now be aware of his violent heart, his merciless eyes. Would this realization not fall under the category of... an opportunity?"

"Well see now there's the thing about all that," I said, "regardless of the employer's spirituality, regardless of the view from his bedroom, whether it's Ostrander or anyone else signin' my checks, I have my word to honor. My line of work is contingent solely on my own reputation. If I break that word once, just once, there's a very high chance that some future employer might catch wind of that. I can live off the land fine, but that's not always gonna be enough. A man needs to earn a livin' somehow. Eventually, if he doesn't have a means of income, that lack of income turns into a lack of purpose, and that is one kind of Hell I don't ever intend on visitin'. That's madness cured only with a bullet or sharpened steel."

"So, it is the acquiring of money that is the basis for your code of honor," the chief went over it in his head as he spoke, very slowly, broodingly. "It does not matter to you the wake which your path leaves behind. Your horse should be so lucky as to have such a strong man as its owner. Quite lucky."

"I'm not alive today because I stopped to care about the negative repercussions of my actions," I said, "I'm alive because of that *code*. If I took back anything I'd done in life up until this point, I wouldn't be here breathing today."

"We will never know for sure of the potential positivity that sort of rearrangement might or would have," the chief said. "It is obvious this is a sore subject for you."

"You have your way of life, I have mine."

The conversation went on like that for a while; him saying one thing, myself taking the opposite stance with an example as to why I was right and he was wrong. And yet, Chief Tenskatawa had an answer for everything. He too had examples, although some of them were a bit cryptic for my brain to absorb. There were references he made to the weather and the effect it had on the earth and of its many people. Some of these references were dead set riddlesome, and I had to let him know just how much I despised riddles. I despised them more than hunger.

We eventually fell into the subject of his people, and their origin. He explained how the Tuskatawa were merely tribe after tribe after tribe of men, women, and children, all of whom gathered together near the beginning of what they called the New Days, the days following the great collapse of civilization, society, and old law. The people came together from all alcoves and fissures of the world, all of them having the blood of their native ancestors flowing through them, descendants of those who once roamed this land free before a hellbent set of explorers began taking over everything and slaughtering anyone who didn't like it. The Collapse, as the Tuskatawa called it, led to the New Days, a period of time during which at some point, they were supposed to fully take back what had been taken from them so many centuries ago. "It was a sigil from the stars," Tenskatawa said, "reason, and proof that what had taken over the minds of the so-called civilized citizens of the world, was never meant to last forever. And today, my son is the tenth generation from which that root has grown."

The conversation took us out from the hut and to the frozen shoreline, where the tiniest waves of lake water lapped up against the hard sand. The little waves barely made any noise, but if they did, it'd be drowned out by the sound of those digging into the ice-cold water with their oars, cutting across the lake to Blackheart Mountain.

"The reason I wanted to speak to you," he said, "the real reason, is because every man deserves to know what he is up against, should he be tasked with choosing one path or the other. Surely your *friend*, Drange informed you what would have to happen should we let you leave, am I correct?"

"He mighta mentioned something about putting a bullet in my back."

"So you understand the concern."

"I understand it well enough. You don't have to insist on sugar coating the damn thing. It ain't no damn cookie. And if you don't mind me askin', why wait until I'm gone to kill me? Why not do it now?"

"Letting someone you mean to kill believe that they're safe is a powerful weapon. If they know something is coming, it creates a risk that could inevitably threaten the lives of those here who are defenseless. I don't know you well enough to judge one way or the other just yet. My people haven't survived this long on taking chances. Mistakes have been made, of course, but never more than once."

"Then why tell me you'll kill me at all?! Doesn't that defeat the purpose?!"

"It was never our intention to tell you. That was *Drange* who spoke those words. It was *Drange* who felt the need to warn you."

"Why?"

"I can't say. I don't know the reasons behind all of his actions."

A cold wind blew down from the Mountain, stabbing into every exposed part of the skin on my face, neck, and hands, with ice carved into little, perfectly-sharpened knives. Without my newly-fashioned long coat, I might have turned completely to ice. We walked back the way I'd come with Drange, taking to the hill climbing up into the village, where everyone we crossed paths with seemed to acknowledge Tenskatawa in some way. He greeted them back, and all whom he embraced, wore an expression of the most absolute appreciation for him being who he was. He stopped to play with children, picking one of the younger ones up and holding him high into the grey sky. The child laughed, and when Tenskatawa placed him back on the ground he ran to his parents, excited to tell them about the experience. I thought about what it might be like to do that with my daughter one day. I hoped I lived long enough to see that day.

"You see these children," Tenskatawa said, "they have no knowledge of the sort of life you live. They know a peace because we uphold that. They have an innocence we can protect, that's the tipping point. It's not because they are children. We teach our young ones to fight at an early age because that is the world we all live in. But each one of them, until that point, lives in a tiny pocket of time that is more sacred than anything you can be paid with. I don't need you to understand that, because a man chooses his own philosophy. That is simply what I believe."

He walked away back to his hut. His son, Owl Wing shot me a look of revulsion before following suit. Drange took to my side.

"He's a long talker," he said, handing me back my weapons.

"A long talker? You must not have been listening the entire time."

"Any new thoughts," he asked. I checked the chambers of each revolver, making sure the bullets were still there. After I was satisfied, I holstered them both and took a deep breath.

"It's safe to say that... I have never been this in-decisive."

That evening, the clouds pushed off and the sky was clear, and I saw all of the stars come out all at once. I lay on my cot, gazing out of the open flaps of my tent. By the time the sun had set all the way and the night gusts had lowered to an occasional howl, there seemed to come forth a bit of commotion from the outside air. I climbed out of the cot and wrapped one of the tribe's heavy cloaks around my shoulders, a cloak fashioned from some kind of large animal by the looks of it. I stood just outside my tent and looked around. The voices fell low, and again the air became silent. I saw that there were tiny fires lit along the path leading away from me, though the fires did not originate at my tent. They began up a hill far away in one direction, and wound down another path toward the village. Looking farther on, I could see villagers, dark under the night sky, each one of them holding their own light, flickering torches, orange and bright. They stood amassed at the center of the village where a great figure stood over a platform. I stepped out into the night and followed the path of fires toward the village. The closer to the village I walked, I was able to tell that the greatly-statured man everyone looked toward was nonother than Tenskatawa. Next to him on the platform was laid on a wooden table, an older man, laying on his back, his arms flat and straight down his sides.

I picked out Drange standing not far from the platform. I tightened the cloak around my shoulders against a brisk night wind. "What's all this," I asked Drange, keeping my voice low. Drange looked surprised to see me awake, but looked back toward the platform, where Tenskatawa stood over the old man, the two of them sharing the same silence.

"It's a burial," Drange said, "that's the chief's father. He died a few days before your arrival."

"They don't believe in diggin' the hole as soon as possible, huh," I asked.

"When the body dies, the tribe believes it takes the soul a few sun cycles, or days, for it to fully leave the body. If the body is buried before that time, it may never fully leave, causing unrest for the spirit. Tonight, the last day of the ceremony, we light the platform, burning the body which allows the last fragments of the soul to be carried into the heavens. After that, the bones are buried."

"Ah," I said to him, looking all around, "I see. What's with all the tiny fires all over the village?"

Drange continued to look toward the platform,

and I could tell my ignorance made him impatient. But he spoke anyway.

"They are mostly symbolic, to 'light the path' on which any part of the soul may depart upon. But also, they are comprised of the deceased's belongings he cherished most in life. It's another form of release to destroy one's materialism, but in a way that's respectful to the one who held them."

Tenskatawa turned to face the gathering of tribesmen and tribeswomen. From a little ways off, seven women began walking toward the platform, each of them holding a lit torch. At the front, walked Sanuye. She ascended the platform first, acknowledging Tenskatawa and circled around to the back of the platform. Each of the women followed suit, until each encircled the table on which Tenskatawa's father lay.

"The soul of our chief, my father, Askuwheteau, will now make its final ascension above, to where he may keep watch over us all, until it is time to join him ourselves," Tenskatawa said, turning slowly to the women. Sanuye was the first to move forward, lowing her torch to the wood below the dead. She let her torch lay there amongst the other logs and branches, and stepped back. The other women did the same, and at last the fire began to take hold and rise. Tenskatawa, Sanuye, and the other women departed from the platform and all watched as the still body of Askuwheteau caught aflame. The flames began low and burned slowly, but against a brief, cold winter night wind, the flames grew to a roar, bringing the fire high, giving a light to the faces of all who watched.

"They do this for everyone," Drange said, "one day Tenskatawa will be up there, and another day, his son. Sanuye too, and one day, maybe, I will be as well."

VIII.
The RETURN
of MANCINO ROLANDRAZ

The mornings in the village under the shadow of Blackheart Mountain arrived from the east softly at first; a pale hesitance that emerged into a gradient brilliance. The waking sounds were pleasant more than they were intrusive, as most of the time out in the world the things that welcomed you first thing in the morning were either something trying to kill you, eat you, or both.

It'd been a week and a day since the burning of Tenskatawa's old man. I'd only stayed because the snow had gotten so bad around the mountain range, that any otherwise passable road out of the village had been significantly cut off. Whenever I'd been asked why I was still here, that was the reason I gave them. In truth, I could have traversed the deep snows with Eleanor. She and I had been through worse. Swamps boiling with acid. Terrain rockier than a Gila monster's back side. Across tundra so cold, we both had had carpets of fur draped over us. It's safe to say that we could have left the village the very night of Tenskatawa's father's burial. Something else kept me from leaving just yet, and while at first it eluded me, the reason... now... seven, eight days later, going on nine, it was becoming easier to accept: the peace I felt here was not something I wanted to let go of just yet.

Eleanor stood calmly as I brushed her neck and her hair and down her shoulder muscles. She hadn't been dirty enough for a good cleanin' in a good long while, but she always liked being brushed whether she was dirty or not. Her eyelashes seemed to flutter differ-ently with each stroke and I swear if I looked at her while I brushed, she actually made eye contact with those shiny black pearls of hers.

"What ya thinkin' about girl," I asked her, giving her head a rub, scratching behind her right ear, which she absolutely loved, "you as confused as I am?"

Some of the tribesmen and women had begun to cease their dirty lookins at me as well. Now, they simply disregarded me, seein' as I was stayin' longer than what they probably expected. Owl Wing, Tenskatawa's son still shot me the occasional repugnancy, but every now and then, particularly when I was tendin' to lovely Elea-nor, he seemed to show a different side. To him, I was probably like that of a mole, a growth of some kind he one day found attached to his skin, something he found unsightly and by all manner of presence, rude. But he'd lessened his disdain towards me long enough to ex-change the occasional passive, if not completely disinter-ested dialogue.

As I stroked Eleanor's mane, he approached from the north road, with a pack slung over his right shoul-der. His face was darkened. Not by paint, but by dust, as though he'd been underground. He wore a tired man's face, but of a man satisfied with the work he'd just put in.

"What's interestin' to me is that you people seem to have this unmatched hatred for my employer," I said, focusing on Eleanor as Owl Wing began walking passed, "and yet you have your own quarry just across that lake there. Yes, I know, the circumstances are different. It's just too coincidental a thing to ignore, 'sall I'm sayin'."

"Just because we sometimes speak to one an-other does not mean I care to hear your voice whenever you wish to use it," he muttered, continuing on his march. I chuckled, but left it at that. As he left, Sanuye shoed away two kids who had apparently been staring intently at me while I cleaned Eleanor.

"What is it with the kids in this place," I asked her, "there somethin' about me they find so interesting? I smell different to 'em?"

"You're an outsider. Outsiders are always a point of interest. The youngest ones haven't left the village yet, and so they've only heard stories from the older ones about the people who live out there. The good, the bad, and... every kind else in between," she said to me. She walked closer, gently touching the other side of Eleanor, feeling her mane and admiring her shiny brown colors. "Have a way with animals, Mr. Mahoney? You seem to have a bond with this horse."

"We go back a ways," I said, "I trust her with my life. As she probably trusts me with hers."

"It's a trait quite common amongst the Tuskatawa men and women," she said, "even amongst the most humble, it's something to be proud of."

Before leaving, she hesitated for a moment, as though there were something else she came to say, but at the last second she decided against it and instead acknowledged me one more time before going back to whatever it had been she was working on.

"What ya doin'?" I asked her. She stopped in her stride, turned around and motioned for me to follow her.

"I'll show you," Sanuye said. She walked into a hut longer and wider than Tenskatawa's and I looked at Eleanor into her big, beautiful, shiny, black eyes.

"Yea, I know," I said to her.

I placed the brush in her saddlebag and followed Sanuye into the hut. Inside, she had a long table set out, topped with narrowly-carved and cut pieced of wood, like long twigs. On the ends of some of the ones set off to the side, there'd been fashioned brightly colored feathers. This continued on down the table where more of these long sticks had been placed. These ones were fixed with arrowheads on the end opposite of the end where the feathers were placed.

"Makin' arrows," I asked to no one in particular, because the answer was obvious. "You're into bows and arrows and all that fancy weaponry? Some people say archery is a lost art."

"It is if you aren't Tuskatawa," she said, "many of the women choose to fight when the time comes but are not skilled with spears or clubs or even rifles and other firearms. So, they master another method." Sanuye held up a bow and tested the structure, the string and the evenness of its craft.

"Do you shoot them as much as you craft em?"

"I'm not a horrible shot," she notched an arrow, aiming at nothing with intent to kill, but rather simply testing the sights. The muscles in her forearms and her biceps flexed appropriately and didn't tremble one bit that I could tell. Her form was straight and the ends of her elbows were as white as the snow.

"I'm more of a rifleman myself," I said, "revolvers too. Sidearms. Anything with a trigger really."

"What's that going to do for ya once you run out of bullets?"

"What use is a bow once you run out of arrows?"

"About the same as a rifle I suppose," she said, shrugging.

"Well," I continued, agreeing that both of our quips had their own merit. I sighed, unsheathing a mid-length knife with a jagged inside edge, "not every fight can be won with bullets and arrows."

"No they can't," she said. "are you stayin' or ya leavin', Mr. Mahoney?"

"Who's askin'?"

"Myself. And I'm sure the rest of the Tuskatawa. To be quite honest, I'm not sure what I think of ya yet. Til seems to think there's something to ya worth waiting for, whatever that means. He, uh," she lowered her voice, "he wouldn't want you knowing I said that."

"You guys talkin' about me with your heads on your pillows, that's precious," I grinned.

"Well? Is he wrong?"

"I don't think it's as simple as that," I said, picking up a fully-constructed arrow. I felt the edge of the feather on the back end, running my thumb up and down. They were good and firm, with just enough softness along the outer edge to allow for a nonconstructive flow of air. The arrowhead was a carved piece of stone, the sharpest stone I'd ever felt. "I haven't thought about it long enough, I suppose. But I will need to return to him soon, my boss, that is. I'd been away for months at a time, but I'd always found a way to let him know of my whereabouts and my business, whatever I was dealing with. This right here is the longest I've been away without havin' sent word of any kind. Though I wouldn't worry too much since he has no idea where this place is, unless for some reason he lied to me about that too."

"He lied to you."

"Well, not exactly a lie, more of an omission," I said, "your hubs was involved in it. Part of a plan to put a bullet in this asshole's head, goes by the name of Mancino Rolandraz. Real mean mug."

"I've heard of him. Most of us here have. To the children, he's... something of a nightmare creature to them. A monster to keep them from straying too far from the village. You know how curious children can be."

"Yea, well, their fears are not unwarranted."

"I've never met him," she continued as she sanded what would eventually become a new arrow shaft to join the others, "if I had, I might have broken the Tuskatawa Law, and killed him myself, based simply on the things he's known to have been behind, and the more horrible, terrible, grotesque things he's only rumored but in reality, more than likely to have done. The children know him as a monster, and yes, a child's mind can exaggerate the true nature of one's self, but in the case of Mancino Rolandraz, they would be wise to keep their assumptions. Their imaginations are not far off from the literal truth."

"Your chief mentioned something about how you people go about handling justice. I guess people like Rolandraz is why you have that Law."

"*Creatures* like Mancino Rolandraz are why we do not trust outsiders like yourself without good cause," she said.

I left the hut, and Sanuye's company, not long later. I returned to Eleanor's side and we looked at each other contemplatively. She already seemed to know, just as she always did.

"Well girl," I said, petting her mane gently, "maybe we ought to let this dream go. There're too many laws here. Too many ways to... do something wrong." It didn't take long to gather my things. I didn't have much to begin with. I slid my rifle in the saddle sheath and wrapped my long coat just a little bit tighter. I mounted Eleanor and patted her neck. "That's right girl," I said, "the snows can't hold us back anymore."

I slowly rode through the village, the many sets

of eyes of tribesmen and women giving me one last look, some of them continuing to watch as I rode passed them. The entrance to the village was marked by nothing other than the path arching at the top of a hill and then winding away sharply into a mountain pass, where I presume would lead me out of the mountains at some point. South would not be hard to find once I made it through there. And the road was clear for me, save for one man. The man of the hour.

"You've got the look of a man who's on his way out," Drange said, standing to the right of the roadway, just at the top of the hill.

"You seem saddened by this," I started, "does my leaving sadden you?"

"Is it a stupid question to ask if you're going back to reveal information that would threaten the lives of everyone here? Or am I really going to have to put a bullet in your back?"

"To tell ya the truth, Drange, I haven't decided on that first one just yet," I said, "I figure I got me a long enough ride back to come to a decision. As far as the second part of that question goes, you can try all you like to kill me, it ain't gonna make any difference."

"It ain't gonna be like that silly fist fight we had a while back. I won't be in chains. And we won't be usin' our fists. You won't even see me at all, that's what I'm tryin' to say. You leave, you *will* be killed."

"To hell with that Tuskatawa mantra then, huh." I started riding passed him.

"For the sake of protecting the secrecy of this place," he nodded, "I'll kill any man."

"Well then I guess I better get goin'," I laughed, my back now to him, "wouldn't want to stop ya from doin' what's right! Oh, and tell your lady thanks for what she did to my coat!"

With the village behind me, and the dark loom of Blackheart Mountain farther back, I took to the winding road of the mountains, the snow as high as Eleanor's knees. But the skies were clear and blue, and I wagered by midday, most of the snow would melt in our favor.

The road through the mountains only took us the remainder of the day to get through. The rocks and the snow led down a steady slope for most of the way, with occasional breaks to either side of the path giving an outlook over the land. From the view along the highest points of the road, I could see the snows had melted more and more farther down the road, and when the land flattened out there was nothing but dirt, dead grass, and the rare, stagnant trunk of a dead tree. There were only a few groupings of clouds overhead, and through these, columns of white-yellow sunlight burst through until they lit the ground they touched down upon. Once out of the mountains, around the time the sun began to disappear from the sky, that was when I told Eleanor to stop. A mile from the mountain range root, just passed the foothills where the last bit of snow edged off until all the remained was dirt and miles of flatland, I made camp.

With the fire low and to my right, the sky to the east a purple haze and the stars out and bright, Eleanor neighed quietly to herself, giving the solitude a brief tune of music. There was something eerily calm about this land, even outside the confines of the village. Here, on the ground, in every direction save back toward the mountains the land stretched out flat. You couldn't see where the land stopped and the sky began, but wherever it may be, the point in which they intersected was far off enough to strain the eyes. I kept an eye on the pass from which I rode. I kept watch for Drange, as I never doubted for a second he wouldn't uphold his promise. I couldn't be angry at him for it, there was no emotion behind it. He was right to task himself with the responsibility of making sure I didn't make it back to Ostrander. I'd do the same were I in his boots. But every time I looked back towards the mountains, there was nothing. No differentiation in the dark of the land and that of what would be a man riding his horse. He must be stealthier than I thought. He must have taken another way, otherwise I would have heard him by now at the very least. It fell upon me then, that he could have elected any strategy and I wouldn't know it. I didn't know him that intimately, and if I wasn't careful, I never would. Part of me wondered why I didn't have a bullet in my back already. And another part of me wondered how in the world I could have missed such an easy road into the mountains on past journeys to find Blackheart Mountain. The road quite literally, swiveled down from the rocky hills like a zig zag. I could see it from here.

I ate what little meat strips I had left from the supply I could scrounge out of the Tuskatawa village. That was all that was there, so tomorrow during the ride, I'd have to find a familiar landmark to aid in traversing my way back to New Canterton, all the while hunting down some kind of food. Wouldn't be hard, it'd just take time. And so, with those thoughts in the back of my mind, I laid my head back on a rolled blanket. If Drange was going to kill me, he was going to kill me while I slept. I couldn't pay any mind to something that I wouldn't be able to change simply by worrying about it.

I was still alive when the sun came up. But with that waking inhale, came a sense of apprehension. My left ear twitched but that mighta been because of the pair of flies buzzin' over my head.

I was still alive when I awoke to the sound of something being sharpened. And I when I opened my eyes, I found myself to be in the company of Til Drange. He'd chosen a perch atop the nearby boulder formation, sharpening the outer edge of his knife with a smaller hand-sized rock. When the rest of my senses came to me, however, I saw that it was not a knife he was sharpening, and it was not a rock he was using to not sharpen said knife, but rather it was an apple he was cutting into slices so that he could pop them one at a time into his mouth. Beside the boulder formation, exactly next to Eleanor stood his own horse as if they were best friends.

"You snore like a crocodile," he said, tossing me a slice. I caught it. "Glad you're awake, finally."

"You don't find that as peculiar as I do," I asked, smelling the apple slice, looking it over on all of its sides for discoloration, texture changes which would imply infused poison, perhaps a poison Drange had grown himself accustomed to enough to ingest safely and without self-harm.

"It's ripe," he jested.

"You can never be sure," I jested back, still cautious.

"Calm your thighs, man. I'm not the sort of fella who'd kill your type with a damn poisoned apple," Drange said to me, eating another slice. I popped the slice he'd given me into my mouth and enjoyed the tanginess. It crunched with juicy chunks that tasted sweet and made my own senses feel good about it.

"Which begs the question," I started, picking myself up off the ground, "why am I still alive? Unless that delicious piece of apple was your idea of a last meal."

Drange finished the apple, but not before tossing me one more slice, which I ate. He wiped his fruit-wet fingers over his long coat and adjusted his hat, taking a leap down to the ground from the boulder.

"No," he said, taking a deep gust of a breath, "it's more along the lines of, giving you one last chance to reconsider."

"You tryin' to appeal to this good side of me is startin' to get tirin', Drange," I said, "I don't have one. Not one in the way that you think I do. I've got a mind for keepin' to my word. My word is impartial, and right now that word is held by the good graces of Gunther Ostrander."

"You don't have to be a good person to do the right thing, Mahon. If you do the right thing, well... that can change things," Drange said, "Now, I don't wanna kill ya. I will, of course. But I want ya to know that I don't wanna."

His eyes fell low, toward my waist, right where my revolver holsters rested on my hips. My hand had been there on the handle of the right one since I first opened my eyes that morning. All things considered I should have drawn on him as soon as I saw that it was him. It wasn't like me to let a man who aimed to kill me talk for this long.

"I see," he said, acknowledging the placement of my hand.

I noticed he too had his hand on the top of his sidearm.

There was a quietness about us. Eleanor let out a tiny, disconcerted neigh, but other than that, there was nothing but an early morning breeze.

"Do you really want this to go down this way," Drange asked.

"Why haven't ya drawn yet," I asked him, "what

ya waitin' for? The sun's up, and I'm right here in front of ya."

Drange breathed.

I breathed.

I didn't have to look down to see that his wrist had tightened and his fingers had loosened.

The abrupt *click* of a gun being cocked that didn't belong to either myself or Drange made both of our heads turn.

"Well, well, well," the man's voice spoke, and out from behind the other boulder formation, the trigger man stepped into the space: Mancino Rolandraz, a decayed-toothy grin spread a mile wide across his ugly, monstrous face, "ain't this just romantic. The bastard who shot and killed a handful of my men, and the snide stranger whose belly I put a bullet in, the latter of whom *should* be dead." He already had one revolver aimed at Drange. He moved around the clearing until there was an even space between all three of us, and then he drew a second sidearm, aiming it for myself, although I was willing to bet his aim was not as good with his left hand as it was his right. "Now, now, don't go and stop your little chit chat just for me," he kept on smilin', having found something incredibly enjoyable about the whole scenario, "you girls go on with your conversation, it was just gettin' interestin'. I'll be right here, don't pay me no mind. Think of me as a spectator."

Neither Drange nor myself said anything. Whatever had been goin' on between Drange and myself, we seemed to both simultaneously agree to put it on hold. We both stared Rolandraz right in his face.

"Oh," Rolandraz continued, looking down at his drawn weaponry, "oh well I guess these here guns might be a bit distractin'. My guns distractin' ya fellas? I bet you wonder how loud they are when I pull their triggers. Am I right?"

We didn't say anything. Rolandraz's smile began to flutter away as his gaze fell back to me.

"Rancid Mahoney. Jesus, what a name. Speakin' of names, I been meanin' to ask just what in the hell inspires someone to name their kid 'Rancid'? Ma and pa must've been mixin' medicinals the night of your unholy birth. I dunno though, I been a lotta places and heard a lotta crazy stories. The idea that you were named somethin' like 'Rancid' right outta the womb just... doesn't sit too well with me. I guess it don't really matter anymore. Crazy world we live in and all. Anyway, I see you standin' there, and you look as healthy as a fruit bat. I shot you in the gut, pretty clean shot, woulda killed any man eventually if he didn't bleed out right there on the floor. You look like a tough guy, but not *that* tough. Go on, lift up your shirt, let's see that wound." He waved the gun held out in my direction, motioning for me to do as he said. When he saw that I would not readily oblige, he pulled the hammer back on the gun aimed for me. "Pull up your shirt or I'll shoot your goddamn pecker off." I lifted up my shirt slowly, and he saw what any man would: the mark in my belly where the bullet went through... a wound, accented by faint, almost invisible black veins trailing off like roots digging deeper into soil. "Ah," he grinned, "that's what I thought. Beautiful to see a miracle in the flesh, don't ya think? Yea, boys. We know all about your Mountain, just haven't found it yet. Tell ya the truth, bunch of my boys have been beginning to talk like it ain't real. Fancy that. I'm thinkin' I'm lookin' at livin' proof said Mountain does exist."

"You can't kill us both," Drange was the first of us to talk back. I didn't agree with his statement entirely, given the situation. Best I could figure is he gets two shots off nearly at the same time, but only one of them hits either one of us, while the either myself or Drange nails him right between the eyes with our own shot. Drange and I both still had our hands holding the handle of our own gun. And that was a fine-enough chance in my book any day.

"I could have killed you without you two havin' a second's moment to ponder the sanctity of a quiet death," Rolandraz spat. "It's just, my weakness I suppose, drawin' things out. Makin' the soon to be dead hurt just a little longer. Makes the last gasp something truly incredible to behold. Though, if I were you, seein' as you two are poised for a quickdraw, I'd first like to just let you know that while it may seem as though I am alone... I am indeed not. Yes, you see, whether it's me who shoots first or one of you, the rest of my men will come ridin' out. Because I told em, I said 'now chances are there will be some bullets flyin', and as soon as you hear em, that's your signal to come ridin' out like a bunch o' banshees'. Take me down, fine. I promise you won't take *them* down. So, here's what we're gonna do. I've been watchin' ya for a bit, as soon as I saw ya come outta them there mountains... Oh yea. And then this fella over here thinks he's sneaky, waits until nightfall to give pursuit. Well now, I gotta be honest, I ain't never been up in them mountains. What's up there? Somethin' special I'll bet. Something worth the weight of the conversation you two lovebirds were havin' 'afore I showed my pretty angel face. Now, I'm not too partial to just blind guessin', and guessin' ain't never been my strong suit. I'm a terrible card player. I lose every dime every time. Poker face ain't so good either. People just seem to know from a mile a way I'm up to no good. Only every once in a while, do I guess and come out guessed right. I'm bettin' this is gonna be one of those times. So… up there, in those mountains," he pointed to my belly area where my shirt had been pulled up, "that's where I'm gonna find your fuckin' mountain, the biggest ticket item of the world, ain't it?"

"Drange," I said, keeping my eyes trained on Rolandraz, "when I say go, you get on your horse and start ridin'."

"What?" He asked, suddenly looking at me as though I were some kind of directionless idiot.

"It's my plan," I said.

"Just what in the hell kind of plan is that, though? You see what's goin' on here, right? Are ya blind, deaf, or just plain stupid?!"

"My guess is all three," Rolandraz muttered under his breath.

"Just listen to me, goddamnit!"

Meanwhile, Rolandraz got a kick out of the banter. He let out a cackle and a full-length laugh, and while I kept Drange goin' with my "plan", Rolandraz laughed so hard his head tilted back. It was the split second I needed.

I drew my revolver and fired, but the motion wasn't fast enough, as Rolandraz was ready. He fired with his left gun at the same time I fired with my revolver. He missed, the bullet hitting the boulder behind me. I missed too, as in my swerve while aiming, I shot too low, catching the outer seam of his coat. Drange drew his own weapon and fired, catching Rolandraz in the thigh with a dark red burst. Sometime during the scramble, the moment came in which Rolandraz's men rode out from a short distance away. I may have been wrong because I mounted Eleanor faster than I shot and missed, but I counted at least ten riders, Crimson Collars, all riding full speed on dark horses shooting excitedly into the air with their weapons. Drange shot again but missed, and instead opted to crack Rolandraz over the head with the butt of his revolver while mounting his own horse. In the same motion, he mounted so quickly he didn't take notice of Rolandraz slashing out with a dagger, which caught his hand holding his revolver. The gun went flying into the air. With Mancino's men making short work of the distance between us, Drange didn't have time to debate; he took off in the same direction I had. Rolandraz let out a furious scream as his men closed in. He screamed high into the air for them to get us and to shoot our bodies full of bullets, and then to tear our bones right out of our skin.

"Give me one of them guns!" Drange yelled out as he raced on, quickly catching up to me.

"You only brought one gun? What the hell kind of a green-toed assassin are ya?"

"I only needed one gun to do what I came out here to do, it's called the art of conservation!"

"It's called the art of bein' a jackass, ya jackass!" I kicked Eleanor to gallop faster. The flatlands stretched out before us, and endless plane with nowhere to take proper cover. Behind, Rolandraz and the Crimson Collars began race after us, though they still had quite a long stretch to catch up.

"You can't get away from em, and you can't kill em all yourself!"

"The hell I can't!"

He pulled up next to me and reached out with one free hand. "Mahon!" The sound of bullets whirring passed our heads rang out through the air. Eleanor let out a cry as I kicked harder. I didn't want to but she had to know that the only way out of this was to go faster.

We kept on the chase, riding alongside the edge

of a dried-up riverbed. Drange took a chance and pulled out in front of me, forcing me to stop.

"You don't give me a gun we don't have a chance," he said, panting. He held out his hand again. I looked toward the crowd of monstrous men riding their horses as fast as they could. Behind them, a billowing cloud of dust kicked up high into the air. I took out one of the revolvers and opened the chamber. There were six bullets.

"Please," Drange panted.

"This revolver is important to me, not a damn bit less than its brother. Don't lose it, and don't tarnish it's feelin's by pullin' the trigger prematurely." I said, slamming the chamber closed and tossing him the weapon. He caught it, a half grin on his face silently thanking me. "You better not miss."

"I never do," Drange replied.

I drew my other revolver and we pulled the hammers back. Together, we both turned our horses around and faced the oncoming horde. We kicked heavily and took off, each of us aiming ahead, riding at full speed. The Crimson Collars began firing back at us, bullets pinging and whizzing and zinging passed. I aimed at my first target and fired, blowing the side of his skull into pieces. The body flung off the horse and crashed to the ground. Drange pulled the trigger twice, taking two more out with perfect accuracy. I aimed and fired again, this time catching my target in his chest. "One other thing," Drange cried out over the sound of horse hoofs pounding the dirt and guns blazing through the air, "don't kill Rolandraz!"

"What?!"

"He deserves the Law, and he'll get the Law!"

We rode toward the oncoming men at our horses' top speed, charging into them head on.

Rolandraz let out a hideous cry as he swung his gun but missed. In the confusion, I emptied my revolver, each bullet landing its mark. Drange got off the rest of his rounds, but didn't get a chance to fire off the last. Rolandraz, in a rage, jumped from his horse throwing his body right into Drange's knocking him out of his saddle and down to the ground.

With only one member of the Crimson Collars remaining, I turned Eleanor to face him. He was perhaps the ugliest of them all, fat with a hairy gut hanging over his belt. He aimed a rifle right for my head, but when he pulled the trigger, the gun went *click*. Out of ammo, or jammed, or just poorly-kept. I took off towards him, drawing my knife in the same motion. He swung the long end of his rifle out at me like a bat, but missed as I ducked. I swooped behind him, sticking the cute end of my knife all the way into his back. With the other hand, I pressed on his chest, which shoved the knife even deeper until the tip stuck out of his ribcage. I tore the blade from his body and kicked him off his horse. It was then that I saw Rolandraz had engaged Drange in fisticuffs, the two of them sending fist after fist into each other on the ground. Rolandraz was too fast though, and Drange must have been tired. Rolandraz swung out with a heavy fist, catching Drange in the side of his head. Drange collapsed to the ground, utterly defeated.

"Now," Rolandraz said to him, as he stood over the limp body of Til Drange, "I'm going to stick this blade into your belly and rip all the guts out of ya until they're all outside and on the ground. It's gonna look like there was a party here, and no one cleaned up after themselves. The wildlife will come in and eat you little by little, until there's nothin' left of ya."

"ROLANDRAZ!" I called out, descending from

Eleanor with a thud. I stood a good sixty yards from the two of them by this point. But Rolandraz heard my call and turned to face me. "Rolandraz!"

He stood, holding his knife upside-down, the near lifeless body of Drange laying still beside him.

"How about I kill you instead, you ugly son of a bitch," I walked closer. Rolandraz spat blood on the dirt at his feet. "We're the only ones left. You and me, and... poor Drange down on the ground. But he's nothing to you. He's not a fighter. You can be sure of that because you overcame him so easily," I removed my long coat in my approach, feeling its weight vanish. I unbuttoned the top buttons of my inside shirt and swung my arms to stretch out the muscles, "surely, you're a fighter too. Brutality is in your blood, because you're a monster. The human side of you has been long gone. I don't care why, I don't care by what or by whom. It doesn't matter. All that's left, is something too deserving of a better sendoff. Bare fists, and only fists, like the men we both used to be."

"You are not yet a monster," Rolandraz called out. "You are still so frail, and untouched."

"You don't know enough about me to make such ignorant claims. It's time you found out just how wrong you are."

Rolandraz muttered something to himself. He looked down at his knife but quickly tossed it to the ground. He too removed his coat and tore off his shirt, revealing a layer of bare, sweaty skin, a myriad of scars carved in all manner of horribleness, nothing less than what I expected. Rolandraz was not just a man mad in the mind, but a man with a body that'd been torn to pieces, ripped into and nearly destroyed entirely. But he survived whatever had come his way thus far. And what was left behind in the wake of those experiences, was this brute of a beast ahead of me. His muscles surged as he relished the idea of my challenge. And as I tore my shirt from my own person, revealing my own scars to him, I walked faster.

It was cold, but the sun above beamed down, and we each sweat like summer babies. I remembered Drange and his words, not to kill him. Tuskatawa Law must be upheld. Whatever awaited Mancino Rolandraz should he face judgment at Blackheart Mountain... as much as I wanted to crush his throat with my bare hands, I would make sure he made it there alive.

Five feet from Rolandraz, I made the first swing, taking him off guard. I caught him in the lip, breaking it open immediately. He stumbled back, unsure of how to take it. Surely, he now understood what I'd said to him. He would have to adjust his assumptions, and put aside ignorance if he was going to win.

Rolandraz spat more blood and came toward me, unleashing a flurry of faster fists than I admit having ex- pected. I blocked with my forearms, but he pounded those with sledgehammer-like force, moving next to my biceps. Landing each fist as if they themselves fell from the sky. I heaved my shoulder into the middle of his chest and pushed back against him. He crashed back- ward against the trunk of a tree, and I took this moment to send my fists out again, each one landing against the sides of his face, his head, cracking dead on into the bridge of his nose. His face bloodied and bruised, one of his eye sockets broken no doubt, he screamed in a rage, bleeding saliva and blood all over me. Desperate, he bit into my shoulder, digging his teeth in as deep as he could. I couldn't help but cry out against the pain, his teeth must have dug down just shy of the bone.

I sent a fist upward, catching him in the gut and

loosening the grip his teeth had on my shoulder. He stepped back by surging forward again, slapping my fists away as he sent his own into my face. His fists felt like trains at full speed, his knuckles were like individual bricks all hitting me at the same time in a row. He cracked them against my lower ribs, sending his left fist up beneath my jaw, almost breaking my neck as my head flung back from the impact. He raised a leg and kicked straight out into the middle of my chest.

I stumbled back into the dried-up riverbed, stumbling even more as my feet tried to balance them-selves over the uneven rocks. From the top of the hill, Rolandraz leapt down, letting out an animalistic growl, blood and saliva flaying from his wide-open, dark crim-son mouth. He fell on top of me, knocking me all the way down onto my back. The rocks on the riverbed made for an agonizing landing, and I felt as though my spine might actually have been broken.

Rolandraz gripped my throat with both hands, slamming my head down against the rocks. He knew he had the upper hand now, and he didn't care what he had to do. He sent fist after first down onto my head and into my face, each one heavier than the last.

I saw Cassandra.

When someone hits you with enough force, the impact is so hard there is a brief flash of light that fully encompasses your sense of sight. And in the brief flash, I saw her.

She had no emotion that I would later be able to remember. It was just her. And maybe I wasn't actually seeing her. Maybe I just felt her presence.

Rolandraz continued his barrage for a moment longer and then stopped, and through the slits of my somehow still-functional eyelids, I saw that from his balled fists, my own blood dripped onto my bare chest.

The structure of his own face bent under the weight of my own attacks, and he bled from his lips, his mouth, his nose and several open gashes elsewhere. But he was still the one holding his own fists like trophies. Without a word, he stood up, breathing like a starving wolf, and climbed the hill at the edge of the riverbed. I could barely move, let alone breathe, and so I rolled over to my side to spit up my own blood. I couldn't feel my face, I could barely feel my arms from having swung them so hard, and I was pretty sure several of my lower-most ribs had suffered fractures of various severities.

Rolandraz returned to the top of the hill, now holding his knife in one hand, and my own in the other. He breathed with his bloodied mouth open and slowly descended the hill. He stopped once he was over top of me, and nodded, acknowledging that he knew as well as I did that I was completely helpless.

"You were right," he said, "you put up a much more satisfying fight. And even if you were to be standing where I am now... I'd have been satisfied with that being the ending to my own story. However, I... am going to kill you now."

"Good," I spat. "I been waitin' for this day to come."

"You been waitin' to die, eh?" He asked..

"Haven't you?"

He cocked his head to the side, barely a little, but for that one moment it felt as though we understood each other. It felt like we'd come from the same place, or at the very least, scarily similar walks of life.

But before he could do with the knives what he stood poised to do, he lurched forward from a rear attack. He made a guttural noise as though he'd been hit in the stomach. But through the skin and muscle above his collar bone, there stuck the iron tip of an arrow. He let out another scream as a second one landed into the back of his left thigh, in turn falling to his knees.

"AH!"

He tried pulling the arrow from the back of his leg but it stayed dug into the muscle, and the arrow protruding through above his collar bone could not be removed either.

"What in the hell is this," he turned and saw a figure riding on horseback, approaching quickly. "Oh my god, a bitch really took me down. Oh, she's a pretty bitch, too. I take back my disgust. She's very pretty, I'd let her kill me, sure, any time anywhere. Come on, you pretty bitch, kill me, I want you to do it," Rolandraz laughed through bloodied teeth. But the woman on horseback did not share his amusement, and rode up quickly swinging underhand with a club, catching him square in the face. He fell backward, either dead or unconscious, I couldn't be sure. The arrow in his shoulder snapped in half as his back hit the ground. The horse with the rider trotted closer, and through my hazy eyes I saw that it was in fact her.

"Sanuye," I said.

She dismounted, paying me a momentary acknowledgement while bending down to check Rolandraz's pulse. She nodded, probably signifying that he was still alive, keeping in line with her people's Law.

"Are you dead," I heard her ask me. I tried to move but could barely pull myself into a sitting position. "You look dead, or pretty close to it."

"Well I guess I should be, shouldn't I? You might want to look up there and ask your husband the same thing. He got his ass kicked almost as bad as I did."

Sanuye immediately left me, taking to the hill and checking in on Drange. I pulled myself to my feet, despite the agony. I had to stand. I couldn't be that close to the ground any longer. Rolandraz lay there like a dead fish, which made sense considering he was on a dried-up riverbed. Maybe when the waters dried up, he had nowhere to go and just ran outta air, floppin' around until his gills stopped screamin'. Back over the hill, Sanuye had Drange sitting up drinking water from a canteen.

"How come you didn't give me any of that," I asked, approaching them.

"I'm sorry but the love of my life is just a little more important to me," she said, helping Drange drink.

"I see that. Love him so much you followed him out here. Sounds kinda clingy, actually, not necessarily love."

"Not exactly," she said.

Drange let out a chuckle through bloodied lips.

"See," he started, "I'm not an idiot, Mahon. In the event the confrontation with you went sour, well... it's not a dumb idea to have someone as good with a bow and arrow as she is covering your back. It's always been that way with us."

They looked at each other then and I thought that if I didn't have my Cassandra in the back of my head, I might have to wake old Mancino Rolandraz up just so he could finish the job.

"That's a hell of a relationship," I said. I looked back at the still-motionless body of Rolandraz. He lay there, and only when I winced my eyes could I see that he was still breathing. "So what exactly is this Tuskatawa Law going to do for him what we aren't allowed to?"

"He's going to get exactly what he deserves," Sanuye said, "I don't take pleasure much in the ways of dealing pain to others, even those who deserve it. But him right there, we just caught ourselves one of the most horrible creatures to walk the face of the earth."

I thought that sounded good, actually. At least in words. I knew I'd be feeling these pains he inflicted upon me for a time to come, but the way she made it sound, he was in for much worse, and whatever "much worse" entailed, I was fully on board with.

"So then," Sanuye said, helping Drange to his feet. She looked to me, "What will you do?"

I presumed she only meant one thing, if I was to continue my ride back to Ostrander. That would be the honorable thing to do. To follow through along the course I originally set out to reach the end of. I'd located the Mountain, albeit unconventionally, and I knew for a fact that Ostrander's men had more than the needed capability to secure Blackheart Mountain without much hindrance from the Tuskatawa. It wouldn't take long. A day, maybe two, maybe less. But no matter what, Ostrander's men would walk away from the ordeal nearly unscathed.

"Well now let me see," I started, "I suppose going back to my... employer... would keep in line with securing my reputation for future endeavors, and by extension, payment. Right? That's what I ought to do. But I gotta say, seein' you two, what you do for each other... I can only assume that must carry over to everyone else who's... Tuskatawa," I hesitated, repeating the name of their people over in my head, and I hoped I'd pronounced it correctly, "Ostrander is a good man to work for. He never skimps out on payment. And he makes sure his employees are well-accommodated," I turned around to face the out-cold form of Mancino Rolandraz, he lay there still, his mouth hanging open as if he really were dead. I thought about all the reasons why I should return to Ostrander. And at the top of all of those reasons, there was only Cassandra... pregnant with our daughter. If I didn't go back, it would heighten the chances of me never being able to see her again, and it may completely sever the opportunity to lay eyes on my future daughter. "I'm gonna paint a bullseye right in the middle of the back of my head if I go back with you two. It's going to be a big, bright red goddamn bullseye."

I didn't have to say anything else to them. Both Sanuye and Drange knew what I was going to do.

We tied Rolandraz up with enough rope to hang fifty men, and then tied him to the back of Sanuye's saddle. I retrieved my clothing and Drange handed me my revolver back. We mounted our horses and Sanuye waited for us up ahead. I slid the revolvers into their holsters and shook my head at myself.

"Don't worry," Drange said, "this doesn't make you a good man."

"That's not what I'm worried about," I replied, "you still owe me six bullets."

IX.
The BATTLE
of BLACKHEART MOUNTAIN

When he was a child, Mancino Rolandraz lost both of his parents to a pack of wolves somewhere further west. The group of people he'd been travelling with were slaughtered and eaten as well. There was never any finding out as to how he survived at such a young age, and in all likelihood there never would be. The most anyone ever heard about the story came straight from Rolandraz himself, so even then the very truth of such a tale was something to wonder about. Every now and then, he'd reference his parents' deaths to the wolves just before killing whatever unlucky soul found themselves at the unlucky end of Rolandraz's gun. But other than that, Mancino Rolandraz's true origin was largely unknown.

The Tuskatawa kept wolves as pets, as workers, and for the most part they were gentle and kind to their owners. When we arrived back at Blackheart Mountain with the bleeding Mancino Rolandraz, the smell of his blood enraptured the attention of every wolf in the village. They sniffed the air with their snouts, and by now Mancino had awoken from the nap given to him so graciously by Sanuye's swinging club. His eyes winced against whatever pain he felt, and when he took in his surroundings, he seemed to find it all very amusing. The wolves followed Sanuye's horse from a safe distance, knowing this prisoner was not meant for them. They were still hungered by his arrival, however, licking their jaws and every now and then giving out short whimpers of wishful thinking. Mancino looked at all of them one at a time, making eye contact and giving them each a little grin. He knew he wouldn't be fed to them, so their misery was his pleasure.

"Sorry fellas," he said to them, "doesn't look like you'll be gettin' a bite of me today."

Sanuye took the bound form of Mancino to the top of a hill, where a series of tall posts stood fixed into the ground. She shoved him off the back of her horse and he nearly rolled all the way back down the hill. Drange was there to stop him from rolling away, as he latched onto his bindings and brought him up to his feet. Drange slammed him up against one of the posts while Sanuye tied him to it.

"You think these ropes are going to hold me forever, buddy," Mancino sneered, "I'm going to break free of these, and when I do I'm going to fuck your whore woman until she bleeds from her eye sockets. You'll be watching the entire time, I'll make sure. And when I'm done with her, I'll have the manlovers of my gang go to town on you. You're going to die with cocks in your ass, you bastard! Big nasty cocks warped and mangled by the horrors of the world!"

Drange slapped Mancino across the face with the butt of his sidearm. Mancino laughed and spat blood to the ground. He spat a wad of blood and mucus to the ground, his gaze leading up toward the mountain. "Ah," he said, a warm, gentle smile forming creases in his cheeks, "and there she is. There's your lovely Mountain."

"Your time is over, Mancino Rolandraz," Chief Tenskatawa ascended the hill, followed by an innumerable host of his own tribesmen and women. He wore a look of satisfaction on his face, pleased at the outcome of recent events. He patted a happy hand on Drange's back, but Drange motioned towards me.

"It wouldn't have been possible without him,"

Drange said, "believe it or not."

"Really," the Chief mused, "I find that a little hard to believe."

"It's true," Drange said, "Sanuye put the arrows in him, but Mahon here, held his ground long enough for her to get there."

The Chief approached me and looked me up and down, no doubt taking note of all the bruises, cuts, gashes, and telltale signs of the recent bout of fisticuffs.

"Interesting turn of events," the Chief said, "which makes me wonder why you are back, as weren't you leaving?"

"I'll stay long enough to watch this tall glass of horse piss hang, and then I'll go," I said.

"Hang?"

"Or whatever it is you folk do to your most-wanted criminals," I said.

"Ah yes," the Chief continued, turning to face the man tied to the post, "what we do with our most-wanted criminals, the most deranged members of the remnants of society. For them, death is a blessing, and not the ideal conclusion to their poor, hell-spreading lives." He stepped closer to Mancino, grabbing him by the throat. "Death will come for everyone eventually, it's not a question of *will it* or *will it not*. Bloodshed must only be called for if the situation demands it so, and bloodshed is too good a reward for this man's life of reckless evil."

Mancino spat into the face of the Chief, but the Chief held his stance, his face firm and as immovable as tree bark.

"Like your ancestors you hopelessly try to emulate, your dedication to your traditions will be your downfall," Mancino grinned through the bloodied teeth he had left, "if you don't kill me now, there isn't anything you can do to stop my vengeance, or my people's."

"Perhaps there will be vengeance once day," Chief Tenskatawa said, releasing his hold on Mancino's throat, "but it will not be had by you, or anyone who calls themselves a Crimson Collar. You will stay here tonight amongst the cold, wintered stars. Your body will freeze and you will feel the coldness of death, but you will not be granted it. We will keep you alive all night if we have to. In the morning, we will take your eyes."

Chief Tenskatawa and those who came with him departed. Before leaving, the Chief placed a heavy hand on my shoulder, the shoulder Mancino had sunk his teeth into, and so I bit a lip to quell the pain.

"You did a good thing, Mr. Mahoney," the Chief said, "the Tuskatawa and myself will remember it. With Mancino no longer a threat, this will be the beginning of a new chapter for all those who were once under the oppression of his existence. Now, we can fully focus on the more pressing matters at hand." And with that he left. Sanuye took Drange away to tend to his wounds. She meant for me to follow but I told her I'd be there in a few moments. She and Drange departed to her hut, leaving me alone on the hill with the madman Mancino Rolandraz. Behind me, the packs of wolves sat with starved patience. They wouldn't move because they were loyal, but their eyes never wavered from Mancino either. He looked back at me, hanging forward against the tautness of the bindings, which had begun to make the area around the bare skin of his redden.

"You wanna know somethin', *Rancid*? Gosh, I'd give a gallon of my own blood to know how you managed to earn that. You wanna know how we got our name... the Crimson Collars," he laughed a little as he spoke the name of his gang, "we didn't always have a name. In the beginnin' we were just a group of guys lookin' for somethin' to do. Eventually, the prices on our necks got so high and so tight... well, they started pickin' us off. And ya know, ya know what happens when you hang a man? His neck gets... bruised, red. From how tight that rope twists. That fat fuck of a mayor over in Vermouth was the one who started callin' us the *Crimson Collars*. And honestly, we liked the sound of it. So, we just... adopted it for our own. It felt good to... have a name, a name that everyone knew. It made it easier to convince others to join our cause. Havin' a name. So, *Rancid*, is that close to... how you got your name? Rancid Mahoney. Maybe the last name is real but that first one," he shook his head, suckin' his teeth in contemplation, "no sir. And the way your face is lookin' right now, tells me I'm right."

Off in the distance, several children, desperate with curiosity to see the prisoner, were held by the hands of their mothers, who gently pulled them back into their tents and their huts.

"You, uh, you know what's going to happen, don't you," he asked me, but really he was making a statement more than asking a question, "this cold air won't torture me any more than those wolves will. And whatever these people do to me won't stop me. I am only one. And the rest of the Crimson Collars are bound to me. I don't make many promises in life," he said with the most honest tone he'd used yet, "I haven't gone down that road. People who make promises are too sure of things, and that's a depth of dishonesty I can't allow myself to drown in. But know this, no matter what happens to me, the rest of them will come. You are all going to die. And that Mountain, that mountain will burn. Such power does not belong in the hands of a single people. What moral good could these people possibly offer the world that burns around them, simply because they possess the soul of Blackheart Mountain?"

"Fancy words coming from a man tied to a pole," I said.

"You're strong, Mahoney," he said, "I wouldn't ever deny that after our little bout. I would have killed you if it weren't for that pretty bitch. But before that, you were hard to put down. Much harder than most."

"I'm impressed at how confident you are," I said, "most men in your position would be begging to be let go. Tryin' to make some kind of deal to make his life last just a little bit longer."

"I'm not a fool like them," he said, "I'm at the end of my rope. What I'm trying to say is, you aren't. You were on your way out when I met you back there. Why did you come back to these... savages, who are so set in their ways they've deluded themselves into actually thinking they deserve this land more than anyone else? The world doesn't *belong* to anyone, it belongs to everyone who lives long enough into the next day, and the next day, and the next. Don't tell me you think these tribesmen have a right. You were stupid enough to get into a fight with me, but you've got to at least be smarter than to be fooled by *them*!"

I stood on the hill, not taking notice until then just how close I'd been standing next to him. The wind blew a swirl of fat snowflakes around us. It didn't take a keen eye to see Mancino's bare skin tighten in agony. His lips were already turning blue. I wondered why Chief Tenskatawa had elected to wait until dawn, other than to cause this man more pain. He deserved the torment; I would never question so. But it seemed to me like he wouldn't last the night in his current state.

"The cogs and the gears of your uncertainty are moving at an alarming rate even you weren't expecting," he said, "I wasn't always like this, the way you know me. I've accepted how I've turned out. How I am is purely a summation of everything that's come before. I'm not the only one in the world like myself, and I think I'm lookin' at someone who just may turn out quite similarly."

"I wouldn't worry about this Tuskatawa Law, or the dawn that awaits you tomorrow," I said, heading back down the hill, "you'll be dead in the night long before then."

"Perhaps," he said back, "I'm ready for either. And I will die a man knowing where his allegiances fall. You won't, Mahoney, you won't!"

"So," Sanuye said as she began cleaning my wounds, starting with the area on my shoulder where Mancino had bit into. When she'd cleaned away the scabbing and the rest of the dried blood, I could see where each tooth had broken the skin. "What'd the evil man on the hill have to say?"

"Well, he ain't beggin' for his life," I said, "he's a hard man to figure out."

"The hell he is," Drange muttered. "You just aren't hearin' him right."

"Don't get me wrong, I ain't questionin' the Law here, he definitely is one who deserves it," I said.

"Something else is on your mind," Sanuye said.

"It just seems to me like the world, as broken as it is, would benefit a lot more from his death, and rather whatever it is your Chief here wants to do. It just seems... selfish, I suppose."

"Selfish?" Sanuye cried out, and the stitching she was doing pulled back with her word, tearing open one of the gashes made by one of Mancino's larger teeth.

"Your Chief is upholding the Law of *his* people at the potential expense of the rest of the world. You can't see what kind of problems that could cause further down the road?" I grimaced against the shift in her stitching. Sanuye didn't say anything back. She finished cleaning my injuries as quickly as she could and stepped away. I took it as my time to leave and left the hut. Eleanor waited for me hitched where I'd left her. I patted her neck and scratched the spot where her ear met the side of her head. She gave a little neigh and I nodded in reply.

I lay back in the cot in the tent I'd originally woken up in. I started a little fire to keep the warmth in and the cold outside. From here, I was allowed a view of the hill upon which Mancino Rolandraz was tied to a post. And from here, I could almost feel every bite of coldness biting away at his skin. But he held on to his life, he kept right on breathing. He didn't seem to be hurting at all. From here, it looked like this was just an exercise in breathing for him.

Later, as the sun began to set, the puffy flakes fell a little harder, coating the ground and the pathways of the village with fresh, powdery whiteness. Through the curtain of snow, I could just make out the figure of Mancino up on the hill, a dark shape against the failing light of a sleepy sky. My own eyes had begun to feel heavy, but just as they closed, my hopeful slumber was interrupted. Drange darted into the tent, a look of urgency painted across his face.

"Get up," he said.

"I'd like to sleep, actually, if that's okay. I thought you said I wasn't a prisoner," I said, rolling over on my side, facing my back to him. He kicked me in the ass with the end of his boot.

"Scouts' eyes reported sightings," he said.

"Oh no, sightings you say."

"Crimson Collars. They're in the mountains to the north, and to the east," Drange said quickly. "Tenskatawa has already ordered Rolandraz to be taken to a more secure spot."

But just as he said that, a horn bellowed through the evening air. It blew twice, hesitated, and then blew again. Drange and I both looked out of the tent, our curiosities seemingly matched exactly.

"Damnit," Drange said. Where Mancino Rolandraz had been tied, there was now only a post. No body. No dark form bound to its base. Nothing. There were however the motionless corpses of three or four Tuskatawa men laying about the dirt around the base of the post.

Suddenly, a series of horrified screams rang out throughout the village. Women and children and men cried into the air. Fires began to erupt from a number of tents and huts. The screams were followed by the sounds of gunfire, and more screams followed suit.

"Well, well," I started as I moved to a sitting position. I stretched, and reached for my rifle, slinging it over my shoulder. I checked the chamber of my revolvers and laughed. "Empty," I said, "happen to have those six bullets you owe me? Maybe six more for interest."

"Come on," Drange growled, "the Chief will be marshalling everyone." The two of us stepped out of the tent and into the night air, an air now filled with the familiar sounds of slaughter and massacre. I followed Drange down through the village. He seemed to be heading for Chief Tenskatawa's hut, down by the lakeshore. There, already dozens of tribesmen and women had amassed, all of them arming themselves with clubs, axes, and smaller axes, bows and arrows, and a small assortment of firearms. Their faces were painted for war, their bare arms and shoulders splashed with colors too. Some of them wore hardly a cloth at all, and so nearly the entirety of their skin was coated in dark, menacing paint. Across the lake, the shore at the heels of Blackheart Mountain were already burning, the miners fleeing in their canoes across the lake back this way.

Drange met with Sanuye, who was already armed to defend to entire encampment herself if need be. She passed a grab of her hand to Drange's arm, and briefly they embraced each other.

"You okay," Drange asked her.

In passing, she nodded, "I'll be at the Mountain. Seems like that's their target."

"I'll meet you at the end of this," Drange called out.

"You're damn right you will," she called back as she headed toward the shore with a number of Tuskatawa beside her. They all pushed into canoes and headed out onto the lake, pushing themselves with long oars across the frozen water as quickly as they could.

Chief Tenskatawa emerged from his hut, on his head a crown of feathers sat, the colors bursting out like shafts of light from the dark, and upon his chest was displayed some sort of tribal decorative armor. He held in his left hand a long staff with a heavy bone club at its top, and from the top down its center had been inserted a blade about the length of my forearm.

"Tuskatawa," he called out, his voice carrying over the sounds of death all around us, "in accordance with the Law of our people, the situation calls for bloodshed!" The assemblage of Tuskatawa men and women gave a warcry of one I'd never heard, and all in unison began charging up the hill from the lakeshore to defend their village. Chief Tuskatawa approached me and with an open palm pressed it against my face. I felt a wetness, and when I touched my cheek, my fingertips came away with a dark paint. "So my people do not confuse you for one of the enemy. Tonight, if not any other night, you are Tuskatawa." His hand fell to my shoulder and gave a squeeze of encouragement. I turned to see what Drange was doing, and he too had the painted mark upon his face, so that only his eyes gleamed under the rising moonlight. We took a wordless gaze upon one another, and then together clamored up the hill after the rest of the warriors.

We charged through the village, the tribesmen and women at the sides lashing out at all those Crimson Collars they could reach. The village was being burned to the ground quickly, but the Tuskatawa, even the oldest children, all had weapons in their hands. We came to a long stretch of a path where the Chief halted everyone, but not for long. Ahead, there'd gathered a grouping of the invaders reaching numbers of over a hundred. They stopped to turn and face us. With our weapons drawn, we stood on the frontline inching closer, Drange to my right, and Chief Tenskatawa not far away, his son Owl Wing to his left.

"Tuskatawa," the enraged Chief roared out, both of his hands clenched around his staff, "kill every last one of them!" His orders were met with equal roars of approval, and together with them all, Drange and I surged forward head first into the hundreds of members of Crimson Collars. We clashed, the impact sending various members of either side backward. Blood soaked the snow-covered ground like black tar, with each slit throat, gutted stomach, and bullet wound that came forth, there was no middle ground to the carnage. The Crimson Collars were known for their vicious nature, but against the Tuskatawa, a tribe of equal, if not surpassed ferocity, their strength wavered.

I lost sight of Drange for only a moment, as shortly thereafter, one of his knives sailed through the air into the back of a man who wanted my head. Drange pushed his way through the raging crowd, sticking a knife into the throat, the back, the eye sockets, the stomach, of any and all Crimson Collars in his way. We met on the grounds, and together we took on the assailants. When I ducked out of aim of attack, he came in from behind to take my attacker by surprise, and when he stumbled from being knocked off his footing, I turned around and snapped the neck of he who would have released Drange's blood. But through it all, neither one of us could catch sight of Mancino Rolandraz.

"This is a lot of men to sacrifice to save just one," Drange cried out, the paint on his face already replaced with someone else's blood. Through the haze, I took note of the boats coming across the lake from the Mountain, except now... there were more canoes making their way *back* to the mountain's shoreline. Except none of the people in those boats were Tuskatawa.

"They're going for the mountain, just like Sanuye said," I winced against the hold of an enemy.

"Blackvein," Drange uttered. "That son of a bitch must've had more people earlier today. They must've followed us back here! That son of a bitch!" He stuck a blade into the chest of the one nearest to him and he took flight back towards the lakeshore outside of Tenskatawa's hut. The Chief, neck deep in the battle at hand seemed to have already caught on and was aware of what was taking place. He looked to me and nodded.

"Go!" he said, "we will hold them here in the village! With any luck, other tribes will be here tonight!"

"The *other* tribes?"

"Yes," the Chief smiled as he fought, "a long

sought-after reunion is on the horizon. What was broken long ago will be brought back together, and we will see the beginnings of a new era soon enough! Now, go! Save the Mountain!"

I didn't need his blessing. I was headed after Drange anyway. I pushed my way through the village, which was now sprawling with members of Crimsons and Tuskatawa at each other's throats. Arrows sailed through the air, making their marks, and the smoke from rifles created a fog that would burn out the eyes of the uninitiated and inexperienced.

At the top of the hill leading down to the lakeshore, Drange had taken on nearly a dozen of Mancino's men himself. I took aim with my rifle from where I stood and put bullet after bullet into the heads of those closest to him, before joining him down at the shoreline. In the distance, three to four canoes were making their way across the lake.

"Help me push this into the water and grab an oar," Drange said hurriedly. To our sides, a few Tuskatawa took hold of their own canoes and set into the water. I pushed the canoe into the lake and leapt in after Drange. Together we took hold of a paddle and began racing forward across the lake. My arms were already tired, but seeing Drange as enraged as he was, it gave me back some strength. To our right and left, there paddled canoes with Tuskatawa in them, and ahead, too far to see the faces of who were paddling them, the canoes of our enemy drew closer to the shoreline of Blackheart Mountain, set ablaze with orange fire cutting into the falling snow. As we raced closer, the mountain loomed higher and higher into the night sky, its sides flickering with the glow of firelight from the attack on its shores. Behind us, the sounds of battle in the village rose to deafening levels, drowned out only every other moment from the paddles we dug into the dark water. With the light of the fires both behind us and ahead, it didn't feel like night at all. Mancino's men reached the shore before we could, of course, and already they were fleeing towards the entrance to the mine, carrying with them large crates of something. As soon as we landed ashore, Drange, myself, and the other Tuskatawa jumped into the ankle-deep water. As they gave chase, I saw the contents of the crates, as some of it had fallen out into one of the canoes. I picked it up and knew exactly what they were planning on doing. The Crimson Collars weren't here to steal Blackvein.

"Drange!" I called out. He turned around and looked what I held high in the sky: a stick of dynamite.

"What...?" Drange came back, taking a hold of what I'd found.

"They're here to destroy the mine," I said. Drange looked toward the mountain.

"We better hurry then," he said. We returned to the race, the sounds of the village now farther in the distance, but ever-present. Chasing up the hillside toward the entrance to the mine, the bodies of countless Tuskatawa lay lifeless and mangled, many of them missing their limbs, their blood frozen in the snow around them. Before us, the mouth of the mine opened: a high archway dug into the mountainside the miners used as an entry point. Here, Mancino's men had met with another group of Tuskatawa, who still fought to keep them from entering. And at the head of this group, stood Sanuye, letting out screams of rage so horrifying, I thought that maybe she could win the battle all by herself. She felled the attacker immediately in front of her and then turned to face the next, the man himself: Mancino Rolandraz. We ran forward through the crusted snow, but over it all

I could still hear her cries as she engaged him. She fought with a staff similar to that of the Chief's, except with a longer blade. Mancino fought back with two massive knives, one of which was one he would have plunged into my heart earlier.

Before we could get much closer, on the slopes leading up to the mine's entrance, more of Mancino's men surprised us from the right and left flanks, halting our pursuit. And with Sanuye taking on Mancino, the men we'd been chasing with all the dynamite made it passed them and into the mine.

Desperate, Drange and I and those Tuskatawa with us fought as hard as we could, but they simply kept coming. More of them came down from the rocky hilltops to the east, stopping us again. My view took me into the direction of Mancino and Sanuye, who were still against one another. She seemed to have the upper hand, having knocked aside one of Rolandraz's knives, but that only meant he now had a free hand. He stopped a downward swing from her staff with that open hand and with the blade in his other, locked it onto the staff. He used his weight to counter her balance, causing the staff to snap in half. She lost hold of both ends and he kicked her in the stomach, pushing away.

I was given the opportunity then, a moment allowing me to take aim with my revolver, to put a bullet where it belonged. I held it out and lined up the barrel with Mancino's head.... but when I pulled the trigger nothing came out. Of course, I'd never been able to reload my revolvers since the last I'd used them.

"Damnit!" I tossed the revolver to the ground to block an oncoming attack, and as I dug my knife into the side of that man's skull, from out of the corner of my eye, I saw that Rolandraz had regained hold of his second blade.... and had stuck both of them into Sanuye's gut, pressing them up further into her chest cavity. The look on her face was that of total awe, shock, and agony... and when Drange finally caught sight of the scene, he exploded forward, not caring about the injuries sustained from the attackers around him. He charged through the snow, now falling from the sky at a diagonal slant.

Rolandraz pressed Sanuye back against the side of a wagon, using the force of his weight to dig the blades in even deeper. He then whispered something to her that none of us would ever know, and unleashed a fury of short, deep stabs in through her ribcage on either side with both knives. Before she slid to the ground, he kissed her on the mouth, long and lovingly, giving her lower lip a small nibble. Sanuye slid the rest of the way to the ground and landed in a sitting position, leaned up against the wagon.

Drange swung a long, wooden plank against Rolandraz's back, causing the man to wince in agony. Drange screamed words I was unable to sort out. He swung his fists into the face of the man in front of him, knocking him to the ground.

I dispatched the last of Mancino's men, and with the remaining Tuskatawa, raced up toward the mine where Drange stood over Rolandraz. The face Drange wore was no longer recognizable; it had been mixed and blended by the dark night sky, the mud on the ground, and the light of the fires. Rolandraz lay on the ground, holding his sides and spitting up blood, but he was happy about it.

"I was," Mancino struggled to say, "I... at least I was able to get in one good kiss before I died."

Drange, furious, stepped forward, presumably to end the man's life, but suddenly there came a rolling thunder from up ahead. The sky seemed to crack open with the sound of an ear-splitting explosion, but the flash died down and it was revealed to have been the Mountain itself, flames bursting from the side sending boulders and rocks and pebbles sailing through the air. The mine entrance collapsed, casting a cloud of dust and rock in all outward directions.

When the dust settled, the light from the new fires revealed that Rolandraz was still laying on the ground. Drange's breathing had slowed to a dull hatred, and behind us, Chief Tenskatawa approached the hillside from the shoreline with a host of tribesmen at his side. He stopped to kneel beside the motionless form of Sanuye. He lowered his head, sad, but turned toward the situation that was unfolding. When he reached Drange's side, he put a hand on his shoulder.

"Rest now, my friend," he said calmly, "the enemy has been defeated."

"Has he," Rolandraz grumbled from the ground, "have you taken a look around you? The mine is dead. Your people can never again fowl the earth with life that were meant to have been taken by death."

"You are mistaken, Mr. Rolandraz," Chief Tenskatawa said, "we will rebuild the mine. We will one day dig in again. But as you may not be aware, your people are no more. Your disgusting ranks have been slain. Every last one of them, except for the cowards who fled into the mountains, whom without their fearless leader, will surely succumb to their wounds, or their failing spirits."

Rolandraz swallowed a heavy gulp upon hearing that, but still he didn't want to appear as though he'd been broken.

"We will commence with your punishment now, here, on the slopes of Blackheart Mountain. We will wait for the materials of the Law, and then, you will be punished for your crimes," Tenskatawa said.

While we waited for the tribesmen to return with whatever the Chief meant as "materials of the Law", I found ammunition on the bodies of the fallen to refill my revolvers. Drange stood over the body of his wife. He stared down, motionless, his face expressionless. I slammed the chamber of my newly reloaded revolver closed and slid it into its holster. My second revolver sat snug in its holster with a full belly was well.

"You'll be here, one day too," Rolandraz said to me, being held still by two of the Chief's men. I turned toward him, the fires of the mine burning even brighter than before, black smoke billowing out into an even blacker night sky, "one day you'll be held just like this. And then you'll understand."

"Men like you lead lives that aren't hard to understand," I said to him, "there's nothing confusing about a wolf running in the wild."

"Maybe," he said, "Every wolf has his last meal, though. This victory tonight, won't be my last. Your Chief and his Law will make sure of that."

"He's not my Chief," I said.

"Really," Rolandraz let out a light laugh, mocking me for sure. "If you say so."

Not long later, the canoe returned and with it the tribesmen brought a metal spade and a torch, and with that also, a dagger with a colorful hilt. The blade of the dagger was not straight, but curved. Perfect for digging something out. Chief Tenskatawa received the dagger and showed it to Rolandraz.

"With this dagger," he started, "I shall remove your eyes. Seeing the world will no longer be yours to enjoy. You will live from this day forward, but you will live in a hell which your eyes can not save you from. And with this spade and torch, I shall seal those wounds closed, so that you will not die from certain infection. Thus, is the punishment to all those who Tuskatawa find to be undeserving of death. Thus, is the Law."

Rolandraz was not having this though, as suddenly his calm demeanor was replaced by desperation. In two swift movements, he was able to break free of those holding him. It was my fault for standing so close, but he was able to steal away with one of my revolvers. He immediately aimed it outward, pulling back on the hammer. He aimed the gun directly at Chief Tenskatawa's head.

"Even if you kill me," the Chief said calmly, holding the ceremonial dagger, "even if you use all of those bullets, you will still be taken. Your punishment is not contingent on my survival. If not by my hand, then certainly by another."

Rolandraz backed up toward the flames of the burning mine. There was nowhere for him to run, but if he had his way, he'd leave this earth with six more lives in his back pocket.

"Maybe that's for the best," Rolandraz said, "maybe I'm meant for it all. But killing you would still make my victory today more complete! Killing you, is *still* killing you! The Crimson Collars be damned, they died for the cause we set out believing in. It wouldn't be right if I didn't do the same! It wouldn't be just if I let them all die and I still get to live!" He held my revolver steadily, but the sound of gunfire did not explode from the weapon he held. He stumbled back, looking down at the new hole in his stomach. All eyes turned to me. Smoke rose from the tip of my kidnapped revolver's brother, aimed straight for Rolandraz's gut.

Rolandraz stumbled backward again, losing the

strength to hold onto the gun. He dropped it, and with its loosening, he himself fell all the way onto his back. I walked forward and stopped at his side, watching his black blood bleed out onto the white snow. He held his side where the bullet went through, and looked into my face. If there was anything to be said about this last acknowledgment, it's that he'd been right. I didn't need to tell him that, because even in his agony, he was well aware.

I put another bullet into him, this time into his chest. He let out a groan. I trained my aim for his skull, and put a third round of lead right between his eyes. No one said a word for the longest time. I half expected them all to turn on me. I was aware of their Law. But I wasn't about to let this madman do any more harm to anyone. Not ever.

Drange stared at me, but he didn't seem angry about it. Everyone else, the Chief, the tribesmen and women, they all wore expressions of shock, but also... awaiting their Chief's next command. Owl Wing, the Chief's son, stood in the foreground. I couldn't be sure what he made of it all, he seemed to simply be observing at this point.

"You've broken our Law, Mr. Mahoney," Chief Tenskatawa said, his voice stern, and unimpressed. I leaned down and picked up the revolver the now dead Mancino Rolandraz had taken from me, and holstered it. As I turned around to face the chief, I held my gun out, but only for a moment.

When I holstered it, everyone seemed to regain a state of calmness. "What do you have to say for yourself," the Chief asked.

And I said to him, "I'm not Tuskatawa. It's not my goddamn Law."

X.
HOW WE CHOOSE TO DIE

With the coming of a grey winter dawn, the havoc Mancino Rolandraz and his Crimson Collars got away with before being exterminated was fully revealed. Most of the fires had died out, but there were some tiny flickerings clinging to life in the burned-down rubble of tents, huts, and some of the larger buildings the Tuskatawa had constructed. The Blackvein mine was gone, with its entrance completely caved-in and the fires inside still burning, the smoke steaming out of cracks and vents from the side of the mountain. The exact number of deaths among the Tuskatawa was unknown at best, but if it had been any higher, surely the Crimson Collars would be the ones walking away.

The Chief, solemn and weary, walked amongst the dead and the smoke. He knelt down to examine the corpse of a child, whose face had been burned to an unrecognizable char. A woman, presumably the child's mother, sat on the ground beside the burned child, sobbing uncontrollably. The Chief knew there was no comfort he could give, nothing he could say to put away her tears. He stood back up and continued walking along the burned pathways of his village.

The Chief soon met with a tribesman I'd not been introduced to. They exchanged words and the tribesman explained to him that there'd been more of Mancino's men to the south, charging through the mountains. They were stopped, when another tribe, not residing at the Blackheart Mountain village, met them and decimated them in a short battle. The Chief nodded, knowing that this was the tribe that had come with hopes to reconnect their union "once heavily celebrated long ago". As they spoke, the rest of the members of this tribe began to emerge from the smoke and the fire and then from between all of the burning structures remaining in the village. There were only a few at first, but then there appeared more. Dozens, reaching into the hundreds. The Chief stood tall, adjusting his stance to welcome them. Another man, presumably the Chief of this newly-arrived tribe, strode forth, and the two chiefs acknowledged firmly and sternly as though they hadn't born witness to each other in a time out of thought and memory.

"Tenskatawa," the new chief said. He was as tall as Tenskatawa, but he wore more... traditional clothing. Whereas Tenskatawa brandished more ancestral attire, this other chief wore slacks much like my own, his shoulders draped by a dark leather coat. His face had been painted with whites and dark blues, and his lower lip had been painted with a vertical black stripe down the middle.

"Quan Zao, Chief of the Black Boar Tribe," Tenskatawa said. He turned his head toward me, "Chief Quan Zao is a... courageous man," he said to me. "A long time ago, our people were very much joined together. I would otherwise find it odd that you've decided to show your face now. However, it couldn't have come at a more opportune time. There's a chance we may have been overrun had you and your people not arrived when you did."

"I may not have shown my face at all, honestly, if not for your son," Zao said, placing a hand on Owl Wing's back, "This is a reunion that should have happened years ago, but I am happy that it is happening at all. When you are ready, I should like to speak with you in private, as brothers, as we once were," Quan Zao said. Tenskatawa nodded.

"We may speak now if you'd like," he replied. "I am very curious as to what you have to say."

The two chiefs walked off to where Tenskatawa's hut sat on the lakeshore. This... Quan Zao, his men and women all appeared just as strong and warriorlike as the Tuskatawa, but there was an undeniable uncertainty spread among the surviving members of each tribe. I expected Drange to be standing beside me, but I hadn't seen him since we returned from the Mountain. Instead, Owl Wing stood there, an expression of concern and distrust for the new arrivals.

"Is he right," I asked him, "did you orchestrate this meeting?"

"Under my father's orders. For years, the Black Boar and the Tuskatawa have been at odds, almost at each other's throats. But it was my father who first began to express interest in bringing everyone back together," he said, "they did not part on good terms, my father and Quan Zao."

"You don't say."

"Quan Zao's people aren't what you might call... of pure native blood. Their ancestors come from a land long and far away from here. An even longer time ago than the fall of the world, their country and this country were hard at war. My father and Quan Zao were... friends, coming together at a time of equal strife. Each of them had different ideas as to what unity meant. And so, before they could go to war with each other, as each of them mutually foresaw, they agreed to part ways in relative peace, not wanting to sacrifice the lives of their people over their differences. That was many years ago," Owl Wing said. "and these are strange times, indeed. I did not actually expect Chief Zao to come. I want you to know something, Mr. Mahoney," he said, his tone hinting at an abrupt change of subject, "I agree with what you did. Killing Mancino Rolandraz."

"You do?"

"I do. You see, like my father and Quan Zao, he and I also have our differences. This so-called Law of the Tuskatawa, I don't agree with it. You saved my father's life, and perhaps several others standing there, but he will never see it that way. If you were not there, I may be dead as well. My father believes that there is no afterlife, no Hell to punish those who've lived a murderous life. He believes it is his duty to therefore create a Hell for each person who deserves it. He wants them to live out the rest of their life in fear and agony of a different sort that death cannot give. But Mr. Mahoney," he explained.

"-some men just need to be killed," I finished the sentence for him. He nodded.

"No Hell. No anything. Nothing. I cannot tell you how many men my father has blinded, only for me to find them still spreading their terror late on. I've felled more blind men than I can count. I've no doubt I'd cross paths with Mancino Rolandraz someday in the future, only to finish the job properly."

Owl Wing walked off into the village, joining the rest of his people in searching for survivors. My view again took me to the woman crying over her scorched child. She'd taken on a wide-eyed stare, succumbing to the shock of losing her child in such a brutal, dehumanizing way.

The two Chiefs spoke for quite a while. When they both emerged from the hut, nothing was said about their conversation, but that there would be words following the funeral ceremony of all those who lost their lives in the battle.

Throughout the day, the bodies of the dead who could be found, and that were not hewn to pieces by the now all-but-extinct Crimson Collars, were all clothed in light garments, and placed evenly together. As before, when night fell, little torches were lit along the pathways of the village, all leading like fireflies to a great platform, this one built larger to accommodate more bodies. The ring of men and women holding torches stood around them, and were of a greater number than when Tenskatawa and his people bid farewell to his own blood. A defeated, but accepting Til Drange stood amongst them. He was the first to approach the dead. He stopped just a few inches from her, looking down at the form of Sanuye, whose face now made no expression at all, except that of a woman deep in sleep. He touched her cheek, and I knew not what he thought about; I imagined it was something he was remembering, perhaps the last time he had touched her cheek, before the bloodshed. He ran his fingers through her hair one last time, and then set the torch to her. He stepped back as others stepped up, placing their own torches to the dead. The flames caught quickly, and burned bright into the night sky.

"It is true you are not Tuskatawa," the Chief said to me while the fire burned, keeping his voice low, "but you still must be held accountable for interrupting our culture."

"Ya gonna cut out my eyes?"

"No," he said, "you are not a monster of a man like Mancino Rolandraz. But you are not Tuskatawa. It was not wrong of Til Drange to bring you here, hoping to convince you to join our people, but it was wrong of me to expect that *that* was possible. In that, you and I are both at fault. So I will not have you subjected to our Law, but I must tell you to leave this place."

"And then you'll have someone shoot me in the back, right?"

"I don't think you'd have saved my life if you were only going to betray me and my people immediately after."

"And who says I did it to save *your* life? I put a bullet in his head because it was the right thing to do. Not to save *you*, but anyone else he would most certainly afflict. Maybe putting a bullet in *my* head would be the right thing for *you* to do."

"If that was how I thought of you, then yes, I would break the Law of my people. But I don't think you're that sort of man. Even with all the pieces lying where they lay, I still have a small sliver a faith that you'll make the right choice. But for the sake of my people, you will have to make that choice far away from here."

The bodies of Mancino's men were burned in a separate fire, only so the corpses didn't decay and spread disease. As for the body of Mancino himself, his body was cut into pieces of various sizes and consistencies. Tenskatawa cut the head from the body and cleaned it of all flesh, muscle, and fluids, pulling the brain matter out and burning it with the other bodies. With the skull, he cut the front half of it clean down the middle, and added it to his ceremonial battle armor, at the center of his chest. The rest of Mancino's body was tossed to wolves of the village, who devoured the remaining pieces in minutes.

The following morning, I tended to Eleanor. She'd managed to come away from the battle with a few scratches, nothing worse than what she'd sustained in the past. Still, her eyes had fallen to a twinkle of sadness since the bloodbath. I'd not seen her during the battle, I'd not been by her side. I whispered to her that I was sorry, that I would not leave her again. I cleaned the cuts on her coat, and fed her what food I could find. From here, I was able to see Drange. He stood over by the hut he'd once shared with Sanuye, the same hut she used to craft arrows and bows and other sorts of weaponry. The hut now lay in a heap, half-collapsed, and half completely burned to the ground. I patted Eleanor on her long neck. "I'll be right back, girl," I said to her.

On the way over to Drange, I caught sight of Chief Tenskatawa and Chief Quan Zao speaking at the shoreline opposite the Mountain. From there, they spoke heavily and enthusiastically about... something. Probably strategy, trying to come to terms with each other. In the distance, Blackheart Mountain loomed like a carcass vacant of any soul. The slopes were still encased in veils of smoke, now grey under the winter morning haze.

"Hey," I said to Drange, taking to his side.

"There's word of Tuskatawa officially uniting with Quan Zao's tribe," he said, as though there weren't anything else on his mind, "It seems as though the two of them are legitimately trying to make it work. I wasn't around when the severance took place. But I'd heard that their parting came due to a fear of war. And yet here they are, coming together for the sake of it. It's things like that that make a man worry."

"And contemplate whose side he's on," I said.

"In a way, yea," he replied, "maybe times have changed, Mahon. Maybe it's a good thing this is all happening." It was obvious he didn't want to talk about her. I didn't want to ask him about her. But there was still his mind to consider. A man's mind is patient only as long as it wants to be.

"You ain't lost it, have ya," I asked him. "Hell of

thing happened here last night."

"I only lost one thing last night, Mahon," he said. He gently kicked a piece of burned wood from the pile of in front of him.

"I've decided to head back. Now's a good a time as ever. Well, it's more like I'm being ordered to leave, which I understand," I said, "When Gunth' asks about what I found out here, I'll tell him there ain't no Mountain."

"Well, you wouldn't be lyin'. There ain't nothin' here anymore."

"Your Chief seems pretty confident–"

"It'll take years to get the mine back to what it was," Drange muttered, "and the war will still be going on by then."

"What are you gonna do?"

"There's been talk of the tribes uniting for a long time. And that only means one thing, Mahon. Last night was just the start. The Chief has always meant to go to war, but it's been quite a while since he first voiced interest in the endeavor. I think he just needed a push. Mancino gave it to him. I'd say your boss is high up there on the Chief's list. I'd be a fool not to bet against it as his next maneuver. Taking control over New Canterton would be a smart foothold."

My thoughts came down hard and swift-like, and she was there at the front. Cassandra.

"What are *you* gonna do?" I asked him again.

"Gunther Ostrander isn't the reason Sanuye is dead. But he's the reason a lot of people are, and he'll be the reason more bleed out in the future. He's more organized than the Crimson Collars ever were, has more connections. And he runs a quarry, a mine of his own, both fed with slaves who work themselves to their own deaths every day. It was in that quarry I was nearly broken down completely to my bones. It's not my own vengeance that's important, but you can bet everything you own of value that I'll be there when his factory is laid to waste and everyone in his wallet is dead on the ground."

"If that's how it's gonna be then I've got to leave sooner than later," I said.

"I thought you said you weren't gonna tell him anything."

"I ain't," I said, "I've had a lot of time to think about it all. I don't care if you kill him, cut his eyes out, or let him die old and decrepit. Burn his house to the ground. String up his men and cut their balls off. That's not my fight. And it never will be as long as I can keep it that way. There's another reason I have to go. I have a woman there, Drange. I'm not sure if she loves me, and I'm not sure if I love her. I don't know if what we have is what you and... Sanuye had. But I don't suppose that matters all that much now. I've gotta get her outta there before this whole Hell breaks loose. Nothing else matters now."

"I'd say I'd go with ya," Drange said, seeing as I was headed back towards my horse. "He and I have never met face to face, but Ostrander would recognize me faster than a fly takes his last shit. He would see me by your side, and with you having been gone for as long as you have been... it'd be over before we could start."

"Doesn't matter none," I told him, "I'm better off alone with this sort of thing." I climbed onto Eleanor's back and gave her a heavy pat of encouragement. "If it's possible, maybe you can delay your Chief's attack, assuming that is what he's going for. As long as possible, if any stretch of time at all."

"And what if they decide not to go for

Ostrander? What if my assumptions are wrong?"

"Then I'll still be doin' what I shoulda done a long time ago," I said. I took off through the burned village and out the same way I left last time. With the distance between myself and Blackheart Mountain and the Tuskatawa village increasing by the second, winding the switchbacks of the mountains and traversing the cliffsides and pathways until the mountains themselves were behind me, thoughts of Cassandra rushed in like a flood. The only thing that mattered now was getting to her, and getting her and the baby inside of her to safety.

III

The Breathless Plunge

XI.
NOT ALL MEN ARE GIVEN THEIR OWN GRAVES

For a little while, even after I'd left the mountains behind me, I had acquired a particular accompaniment that kept watch from afar, but every now and then would dart his head out just long enough for me to catch him outta the corner of my eye. The eyes of the spy belonged to that of one of the wolves from the village, probably the same eyes I first woke up to after being taken there. As far as I could tell, he never allowed himself to get any closer than what eyeshot permitted. At the very least, I knew where he was simply by the tips of his ears, habitually perking up from behind mounds of dirt. At his most revealing, he would stand tall and proud atop a ridge, looking over the land, pretending to run into me with his gaze. "Oh, hello there," his eyes would say, "fancy meeting you out here in the wilderness, it's quite unexpected." He would howl during the nights for the first sun-setting moments, and then fall silent once the stars started to come out. Each morning since having taken my leave from Blackheart Mountain, I left him a scrap piece of whatever I'd made a meal of the night before. I never looked back to see if he'd taken the food, but I thought that maybe that could be at least one reason why he followed after.

Blackheart Mountain was situated farther away from Gunther's encampment than originally assumed. I'd been on the road for four days since departing, and had only now just begun to take note of familiar landmarks that let me know I was heading in the right direction. About fifty or so miles northeast of Gunther's factory there was a cemetery covering an entire hillside. The names had all since been rubbed off by time, and most of the headstones had sunken into the ground. Near the base of the hill where the ground jutted out into a ridge, several caskets protruded from the hillside, some of which had been broken into by cannibals, rodents, and other meat-eating beasts. At the top of this hill sat a line of trees that had grown to a menacing height, their trunks narrow, thin and underfed, and I'm sure at one time or another the tops of them grew all sorts of greens and were filled with nests for birds of all colors of their own. At present, their gnarled roots had burst from the ground, reaching like tentacles toward the headstones not far off. I stood near the trees and observed the cutout in the land that served as a main road to travelers, leading through a small ruin of buildings once used as homesteads and eventually across a plain stretch of dirt for a few more miles, ending at the front gate of the outer wall which surrounded and served as the regional border of New Canterton. From here, I could see the black smoke rising out of the stacks of the factory. The smoke was only a thin cloud from this distance, but even far away, I felt its shadow.

The first job I'd ever taken from Gunther Ostrander had been a simple one. The peace agreement written decades ago, an article of officiality titled the "Westward Exploratory Projection Treaty", needed to be taken to a man in Vermouth, for what Gunther referred to as a "preservation overhaul". This contact of his residing in Vermouth had reportedly perfected a new method of preserving documents, and Gunther was willing to pay handsomely for the work. Long story short, it had all been a test. Gunther already had the Treaty well taken care of in his vault, and had sent me out with a dupe copy. The man waiting for me in Vermouth had been specifically ordered to accept the "document" and make a run for it. Gunther never expected me to shoot the man dead before he could even leave the building. He bled out of a hole in his back and out of his chest right there in his goddamn doorway. Gunther, dismayed but not unimpressed, revealed the truth when I returned.

Thinking about that now, it had me thinking even harder. Even from the start, the man had been a deceptive son of a bitch. He had the artform perfected, so much so that I never saw any of it coming. I wondered how much more he'd been lying about, or stretching the truth of, or just plain producing bullshit underlying the foundations of whatever his design truly was. How much of my work for him had actually been sincere in its intentions, and how many of the jobs I'd pulled off had been interlaced with nefarious underlying falsehoods and stretched truths?

The wolf emerged from the line of trees not twenty tree trunks away. He perched himself right at the line, adjusting his stance and looking over the land as he always did. He noticed me looking in his direction, but instead of hiding, he remained still, fixing his eyes on my own. It was possible he meant no harm; a wolf alone out here rarely lasted long, the same as any man would. It was possible he had something in him the same as me, that kept him going even when alone. Aside from my ability to hold in my hands a gun, or any weapon to defend myself with, he and I both shared the same chances of survival while alone in the wilderness.

I'd made camp up on the hill. There'd been nowhere else to truly hide myself. Some nights, the risk was not even a risk anymore, but an only choice. Under the night sky anyone could be taken. But the wolf had stayed where I noticed him, he sat along the edge of trees and kept watch.

I walked slowly in his direction, not to meet him, but just to lay some food down for him. He watched me the entire time from the moment I started moving toward him, his pupils wide like coals. About midway between my camp and the spot he'd chosen as his own, I placed some uncooked rabbit meat on the ground. I pointed to it as though he would understand my meaning, and then made my way back to my camp.

I took my seat on the log and went back to my part of the meal, keeping watch from the corner of my eye. The wolf didn't move, but he saw where I'd placed the meat, and he saw that it was meat. I took a bite of my food and chewed it, swallowed it, and wiped my hands clean on my slacks. From the glow of my little fire, I saw his eyes shine. He'd gotten up and trotted over to sniff the meat. He licked it a little, and then took it into his mouth with those white teeth, chewing voraciously. We met eyes again, and I thought that maybe he might have been thanking me. You can tell by the eyes when a horse is appreciative of your care, I wondered if it was the same for all animals.

I awoke to the sounds of galloping horses heading closer up the cemetery hill toward me. Eleanor let out a concerned neigh. I saw that my wolf companion was nowhere to be found. Must've run off either before sunrise or as soon as he heard the riders approaching. I looked on down the hill and counted four men, one of them taking the obvious lead. He wore a style of hat that only an idiot would wear.

"Oh no," I muttered to myself.

I knew exactly who it was comin' up the hill. But my uneasiness was not out of fear, of course it wasn't. On the surface, Douglass Flood was a dumb man with a brain, but that was more dangerous a man than a dumb one without one. If anything bad happened to anyone who happened to be around Douglass Flood, it was only out of the sheer bad luck of being that close in proximity to him.

Douglass Flood rode up the hill accompanied by the three others. They must've already seen me, as they rode at a pace of informed hurriedness. By the time they reached the top of the hill, I'd already had my sidearms ready and my rifle half-unslung. Douglass Flood wore the same idiot grin across his face he always did when crossing paths with me. He gave a light chuckle that evolved into an amused laugh.

"Well now," he said, "ain't this some shit. Come ridin' up this hill expecting to find some asshole, and come to find I was right."

"Hey Doug," I muttered.

"Mahon," he nodded, tipping his idiot hat, "been a while. Almost thought you were dead, seein' as how you haven't shown your face back at Gunther's for as long as it's been."

"I been gone for longer stretches before," I said, "and I still ain't dead. Didn't even come close, not once. It's just been a long road. Was actually on my way back."

"A long road, ya say," Douglass said, sucking on his teeth, "that a fact."

"It's a fact even an idiot can't argue with," I said. Douglass nodded, shrugging because even he knew I was referring to him in the statement. "Although, one could say that's what makes an idiot, an idiot. His inability to recognize fact from rattlesnake piss."

"Well it's good you're headed back, cause as a

matter of fact, we're headed back that way too," he said. "We can ride together."

"Lucky me."

"Lucky us, I'd say," Douglass said, "you're the toughest one here. If anything, you'd be protecting all of us all on your own." Douglass's men seemed to get a kick outta that one. There was somethin' outta place here, and the air was thick with it. Douglass had never been a man hard to figure out; his giveaway was in the way he talked. He hesitated between certain words, briefly pausing because he wanted to be sure what he was sayin' wouldn't give anything away. But he'd never perfected the art, and one wouldn't be wrong to say he took a steaming pile of shit all over the historical heroes of the past who had.

"I think I'll ride it alone, actually. You and your... handsome posse will have to do without me," I said, starting to gather my things and load it back onto Eleanor. I went to mount her saddle when I heard them. The unmistakable sounds of metal hammers being pulled back.

"It might be better if you come along with us," Douglass grinned. I turned around and, along with the others in his company, saw that he had a sidearm aimed for me head, with a trigger finger primed.

"Feels a little like some things have changed since I've been away," I said.

"Nothin's changed in my book," Douglass said, "today is just another day for you. Now," he removed a length of rope from his saddle bag, "we have orders to bring you in should we find you. And find you we have. You can either do with this rope to yourself in a comfortable manner, or one of my compatriots can drag you for the rest of the way to New Canterton." He tossed the rope at me and I caught it.

I looked to where my wolf companion had been the night before. Still, he was gone. Smart pup, that one. Better he get out of here while the goin' was good.

"Around your neck," Douglass said, nodding at me in reassuring jest.

"You know what this means, don't you," I said to him as I began securing myself. I mounted Eleanor, tying the rope around my neck, and then tying the other end to her saddle. With the remaining end of the rope, I tossed it to Douglass, who caught it and tied a knot onto his own saddle.

"No, what does this mean?"

"Believe it or not, I used to lay awake some nights with the sadness of knowing I could never kill you, being we work for the same man. But after today, every night from here on out, I'm gonna sleep real good."

The five of us rode on down the headstone-laden hill, left the cemetery and the architectural ruins soon after behind, and found our way onto the path that would lead directly to New Canterton. Douglass Flood always had a habit of whistling annoying tunes he'd picked up from who the hell knows where. He liked the brag that he once heard a target of his whistle the tune before killin' em, and the tune just stuck with him. But everyone back at New Canterton knew that was elongated bullshit. Still, he liked to whistle. That habit hadn't left him, as for a good portion of our ride together, he whistled a tune that could have slain a sandshark all on its own. The men riding with us I didn't recognize. Gunther hired them himself, as was another of his habits. They seemed to have only been temporarily brought on by Douglass, though; roadies, lackies, someone's to keep his ego high and inflated. I got the feeling Douglass wanted to send the message that he was the leader of his own gang; the way he rode upon his horse, his stature, seemed to agree with my supposition.

Listening to their banter, I learned that there was a Henry, a man who liked to chew more than talk. His face had been blessed with more than one chin, and I guessed it was for the best since there was only so much a man could do with only one. Then there was Ralph, a skinny sort of breed who talked with an accent I hadn't ever heard before. He had a canteen on him but it wasn't full of water. Whenever he offered it to one of the other guys, they spat in disgust, proclaiming how they could never figure how anyone could drink tea from a canteen in this heat. The third member of this wannabe posse, the others referred to as Boon. He never said a word. But I suppose he didn't have to. He had a set of mountainous shoulders and equally-daunting biceps. His best feature was reserved strictly for his face: a permanent expression of hatred for everything around him, all of which got his message across without a single whisper.

Henry and Ralph spent the majority of the time insulting each other's family members, and tossing various scraps of food and snacks at one another. Boon, on the other hand, rode silently a number of yards back. Judging generously with sight only, he must have stood at least seven feet tall, and even his horse, a dark-coated breed with a mutant-like stride, held a similar disposition. There was never a better match seen in my day between a man and his horse.

"Mind fillin' me in some of all this," I said to Douglass, "this all seems a bit unwarranted."

"Unwarranted? You've been away a long time, Mahon," Douglass said, taking a bite out of a light-red apple the size of a tree knot, "You're right about having been away for longer periods of time, but those were different stances of circum. Word is, after the attempted assassination of everybody's favorite land-rapist Mancino Rolandraz, you just up and vanished along with the rest of those... painted-face people. Funny thing really how that all went down. And while you haven't exactly been gone for a *real* long time, enough time has certainly passed to inspire the increased cautiousness of our mutual employer. You know as well as I do Gunther ain't the sort of fella to be takin' many chances. I'd thought you of all people would understand that."

"I've known him a lot longer than you have, and as long as I've known him, he's never taken a chance on you over trustin' me."

"Question is, Mahon, is if you found what he sent you out to find," Douglass said.

"That's between me and him," I said. "The contracts he offers me have always been confidential."

"Maybe," he gave the rope which was tied to my neck a little tug, "maybe it would make things easier for you if you told me about it first."

"Oh good god, man," I let out, "is that what this is about?" He stopped our ride and turned toward me. "You're just tryin' to get outta me any information you can. My guess is you'll shoot me, or have one of your tagalongs do it for ya, and then take the credit yourself. I know that's what I'd do if I were a man in your boots. Because everyone who's ever known ya knows you'll never accomplish anything yourself."

"You didn't have to put the rope around your neck," Douglass said, "if I say so myself, that was very unlike the real Rancid Mahoney I've come to know."

"You don't know a goddamn thing about me, buddy," I said.

"Maybe we've both been wrong all this time," he said, "but seein' as there's no sense in hidin' anything anymore," he gave the rope a sudden yank, hard enough to pull me from the saddle. Eleanor let out a high-pitched neigh, as the rope tied to her saddle tightened while Douglass road enough distance away to tighten the rope taut, with my neck in the middle. Every movement he made whether it was his horse adjusting its stance or him laughing, the rope around my neck squeezed so tight that any tighter and it would cut right through my neck, sawing my head clean off in one messy, bloody fashion. I'd seen it done before. I'd been the one of the dealing end of things. One of Douglass's cronies rode up next to Eleanor, stabilizing her to keep both lengths of the rope tight.

I choked, my knees buckling, because there was nothing for me to do. I could feel my face filling with blood. My sight blurred and very soon I wouldn't be able to hear a damn thing.

"There ain't long left for you to feel the lovin' embrace of that rope, Mahon," I heard Douglass jeer, "Now, part of me is sayin' I should just go ahead and do it. Take your head. Gunther wouldn't be sad for long. He knows how cruel the world is. Even the great Rancid Mahoney must eventually meet his demise. Henry, gimme that bottle."

Henry had been drinking from a small flask-sized bottle of whiskey. He tossed it to Douglass, who then showed it to me.

"That's right, you're a whiskey man," Douglass laughed. He then tossed it as hard as he could at my head. The glass shattered, and while I would have otherwise fallen to the ground from the impact, the rope around my neck held me up. My legs gave out, and I thought that I might be hanged right then and there. I couldn't even feel the whiskey run down the side of my head, mixing and blending with the blood from my new wound. Douglass had Ralph remove the end of the rope that I'd tied to Eleanor's saddle and wrap it around a nearby tree. Henry and Ralph then proceeded to ride on by one after the other, kicking me in the face with each pass. I could barely feel the kicks, and I could hardly see much of anything, but I could just make out the sheer amusement they shared, their laughter rang loud and bellowing. They slapped me around, punching me in the gut and in the ribs. I waited for Boon to come forward to finish me off, but he never did. He stayed behind, sitting on his mountain of a steed.

"Boon! Hey there Boon!" Douglass finally called out. When Boon didn't move, Douglass tossed a small pebble at him. It bounced off his forehead and landed in the dirt. "Boon! Goddamn Boon, get in there and give this piece of shit some muscle. Go on, give him a few of your good punches!"

I spat a wad of blood and mucous to the ground. Douglass had loosened the tautness of the rope by closing the gap between him and the tree by a few feet. I'd fallen to my knees, unable to stand any longer. Boon grunted, but it didn't seem like he wanted any part of what was goin' on.

I lurched forward with a kick from Henry's or Ralph's boot, I couldn't tell who'd done it, and the other of them kicked dirt into my face. When I looked up, my eyesight blurring a little more, the haze thickening, but then clearing after a moment of no physical contact. I saw that Boon had dismounted and had slowly begun to make his way toward me. I'd been right about him; he must really be at least seven feet tall. The top of his head reached Douglass's shoulders even while Douglass was still on his horse. With each step, he lurched forward with a distaste for what Douglass ordered him to do. He stopped directly in front of me, barely a foot between us. I looked up. I didn't care about the pain in my neck. If there was going to be anyone who'd put an end to my life, I told myself I'd always look them in the eye. Seeing as I was still afforded some muscle movement, I wasn't about to let the opportunity pass me by.

Boon looked down, and I saw the darkness beneath his eyes. Here was a man not bound by the lecherous words shared amongst his immediate company. Here was a man who'd chosen to remain silent in patient waiting. I didn't know his story, and so his internal turmoil was not mine to understand. But in the shared moments spent looking into each other's eyes, he silently reassured me of something.

Suddenly, Boon spun around, grabbing the throats of Henry and Ralph, crushing each one in each of his hands. They fell to the ground dead almost instantly. Douglass didn't have time to react with more than an onslaught of obscenities. He tried to flee on his horse, and with him the rope began to pull, tightening around my neck. Boon, however, reached out with both hands and grabbed a hold of the rope. With one yank, he sent Douglass flying back off of his saddle. Douglass landed flat on his tailbone, slamming the rest of the way down to the ground flat on his back. Boon stomped forward. Douglass managed to pull the trigger once, but I didn't see if it hit Boon or not. Boon reached out with one hand and grasped the hand Douglass held his gun in, squeezing so tightly the gun tore through Douglass's palm, blood running down his forearm.

Douglass let out a scream, but it was short-lived. Boon lowered a knee to his chest, holding Douglass firmly to the ground. Boon swung down with a fist the size of any man's head, and completely crushed Douglass's skull with only three blows. On the third blow, I could hear the bones crunch into even smaller pieces.

Boon stood up slowly, taking a moment to look down at the now faceless corpse of Douglass Flood. When he turned around, I wasn't afraid for a second that I'd be next. I knew that look in a man. Whoever these three men were to Boon, they weren't someone's he liked at all. The fury he just unleashed had been building up in him for days, years even. Why he never took the chance sooner was beyond my understanding.

The brute of a man walked toward me, unravelling the rope from my neck and in turn undoing it from the tree. He tossed it to the ground as though the rope were a snake he'd just slain, and then he held out a hand, meant for me to take it, so he could help me to my feet. And when I took it, he pulled up, probably with more strength than he needed. I coughed, wincing against the pains in my chest and my throat.

"I take it you've been meaning to do that for some time," I said. Boon remained silent, as I expected he would. "Well," I coughed harder, feeling the space in my throat return to normal. The rope that had been there had cut into my skin. I could feel the blood seep through. Not a terrible breaking of the skin, but there would be a mark left behind to remind me of this day, and to make all who looked upon me wonder if I'd been lucky enough to survive the squeeze of a noose. Boon retrieved my weapons from Douglass's body, as he'd holstered the revolvers, and as his horse fled, my rifle fell from the saddle, due to an ill-placement on his part. Boon handed me them one at a time, waiting for me to get situated before handing me each subsequent piece of weaponry.

I climbed onto Eleanor's saddle, almost falling back to the ground as the pain of the injuries recently inflicted began to truly set in.

"You gonna be alright, Boon," I asked, as if I really expected him to say anything back, "I don't reckon your plan was to head to where I'm goin' anyway. Part of me wonders how you got tangled up with that fool Douglass Flood in the first place," I started, seeing the immovable expression on Boon's face change without changing, as he looked back toward the body of the men he'd just killed. His eyes did not narrow, his lips did not purse, he didn't make a sound, not a murder nor a grunt. But in that reflective gaze of his, I saw everything I needed to know. "You take care of yourself, Boon." He looked back and we gave each other one last look.

Ahead, New Canterton still waited for me. I don't know how true Douglass's words had been regarding his orders, but there was still Cassandra's safety to consider. Her life, and the life of our daughter still inside of her. Boon and I rode off in opposite directions. Wherever it was he was headed towards, I hoped he found better luck than he had around these parts.

I was met at the massive front gate before the towering stone wall with a bit of scrutiny from the guards. All along the ramparts, they peered down, some of them wearing faces of confusion as if expecting my arrival to have come in a different sort of manner. Maybe they expected me to be accompanied by... the most recent departures. Maybe I wasn't supposed to come back at all. At once, this place I could have probably at one time or another gone as far as to have called my home, didn't feel like home anymore. There was a new air, an invisible fog, a texture none of the senses could physically, or emotionally touch.

The ground guard closest to me walked forward, and recognized who I was with a disheveled exasperation. I recognized him too, although I can't say with an honest heart that I knew him personally. He'd been here nearly every time on my return journeys from wherever Gunther Ostrander had sent me. He was of the younger sort, but not so young to make you think he couldn't handle himself when it mattered.

"Mr. Mahoney," he said, "it's been a while."

"Yea, that's what the last guy said," I replied to no one in particular.

"There's been talk that you wouldn't be coming back at all."

"People think I'm dead?"

"That has been suggested, yes. It's one of the more popular rumors, I'm afraid," he said.

"Well, I'm not dead. All I want to do is check in with the boss," I said. The guard nodded, motioning for the rampart soldiers to operate the mechanism which allowed for the iron gate to be opened or closed.

"Be careful, Mr. Mahoney," the guard said genuinely, keeping his voice low, "Mr. Ostrander has been busy planning something big, bigger than what he's been willing to tell us guards of the outer wall. Mr. Kenroy stopped in from Vermouth not long before you arrived. When I asked what the purpose of his stay was, all he mentioned was something about it being an urgent summons from Mr. Ostrander."

"Thanks for the heads up," I said to him. He nodded, tipping his helmet. "Ya know something, you've been a guard here for a good long time and I've been comin' and goin' a good long time. I don't think I ever got your name."

"It's Ash, sir," he said, "Ash Wilkins. And not to worry. I never considered the lack of knowledge an affront to our interaction."

I rode through the gate, patting Eleanor letting her know we were almost there. She trotted at an easy pace to the other side, onto the great stretch of plain leading up to Gunther's factory. Already I could hear the faint sounds of the.... slaves, working in the quarry to the north. Everything appeared the same as it always had, except for one thing.

Along the single path leading up to the factory, off to either side there had been assembled an innumerable count of rough-looking individuals, all having set up tents and stations for cooking meals, cleaning weapons, and half a dozen areas where their horses could feed and relax. The encampments must have reached numbers as high as the hundreds. All of the men watched as I rode by, as though they'd been given specific details as to "what this Rancid Mahoney man looks like, and if he should arrive, keep a close eye out, he's not to be taken unseriously". That was the vibe, but alongside that vibe came with it the subtext implying that anyone could expect a handsome reward for bringing my severed head to the one who demanded it. The gate closed heavily behind me, and I rode on through the encampments. Ahead, the black smoke stacks rose up higher and higher, their smoke billowing upward and merging in with the grey clouds forming overhead.

I was met at the entrance to the factory by another guard, only this one I know I'd never met before. He wore a metal helmet with a faceplate of some fancy design that hid most of his features, and when he approached, his stride was that of immovable intent. I pulled back on Eleanor's reigns gently and she came to a stop. It was then I noticed the sign that'd always hung up by the entrance. The sign reading: "OSTRANDER and BOOTHE, Co." Except today, it was gone.

"Mr. Ostrander is currently not available," the guard said with a thunderous voice.

"I find that to be a bit unbelievable, but should it be true, maybe you can send word to him that Rancid Mahoney has returned."

The guard hesitated, and again I got the feeling he'd been instructed to keep an extra sharp lookout for me.

"Wait here," he said, turning into the factory through the main entrance.

The guard returned not long after, had me hitch Eleanor, and instructed me to follow him. I tried tellin' the man I knew my way, that I even had my own room of occupancy in the building. But he insisted otherwise. "I'll be right back, girl," I said to her, giving her a reassuring pat on the neck. "Don't you worry about a thing."

I was escorted the entire way up through the many levels of the factory and finally to Gunther's office. The faceless guard opened the doors, letting me inside, and at once I was at more unease than I'd been since arriving.

The door closed behind me and a quietude took over much in the same way the noose at the end of a rope begins to tighten. On the sofa nearest to me sat a thick in the midriff, and rather pleased and at ease with himself, Mr. Kenroy. From one hand he sipped something bronze colored in a fancy looking translucent goblet while playing with the hairs of his mustache. He looked over to me with just the corners of his eyes, his mouth forming into that of an expectant grin. He knew I never liked him, but for some reason, my arrival pleased him.

Standing out on the balcony ledge, overlooking the great field littered with soldiers and their horses and tents and torchlights, stood Gunther Ostrander, his back facing the interior of the office. On his desk lay the sign that had once been outside. "OSTRANDER and BOOTHE, Co., New Canterton", it read. Beside it lay drawings on rough sheets of paper. Designs for a new sign, and a list of words written under a column titled "new name ideas for company".

"I see you've taken down the sign out front," I said, "finally decided to move on, have ya?"

"When the world ended, people eventually regained their footing, but that was a long time ago. We have come so far since then. We still have so much farther to go. Times are changing, Mr. Mahoney," Gunther said, "it's important, if not completely paramount, to a man's personal evolution if he is to move on with those times, if not on a human level, then the very least at the company level, and the rest will follow in suit. Boothe will always be remembered for the wise man that he was, and what he gave to the people of New Canterton. But he's been gone a long time. His memory alone, or his ideas, can't carry New Canterton safely or prosperously into the future."

"I see," I said to him, looking down at Kenroy, his gut overlapping his waistband, "I see you've started to change as well," I said to Kenroy, poking his belly with the toe of my boot, "looks like you've started on that diet you're always talkin' about." He scoffed, half chuckling over his drink.

Gunther cleared his throat, taking a long, meditative breath.

"Over the years, some of my men have brought

me back reading materials. You used to have that job yourself, in fact I believe that task was one of the first things I asked you to do," he began, looking briefly at the now framed copy of the "Westward Exploratory Projection Treaty" hanging up on the wall behind his desk. "I've been brushing up on history, or, what history was recorded. The history before the fall of civilization. The history before that history. It seems that history had been written by many different men and women, all with very different ideas as to how humanity itself unfolded. Some of those ideas conflict with one another on completely polaring levels of opinion. Sadly, I cannot argue with any of them because the ones who expressed those opinions are all long dead. Their graves have been dug somewhere in the world, and their bodies have long since decayed. I can't argue with them, Mahon," Gunther said, turning around, "I can't tell them that each of them in their own way got it wrong."

"Maybe that's a good thing," I replied, "I don't know much about all that history stuff, and I'm not here to talk about it. What I do know is that someone who works for you... *worked* for you, rather, just recently tried to kill me. So before you stretch out this talk about irrelevant history, just what in the *hell* was Douglass Flood and his gang doin' on the hunt for my head?!"

"So he did try and take it from you," Gunther found this amusing, as he always did get a giggle from these sorts of revelations, "Can I assume that being he wasn't the one to escort you here, you overcame him yourself."

"Rather one of his own men smashed his face into the dirt where it belonged long before you ever hired him," I said, "I came here alone. And it seems like," I looked down at Mr. Kenroy and motioned outside the window, passed the balcony where Gunther still stood, "it looks like you've got somethin' pretty big goin' on."

"Would you care for a drink," Gunther asked, holding out a bottle of brown, the stuff I generally took a lovin' towards, only now, funnily enough, I just wasn't in the mood for a drink. I shook my head and Gunther was taken aback. He stopped in his inward-walking stride, exchanging amused but surprised expressions with Mr. Kenroy. "That's a first, even for you. So, you're still alive, after your little adventure. Mr. Kenroy told me you were... shot by Rolandraz, but then taken away by our mutual friend, Til Drange, and a handful of Tuskatawa. It's been a while since then, so come, tell us, what were they like? And more importantly, lift up that shirt of yours. Word out in the world is that you were shot pretty good. A shot that would kill any man weak or strong. So, let's see it. Aw come on, no need to lie. We've long suspected the Tuskatawa to have been the caretakers for Blackheart Mountain, we just never had any real solid proof to substantiate our claims. Nor did we truthfully know where they made camp. I know it must have been a hell of an experience. Your delay can be forgiven, of course. You did have to heal, and that can take time for anyone. So, go on, lift up that shirt of yours. I want to see it. You want to see it too, don't you, Mr. Kenroy?"

"Oh yes, I certainly do," he said, leaning forward, placing his goblet on the table beside the couch arm. I did as I was told, showing them where I'd been shot. They saw the trailing black veins, their eyes widening. "It's so good to know the truth," Mr. Kenroy jeered.

"Indeed it is, Mr. Kenroy. Indeed it is," Gunther said, "to know that your most-trusted employee has slept rather soundly with the enemy."

"But surely, he'll never tell us where the Mountain is, that would be too foolish to assume," Mr. Kenroy laughed, chuckling along with Gunther. "As a matter of fact, I'd be willing the wager the literal foundations of Vermouth itself he probably had it in his head to lie to us, to say that he never found the Mountain at all, heh heh heh, ah-ha, but oh... I'm sorry, it's just amusing!"

"Well now, Mr. Kenroy, let's not assume the worst of my most-trusted employee! Maybe he'll surprise us! Maybe he'll tell all! But hold on, just wait a second Mahon, before you spill the whiskey. Um, oh guard, yes, go on out there and grab the other two, bring em here." Gunther said to the one guard standing in the room. The guard departed as ordered, and when he returned, two more guards were with him. They entered the room, shutting the door behind them, and then they took position behind me, all three of them taking a steady aim with their rifles for my head. Gunther shrugged, "What? Did you honestly think you'd have a warm reception should you return? You've been gone far too long to not have at least considered jumping sides. We go way back, you and I. But I know a traitor when I see one."

"Yea? I'm sure you look at one every day in the mirror," I muttered.

"I've never betrayed anyone."

"What about humanity? What about life itself? The very notion of what you're trying to achieve is a betrayal. You're right, boss," I said, "I've been gone a while, and it's given me a while to think things over. I think it may be time to turn in my cards, and think about early retirement."

Gunther and Kenroy both exchanged more laughs. Gunther eyed one of the guards behind me, and gave him the signal. I'd seen this look before, but I'd always been on the observing end, never receiving. The guard he signaled hit me in the back with the stock of his rifle. The two other guards confiscated my weaponry, and I was hit again in the back, where the attacking guard forced me down to my knees. Gunther stood in front of me, the look of glee and humor far removed from his face.

"So, Mahon," his voice now stern and ready, "where *is* the Mountain?"

Since the confrontation of fisticuffs with Rolandraz, my body hadn't been given the right amount of time to heal. There'd been that little fight, and then the battle when the Crimson Collars attempted to kill everyone in the village, the night they set the Mountain on fire. The encounter with Douglass Flood in turn reopened those old wounds. I was still hurtin' somethin' awful, and now, this asshole's guards were layin' into me with their rifle stocks. I was tired, real tired. And now, all I wanted to know was if Cassandra was alright.

"There ain't no Mountain anymore," I said, "so even if I told ya, it wouldn't do ya no good."

"Oh?"

"Rolandraz and his hounds destroyed it, blew it to hell. There ain't no gettin' back inside of it, and if there was, it would take a longer time than either of you have left on this earth."

"By your tone, it sounds as though you've already made up your mind," Gunther said, nodding, "it's a shame really. I thought you and I had something good goin'. A real trusting, almost imperfectionless working relationship, a real employee-employer rapport. A relationship on the brink of friendship. That's a rare thing to have these days. Which is why it saddens me to have to do this. You see, I don't care about any damage that was done to the Mountain. If what you say is true, my men can bring that mine back to life in no time. All we need is to know where it is. And you can tell us. That's all you have to do."

I was hit in the back again by one of the guards, this time harder than before.

"Hmm," Gunther took a closer look at me, "looks like you've had a tangle with a noose recently. Bruising around the neck there, looks painful. Well, I'll tell ya what. It's not my favorite thing to do, but it has worked in the past to get outta whomever what I require. Maybe a little time down in the quarry will shake you out of this so-called rebellion your nerves have convinced you to succumb to. My money is on you'll be begging within three days to tell us where the Mountain is. But just to be safe, we'll keep ya down there for two weeks. Fourteen days of hard, bloody-knuckled labor to get your thoughts and your allegiances back on the right track. It's okay, Mahon, really. Some people just need that re-adjustment. That sound good to you?"

"Sounds like shit," I muttered. Gunther laughed.

"I thought you might say that. Alright, take him away," he said to the guards, "oh and, all this hosting of our guests outside, I'm sure you saw them on your way in, it's really put a heavy hit on our supplies for horse care, not to mention accommodations for the men themselves. I'm afraid we won't have room in our stables for your dear Eleanor, nor will we have enough feed to keep her belly full. And to starve an animal like that is just too cruel a thing. So, guards? After you've dealt with Mr. Mahoney here, or before, whichever is more convenient, put a bullet in his horse. Might as well end her misery before it even begins."

"You son of a bitch," I growled, "you touch her and I'll rip your fucking head off! I'll cut you wide open and let the wolves on ya!"

I was dragged by two of the guards while the third led the way. On the way out of the factory, the two guards dragging me took a sharp right, pulling me toward the quarry. The third guard moved to where I'd hitched Eleanor. I fought back against the guards but together, they were stronger, their hands were like vices, dragging me away from her. I cried out, trying to warn her. I saw her turn towards me though, a look of confused concern in those black shiny marble eyes of hers.

The guard standing beside her checked the chamber of one of my revolvers, and closed it when he was satisfied. He pulled back the hammer, placing the barrel against the side of Eleanor's head. I tried. I tried. I cried out her name, trying so hard to free myself.

The guard pulled the trigger and her lifeless body collapsed to the ground.

"You there," the guard who pulled the trigger said, pointing to one of the men in the encampment out in the field, "grab a few extra pairs of hands and have this beast taken to the butcher. Should make a good meal for at least a portion of ya."

The soldier nodded excitedly, waving to some of the men he knew. They put her on a wagonbed and with two horses pulling it, they carried her off into the encampment. The blood from where her head hit the ground remained behind in the dirt, and the guard who shot her kicked granules overtop so that it was no longer visible.

My legs seemed to forget how to move, and so I fell limp under the hold of the men dragging me toward the quarry.

XII.
The SLAVE
and the PROSPECTOR

I was tossed onto the rocky, dirt-coated floor of a cell with an equally rough-surfaced concrete on all walls and when the cage door slammed shut, everything seemed to fall into a dark, final quietude.

The only light came from down the other end of the corridor, and from what I had gathered while being escorted, the area I was in was specifically meant to house the workers, or as the unfortunate truth turned out to be, the *slaves*. From here, I could hear the sound of rock on metal and metal on rock, and the occasional screams of those who either refused to work, or simply did not have the strength to work anymore. The sound alone brought with it a flood of long-ago and far-away memories, trailing away as quickly as they arrived, leaving behind the essence of their existence whenever and wherever they chose to present themselves.

It wasn't hard either for the nose to sift through the air thick with dust, finding that the only scent drifting in and out between the cage bars, was the unmistakable odor of human sweat, urine and feces. Each cell I caught of glimpse of while being dragged to my own had been packed with workers, three, four, some of them containing five, and possibly more out of sight in the back. There wasn't a single bed to be found, and mine was no different. Except my cell was strangely empty. I couldn't decide yet if that was good fortune or ignorant bad luck. My good and kind employer didn't want me dead; I still carried with me the knowledge and the whereabouts of Blackheart Mountain. And so he probably wouldn't want me to experience the worst of this place, just enough to get a taste, a passive threat letting me know what awaited me should I decide to indefinitely keep said information to myself.

When the iron, barred door slammed shut, the guards who dragged me here took one last look at me. They both grimaced. The one on the right spit at me, his big fat glob of saliva smacking against my cheek. "Traitor," he mutterd. The two of them gave out a little satisfied chortle before taking off back down the corridor to whatever post they'd been assigned to.

I let it out, sighing silently, telling myself how much of an idiot I was for even thinking returning to this place would have gone much differently. And now, with Eleanor dead, the only thing left for me here was Cassandra, and yet I hadn't seen her yet. I hadn't even caught the familiar scent of her form, the sweet smell she left behind her in her wake, because she was not like other people. She had, of course along with being the wife of Gunther P. Ostrander, been afforded certain luxuries that enabled her to most always be clean. Whenever I'd see her, whenever I knew she was walking from down the hall, I'd known she was near. But not this time. She could be as far away as Vermouth for all I knew.

"Hey," a scratchy, dehydrated voice clawed from the cell across the corridor, and when I looked in its direction, I saw two hairy-tanned arms hanging out of the bars of the cage like weary tentacles. Looking harder, I saw the outline of a face with a chiseled jawline and a mouth without too many teeth, not as many teeth as he probably had as a child, at least. "Hey you," he called out again.

"What do ya want?"
"What's goin' on up there?"

"What's goin' on up where?"

"Surface level! Come on, tell me somethin'! I've been down here for a million years! They haven't put the rockslingers in my hands for a while. I've been startin' to think they've forgotten about me, except every now and then the guards toss slopmuck into my cell, so they at least wanna keep me alive. But not long ago there was a lotta rumblin' up there."

"War," I muttered, taking a seat against the farthest wall away from the voice that I could.

"War? Really? Nah. Can't be."

"Could be, probably is," I said, "Fuckers shot my horse just to feed the soldiers."

"Those sons of bitches," the voice said, "monsters, really. All of em. I mean you'd have to be to be working for someone like Ostrander. They like to walk around wearing the faces of men, but we all know what they really are."

I sat quietly, not wanting to converse with anyone or anything, not about anything at all. I just wanted the courtesy of being able to gather my thoughts, calm my nerves, and figure out just what to do. Drange had found a way out of here, or had Sanuye been the one to rescue him? I couldn't remember the exact chain of events. But somehow one of them escaped. There had to be a way to replicate that. There had to be something that could done.

"You look like a rough guy," the voice across the corridor said, ignoring my silent wish to be left alone, "you'll probably do alright down here, for a while anyway. Better than most newcomers, anyway. At the very least it'll probably take a while to wear ya down to bare bones. Do you even know where ya are? They pull ya outta the wild like me?"

"It was my fault," I said, "I came back knowin' I

shouldn't have."

"Came back? So, you do know where ya are, then."

"I worked for him. Ostrander. I worked for him a long time."

"You worked for that asshole? And he threw ya down here? Must've done somethin' awful. But honestly you ain't the first of his former employees he's thrown down here. Honestly further, not may of em are still alive."

"I'm sure you and I will have more opportunities to talk and get to know each other, bein' we're neighbors and all, but... I just lost my horse. If ya don't mind I'd like to just... be left alone."

"Sure, understandable," he said, "not a problem. I get it. I've lost people too. They say time is best cure for pain, but time ain't nothin' without silence. Name's Hoxford, by the way. Maurice Hoxford." He tapped the cage of his cell with his knuckles, signifying he was gonna be quiet, and then he disappeared into the darkness behind him.

I leaned against the far rock wall, letting the back of my head touch the roughness, with thoughts of Eleanor being shot pressing down on my chest like a vice.

At dawn, we were brought out of our cells. I wasn't given time to immediately figure out the system, but it seemed like whoever was working in the quarry, the group who'd been working before them were then sent to occupy the cells; an exchange. My neighbor Maurice Hoxford walked behind me, whispering to himself how strange it was to be brought back out into the daylight. As we marched on down the corridor along with the other workers, those coming back from the quarry marched back down the corridor, filling up the cells we'd just been held in. Someone returning from the quarry screamed in anger about the state of his cell, crying in a rage that "this shit really needs to stop" and "this isn't how I left it". I didn't know what he meant by that specifically, but the cell he'd returned to did emit a strong odor of vomit and shit. Then again, that could be said about every cell.

We were pushed and shoved by the guards, some of them whipping us with long curls of leather that cracked like lightning. We climbed up a mostly flat incline of rock, dirt, pebbles and mud, while the guards along the sides of the ramp had the comfort of ascending or descending via steps carved into the stone. Every time someone stumbled or slipped on the unreliable surface, it gave them another excuse to lash out with a whip.

The sun pierced through a veil of bumpy-looking snow clouds, and from the sky a thin hail of icy pebbles fell. The air was cold, as it should be in winter, but none of us were allowed the proper clothing, and so as soon as we climbed out into the open air, we all began the slow process of freezing to death. We followed a white, granular path cold to the touch even to our boot-covered feet. Ahead, the dust bowl opened like a mouth, the widest circle ever carved into the earth, like a crater left behind after a celestial impact. The quarry must have dug down a quarter mile, maybe deeper. And the line of workers emerging from the depths was like an endless parade of the slowly dying and almost dead. Their faces were gaunt, the skin of their cheeks sucked in so tight you could count their teeth. Their eyes might pop out from their skulls if the wind blew a certain way. Their legs wobbled and their arms hung low as though they'd been stretched by some terrible mechanical device. As they walked past, whether by choice or learned automation, they refrained from acknowledging us going to work. They walked passed, quietly breathing breaths of relief that their shift had ended, their brows cursed with an accepted sadness that it would not be their last to serve.

"I heard that this whole place started because Ostrander had this obsession for this particular mineral. He caught wind of a vein being somewhere down here in the quarry. But when he couldn't find any, he ordered the start of the mine, to dig deeper into the earth. That's where these people are comin' from, and that's where we're goin'. Half of these men and women will die in their sleep today," Hoxford said, "and half of the dead will be sent to the grinders, where their bodies will be reduced to the slop they serve to us on silver platters. The other half will be burned and their bones converted into mortar."

"You mean to tell me," I started to reply, continuing to look ahead, "that spoonful of shit they feed us, is the old workers. I'm goin' to be eatin' ground up human meat?"

"The meat, the guts, the bones," Hoxford muttered, laughing, "how do ya think we all maintain our sanity? It's actually not so bad, they throw in some spices that help our digestive system do the work so we don't die from toxicity. At least that's what I've heard."

"You've got to be bullshittin' me," I insisted.

"What? Didja think they fed us fall-off-the-bone ribs down here? The best accommodations are saved for the folk who either turn their heads to this place or the people who've just flat out convinced themselves we don't exist. That cute little town up there thrives on its own ignorance. Then again, who can blame em? A little ignorance is a small price to pay for security, I suppose.

Hell, I'd probably be one of em if I could."

"Tell ya the truth I don't know what I used to think," I said, "you have to understand, Ostrander never talked about the truth of this place."

"Of course not," Hoxford said, "it's how he keeps his employees happy. There aren't too many good-hearted folk out in the world, but if even just one of 'em caught wind of this place... hell, there'd be situations to arise."

It took us an hour to reach the bottom of the quarry, marching down the decline that wound all the way around the outer wall, scaling switchbacks and sometimes taking metal walkways across collapsed pathways. The air grew heavier, but thinner, and colder as we made the descent. The lower we walked, the higher the sunny clouds above climbed away. It got to be so dim down below the earth's surface that tiny lamps lining the walls gave us a golden light to follow. Until at last we came to a large opening in the wall, where we were given pick axes and helmets with flashlights soldered onto them. The guards did not hand us the pick axes though, they tossed them to the ground. One of the taller, more muscular beasts belched out orders close to the entrance, giving a few of us kicks and shoves and slaps to get us moving faster.

"And for all of you newcomers," he grabbed me by the collar, pulling me in close so that our eyeballs almost kissed, "you dig, and you dig until we say stop. And don't even think about getting' cute with them pick axes. Get cute, and you get the rack."

He was addressing everyone, but he seemed to be talking mostly with me. So, I asked him: "Oh yea? What's the rack?"

"What's the rack, he asks," the guard said. He let go of me, and proceeded to grab a random worker by the back of his neck. He picked out a scrawny man, impossible to tell his age by how worn out every inch of his skin appeared. The guard dragged him and threw him onto a wooden table, strapping his arms and his legs down. The worker didn't protest though, he didn't scream or plea, or beg to be let go. He just lay there, quietly, and only let out a systematic gasp that I'm sure anyone would let out, when the wooden table he was strapped to folded in half backwards, snapping his spine in two. The table returned to its original shape and the dead worker was unstrapped and tossed onto a pile of other dead workers I could only assume had accumulated from the last shift. "That's the rack," the guard bellowed, "and yes, you can have it if you'd like. You don't even need to get cute with a pick axe. If you want it, all you need to do is ask. Mr. Ostrander doesn't want anyone working down here who doesn't want to be here."

"Fancy flavor of psychological torment," I said, "makes sense, knowin' how the mind of the guy really works." The guard pointed to the mine entrance, and I picked up my pick axe from the ground. The handle was a nice, heavy make, but the wood had been stained many times over with several different person's blood. The oldest stains had darkened to a brown hue, whereas the newer splotches still gave off a bit of sleek crimson, feeling sticky at their centers. Hoxford held his own, showing me that his too had its own history to tell. As we stepped into the darkness and the light of the world disappeared from view, he patted me on the back.

"Relax," he said, "this place really ain't so bad. Well," he chuckled, "that's a damn lie. Smells like shit up top, smells like shit down here. Up top it's the voluntary shit, ya know when ya squat down and let it all out. But down here," he shook his head, lookin' around as if checking out how the place had changed since the last time, "it's the involuntary kind, the kinda shit that falls outta your asshole when you die. But truthfully, there's only a few things that can kill ya down here. We haven't had a collapse in a few years, so the worst ya have to worry about really is the dust in your lungs, and maybe if one of the other workers gets a little crazy, and snaps. You don't wanna be in the way of them when they snap."

"And why haven't you snapped yet?"

"Because at a very early age, I learned to find humor in just about everything life has to offer, no matter how horrible a situation may seem, believe it or not. Or maybe, I was just born crazy, and all this is really nothing at all for me," he smiled.

The faces of everyone digging reminded me of skeletons, minus the grin. Their gaze, if they could see at all, shot out straight ahead. Not many seemed to give a sign of a functioning brain other than the motor skills they'd been restricted to operating. It seemed this was all they'd done, their whole life. It was just another day in the dark for them. Digging into the rock for, who knew what anymore. Gunther had sometimes said they mined for coal down here. But I got the feeling that was all bullshit. As Maurice Hoxford had mentioned, the rumor had been Ostrander caught wind of a certain mineral, and I knew what that meant, maybe I was the only one who knew what that meant. Maybe he really did think there'd be Blackvein to be found down here. He must know by now that the only source was Blackheart Mountain... so why did he keep the workers digging?

Small wagon stations were set up in the mine, each one being piled heavy with rocks and boulders and pulled out by two horses each. I followed Hoxford, because he seemed like the right person to know in a place like this. He showed me where to dig and then took a spot a dozen or so yards away. He showed me how not to angle the pick axe, and if I saw what he called a "cavity" open up, to stop swinging right away. Check it, and if all possible, take out the rocks above the opening to "even out the playing field". According to him, the last person to cause a collapse did just the opposite of that. He saw a cavity open up, and kept right on diggin' down until the whole world started shakin'. The mine claimed eighty-some lives that day, but Hoxford, and many of the other workers saw it was a good thing. They saw it as eighty-some workers gaining their freedom, more specifically: eighty-some workers giving their lives so the rest could sleep with full bellies.

There were no breaks, but the guards didn't seem too terribly concerned if some of us stopped for a moment to catch out breaths. In fact, I couldn't see any guards at all. It was almost as though they just threw us down here, and while given a task to accomplish, they really didn't care what we did as long as the wagons kept coming out with full carts. Hoxford took as many breaks as he could, frequently strolling over just to shoot the shit. He told me that a little further in the mine, before the last collapse, there'd been a small corner where workers went to fuck if they felt the urge. He said the guards never did go down that way, and so the only challenge was finding someone who wanted what you wanted. But sometimes you were taken anyway, whoever took ya took what they wanted from ya. Hoxford said: "once someone down here wants somethin', and that somethin' happens to be between your legs, you can bet the rest of your years they'll get it from ya."

"You're not tryin' to hint at me somethin', are ya?"

"What? No, I'm not like that!"

"Cause if ya are, I put this pickaxe through the side of your head."

"No, no, you don't need to worry about me. I'm just lettin' ya know. This place is funny like that. Nooks and crannies and all."

During that first day down in the mine, I'd noticed an older man just sittin' away on his lonesome. He never once picked up a tool, nor made any inclination to engage anyone in conversation. From his face grew a grey beard down to his chest, and he seemed to be content right where he was. He'd been down here when Hoxford and myself arrived, so I presumed he'd been a part of the last crew, only he never came back up with them. When I asked Hoxford about him, he just shrugged disinterestedly.

"That guy? That's just Two Seas. He doesn't do shit down here and the guards really don't care. Sometimes he'll spend days sittin' right there without ever goin' back up to the surface. He's been here since the beginning I think, at least that's what some of the older workers say. He's just an old guy, probably close to snappin', if he hasn't already to be honest. I mean maybe that's what *snapped* really looks like. Dead in the face, maybe the mind. Just sittin' in silence all the time. So, while I'd say not to worry about him, I don't think it'd particularly hurt to just keep him in our sights. Ya never know down here, Mahon, ya never know. People are funny out there in the world, but down here, everyone's their own comedian."

Two Seas had been staring at me, and it was when I first made eye contact with him that I started to make the connection. The name "Two Seas" sounded oddly familiar, like something that belonged in a dream and only in a dream because you knew it couldn't possibly be real. I asked Hoxford if Two Seas was just a nickname for something else. Hoxford shrugged, not sure, telling me he'd only ever known him as Two Seas, but that was only because anyone who ever talked about him referred to him as such, and not because the man had ever introduced himself with the name.

That night, I awoke to the sound of someone clearing their throat. I opened my eyes and saw that a man was sitting on the other side of the bars. He held a revolver in each hand, his elbows resting on the top of his thighs. I didn't have to wipe away the sleep sands from the corners of my eyes to see that it was Ostrander, sitting in a metal chair holding both of my revolvers.

"Are you hidin' a bottle of the good stuff," I grunted, "or is that whiskey I smell on your breath?"

He smiled.

"Do you remember when I gave these to you?"

"I remember you got a little sentimental."

"I had the first twelve rounds painted red, hoping you'd kill twelve members of those Crimson Collar sons of bitches. I suppose it's a good thing I never went ahead and got the damn things engraved. Maybe someday I can give them to someone who'll appreciate 'em. Maybe *then* I'll have them engraved."

"I'm surprised you can remember that far back."

"I said to you: 'these aren't typical pistols, Rancid. They're special. You might say they're a little like brothers, and if they're ever separated, it could spell certain... doom.' That was the story, anyway. I know you don't believe in that sort of thing. Regardless, there was sentiment behind my giving them to you. And now, here we are." He looked over the revolvers, a drunken sadness just barely visible on his face from behind the dark shadow of the corridor. "What do you have to say about that?"

"I ain't got nothin' to say to you."

Gunther nodded, "You've killed a lot of people with these guns, Rancid. You three have had a hell of a ride together."

"That your way of lettin' me know I'll never get outta here?"

"I haven't decided," he got up, tucking the revolvers away under his belt, "but I'd be lyin' if I said I wouldn't be disappointed to know that the grand story of Rancid Mahoney reached it's conclusion in a place like this. You don't strike me as the anti-climactic sort." And then he left. I listened to his steps fade into the distance, and wondered why he came down here at all.

A week went by and it felt like a month.

Two weeks went by after that and it started to feel like I'd been born in the mine, living here all along; the memories and the history of my life once existing before being dragged here was now all but-realized as having actually happened. Everything just started to feel distant, and a part of me which grew bigger every day, was starting to really not care.

In some ways I'd been born with shackles and in others I'd been born just for those shackles to find their way onto me. I ate the food, the slop, the ground up remains of who came before. The slop had a flavor, oddly enough, that wasn't altogether unpleasant. It was the texture that forcibly brought up the contents of my stomach. It was gritty, like water-soaked sand. Every now and then you could bite down and your teeth would make something crunch or snap. It could've been a small bone that hadn't been ground up all the way, or a piece of cartilage still rubbery and solid. The first few mouthfuls I couldn't help but spit out, I couldn't take it. The thought of what I was eating and where it came from. One day, some poor soul down here could be taking a spoonful of this into his own mouth, and in that spoonful would be the blended up remains of my own body. Eventually, he'd shit it all out, and I'd be forever stuck on the rock floor of his cell, a permanent fixture of excrement which would one day, if undisturbed, petrify under the weight of time. What a future to look forward to.

At first, I'd thought Hoxford's warnings against bein' dragged off deeper into the mine by sex-starved individuals was just a way of pullin' my legs, until I saw it happen. The slaves had at one time or another forgotten that they were slaves and instead took from each other in perhaps the only worse way than what Ostrander had taken from them. Every day someone was dragged away by a gang of three or four or more. Their victim's screams echoed through every tunnel of the mine so horribly, I thought they might bring down the ceiling on us all. No one ever approached me. I'm not sure if they were just biding their time or I just wasn't their type. I thought maybe I'd wake up one day in my cell and it'd be my day, but that day never came.

On the twenty-fifth day, I suddenly realized that Ostrander had said I'd been sentenced for only two weeks down here. Twenty-five days was much longer than two weeks. In fact, it was more than three. Two Seas unexpectedly approached me, taking me out of my contemplative trance. I asked him if he'd come to fuck me, half-joking, half-serious. In the darkness of the mine he looked like a ghost who'd forgotten how to contort his face into responsive expressions. He stood there and looked over me, as I'd taken to sittin' my ass down on a pile of broken up rock. Hoxford stood alert and entirely invested in the situation, staring at us from the other side of the chamber.

"Rancid Mahoney?" He asked.

"Uh," I stammered, not being able to figure out just how in the hell he knew my name, "sure."

"Come with me," Two Seas said.

Normally, any stranger who comes into my breathing space and starts barking commands and demands, I either ignore, laugh at, or shoot. For some reason, I wasn't in the mood to ignore him, or laugh at. And the last gun I'd really gotten a good look at had been used to kill Eleanor. I stood up and he started walking towards the back of the mine... where the slaves were "taken".

"I gotta stop ya right there, old man," I said, "and it's not that you ain't my type, I'm just not what you would say to be... emotionally available."

He kept on walking, and oddly, I continued following him. We wound around a corner and the corridor began sloping upwards. Ahead, the darkness began to thin. He stopped at what I thought might be halfway up the sloped pathway, and suddenly he vanished to the left, squeezing himself into a gap in the rock wall.

"Come on," he said. I looked back down the pathway. Hoxford stood at the bottom of the slope, a nervous, but curious look under his brow. I looked back where Two Seas had gone through the rock wall, took a second more to consider my options, and went ahead anyway. I was barely able to scrape through, the jagged surface of either side of the fissure scraped my back and my front, sometimes catching on my beltloops. I slid and shimmied for a good while, it seemed. But once on the other side, I stumbled out into a high-ceilinged chamber where several other pathways and tunnels branched off into more darkness. Two Seas stood in the center, with a waiting gauntness about him.

"What are we doin', old man?"

"Someone wants to talk to you," he said.

From one of the tunnels off to the right, a hooded and cloaked figure walked in. It didn't take me any more time than it does to skin a swamp gnat to recognize who she was.

"Cass," I thought I heard myself say, but I don't exactly remember saying anything during those few moments. She removed her hood and at the same time we embraced each other. We kissed and I looked down to her belly. She nodded, letting me know the baby was still okay. "What are ya doin' down here? And also," I looked to Two Seas and looked back to Cassandra, "what's the story with *you* two?"

"That would take a while, I imagine," he said.

"We," Cassandra began, "we knew each other before he was thrown in here. I didn't know what Gunther had actually been trying to hide. I thought I saw Christopher one day during a shift crew transfer. Looking into it a little further, I found that I was right. And, besides Gunther, and now you Mahon, we're the only ones who know he's still alive."

It all clicked.

"So you *are* the Two Seas I know of," I said, turning my head towards him. "Gunther has spoken of you in the past. Of course, in his stories you're dead."

"My real name is Christopher Carl Boothe," he said.

"Yea," I said.

"I heard you'd come back," Cassandra changed the subject, I felt the tips of her fingers clawing at my sides desperately, "but before I had the chance to see you, you were thrown here, into this hole. I heard what they did to Eleanor," she said sadly, "Oh Mahon, I'm sorry." I let the conversation about Eleanor end there.

"Cass," I started, "I found the Mountain."

"What?"

"I found the Mountain," I said. "I found the Mountain and its people. It took a little while but I've come to the realization that my employment with Gunther needs to end. Being put in this place, though, I suppose that goes without sayin'. Except there's still you. And the baby. And the war that's coming."

"War?"

"I knew he wasn't... a *good* man, by any means," I said, talking about Gunther, "and maybe I was wrong to have turned face to what I knew was probably true. While... doin' all these things for him, I've had the chance to see more of the world, Cass. And with that I was able to see first-hand just how far the reach of his twisted hands go. But I am not a man of war. I can't just... take a side and kill in the name of some idea that may or may not be what's right for the world. That's too much I'm willing to give up. So, I came back to get you out. But... as you can see, I didn't exactly succeed in that endeavor."

"Well, we can go, if you want," she said slowly, "I mean, that's what I came to do. Or to suggest. There's a way out of here. We can leave, Mahon."

"No, we can't, Cass. Not anymore. Not we. I don't know why I ever thought it could work. You see, if I leave with you now," and it took me a moment, because I suddenly realized the truth of what I was about to say, and how important it was, no matter how much I didn't want it to be true, "you aren't safe with me. If... Gunther ever found out, which I promise you he would, that I escaped and you were with me... I couldn't let that be the life we pass down to our child, even if we somehow survive long enough to witness her birth. We wouldn't get very far even if it was just the two of us."

"I'm not safe with you, and I'm not safe without you," she said, "what exactly are we supposed to do then? You say war is coming here. So, what exactly is it we are supposed to do?"

"There's nothing really to do. We're stuck where our paths lead us. It's just how the world is, sometimes, Cass. It's the hardest truth that's out there," I tried to sound as honest as I could, because it was true. The world doesn't always work out for the best of things, and there isn't always a way out. The world is a vice, I've found, and whoever is turnin' that vice doesn't answer to anyone.

"So the man upstairs throws you in the trash can and you give up," she said, "that... that doesn't sound like the Mahon I know."

"And livin' with the knowledge that her husband is a psychopathic slave driver without ever sayin' a word doesn't sound like the Cassandra I know."

"And what was I supposed to do once I found out," she yelled back, "you were always gone on the road. But even if you were here, what could the two of us have done? Have you seen the size of this place, Mahon? All the people he has under his belt? The man is a war-lord, Mahon. It was better when I didn't know, and I kept it that way by not letting him know that I knew," she looked down at her belly, placing both hands over it and gently caressing the surface with her thumbs. "But now, all that clearly doesn't matter, seeing you the way you are now. The *new* Rancid Mahoney."

"The world doesn't ever change, Cass, but eventually people do," I muttered.

"And what am I supposed to tell our little one, that her father was a coward? That he bellied up and gave in just when everything started to feel hard? What am I supposed to say?"

"You aren't supposed to say anything about it! You don't seem to get it, or maybe you do, but you're just too stupid to accept it. Gunther can never, ever, EVER know about you and me. And by extension, our child can never, ever, EVER know who their real father is," I said, "Gunther may be a real bastard, and war is comin' this way... but you know what? It's still safer here than it is out there. You're safer behind these walls, because he does have enough people working for him to protect this place. He's got an army and a half. Our child is forever safer behind these walls than any given day out there in the wastes."

"I don't believe you," she said, "I really... what happened to you? You're not gonna fight for us? For our child? There's a way out of this, now, Mahon, and it's not gonna be easy! But it's still a way! A possibility! Maybe I did fuck up by keepin' this place to myself from you, and I'm sorry about that. But is that really the basis for what you want to dwell your emotions on when it comes to you and me... our child?"

"My mind is made up."

"And your word is law," she spat, "and who does that benefit, besides yourself?"

Cassandra returned the hood over her head.

"Cass," I called to her, and just before she would have vanished down the tunnel she'd come in through, she stopped and half-turned her head towards me, "this right here is your chance to escape," she pointed down the tunnel, "it's important, *important*, for our child."

"Is it more important for a child to live in a world without knowing her real father," she asked, "for her to exist in one in which she's taught the lessons held dear by someone like Gunther Ostrander?"

"You married him."

"I wasn't the only one fooled by him," she said, "you could've killed him years ago when you found out who he really was."

"Maybe we both could've," I said.

She nodded slowly, mulling it over in her head. And then she was gone. Her footsteps echoing through the tunnel faded and I was once again without her. Two Seas... Christopher Carl Boothe, walked to my side.

"She's right you know," he said, "she wasn't the only one. Gunther P. Ostrander is a master of the spoken word, it's how he got to where he is. He and I were friends for a long time, until I realized what sort of man he truly was."

"I had to do what I did," I said, "here, I mean."

"I know. I agree with your decision. If you left with her now, it would have been for her, and for *you*. That would have been okay if it weren't for-"

"-yea."

"Perhaps the reason why I don't leave this place is similar, even though clearly I know of a way out," he said, letting out a gentle chuckle, "I could leave right now, take my chances against the world. I certainly don't have the strength to last all that long, but at least I'd be rewarded with the knowledge that I didn't let Gunther P. Ostrander be the reason why I stop breathing. Maybe that little piece of knowledge would be worth it."

"So why don't you leave?"

Two Seas looked on down the tunnel Cassandra departed through. He started long and hard, contemplating the very notion of leaving, probably for the hundredth time.

"I too am aware that... war is coming. It's been coming to this place since before we slaves began digging deep into the mine. Ostrander may not have always been the man he is now, but he always had a strangely delicate way of making enemies, unintentionally or otherwise. It was like he knew right from the beginning how a relationship with someone would turn out, so he'd plan ahead for that decisive confrontation. And when it comes to running a business, offering a place of safety to people, and families, it's not uncommon to cross paths with those who disagree with your way of life, even just because they can... because as you know, there is no true law of the land anymore. I knew Ostrander when he was a man of truth and goodness. Time changes a man, and for that he does have my sympathy. Eventually, our ideas as to what this... New Canterton was supposed to be, began to twist away from one another, until one day we realized our concepts were not at all the same. When he sent me here, he said to me that, news of my death would go over better than if the people knew about... the truth. To strengthen the people's faith in his leadership, Gunther had me declared dead, and he took advantage of their mourning. For a while, he even had a memorial built for me. I don't imagine that's around anymore, judging from the confused look in your face. He wants to be known as the man who rebuilt humanity, who brought civilization back to its feet. We both did, only he didn't care who was killed or forgotten about in the process. And then the day finally came when we confronted what we both were afraid of.

"I know that judgment is coming for him, something that he deserves for all the pain he's caused others, injustices, and civil agonies while maintaining this... New Canterton, and if I leave, I'll never see that. I'll never be able to look in his eyes and let him know that what has befallen him, was his doing right from the start. So, I stay. Because I too know the day is coming, and I want to be here for it."

"They aren't coming to kill him," I said.

"That's foolish. Although, ff they don't kill him, the world eventually will," Boothe said, "either way, he'll die. But death is not true judgment, Mr. Mahoney. Death is simply the end. Nothing comes after death, nothing more to suffer. And for someone like Gunther P. Ostrander, judgment and suffering must come in another form. The end for him, must not come with death. He must live as long as he is able, so that true judgment can take root."

XIII.
SIX BULLETS OWED, with INTEREST

"And for someone like Gunther P. Ostrander, judgment and suffering must come in another form," I said the words to myself over and over as I lay in my cell. I knew what the Tuskatawa Law was. I knew what they had planned for someone like Gunther P. Ostrander.

At the moment, though, I was more concerned with Cassandra. It'd been two days since we spoke in that cave. Almost a month down here in the dark. My bones had begun to thin, and I could feel it. I mined when I could simply to keep my muscles strong, but even those muscles were beginning to weaken. With a reliable food supply, my muscles might have been okay, but slurping down the ground-up, blended remains of dead slaves, once the initial vomiting phase had leveled out, had only made me hungrier and hungrier each day for a bullet. Hoxford wanted to know what'd been exchanged but I hadn't felt like explaining it. I gave him the coldest of shoulders and maybe that could be considered rude, and rightfully so, but really, the guy just annoyed me. I didn't care what he had to think about the situation.

He looked over at me from time to time, from the bars of his cell.

"I gotta say," he finally said, "you not tellin' me what was said back there is startin' to make me wonder."

"Just shut up and let me get some sleep. Our shift is comin' up and if I have to kill ya, I'd prefer to have rested a little beforehand."

Before Hoxford had a chance to respond, there came a sound from the entrance like a crash, a groan, and then the unmistakable sound of a body slumping to the ground. Three times. Three bodies. And in from the dark of the entranceway crept Drange, the blade in his hand still dripping with blood from the guards he'd just killed.

"Well," I said, "ain't this a surprise."

"Finally," he said, gasping for air. "Been lookin' all around the grounds all night for ya. I guess you really do find what you're lookin' for the last place ya look."

"What the hell do ya want, man," I muttered, adjusting the way I was laying on my cot. "If you came with real food, I gotta tell ya, I probably shouldn't eat it now. I'd been eatin' dead people for weeks and to reintroduce real food into my system might make me seven different kinds of shitty sick."

"I'm here to get ya out, asshole," Drange said, "you're probably the only person in the whole damn New Canterton I care to say that to."

"Why now? It's been a goddamn month!"

"War takes time to plan, smartypants. The Tuskatawa, Quan Zao and his Black Boars," Drange said hurriedly through the cell bars, "they've amassed just outside the perimeter wall. Chief Tenskatawa and Quan Zao are settin' to attack in the morning. Tomorrow morning, Mahon. And you better believe right there in your rot, that we have enough to take this place."

"We, huh," I laughed, turning over, "so you're going to charge in here on the front lines with your fellow tribesmen. Like saviors."

"I tried to get them to delay-"

"-why?"

"Because you're a damn good fighter, Mahon. It'd be a waste to let you die in here."

"You really think that even if I got outta here I'd

do it just to jump into the deep end of your war? How in the hell does that make any bit of sense, Drange? Your Chief even said it himself, I'm not one of ya. Your fancy *laws* and all that, just dancin' and two-steppin' around the world like it has any chance of settin' things right! Whether I die in here or I die out there, it doesn't matter, but I tell ya this: I ain't dyin' lookin' down the barrel of a hundred thousand guns while the philosophy of a delusional maniac is shoved into my back pocket. War hasn't killed me since I was a boy, and it sure as hell ain't gonna kill me now! You wasted your damn time comin' in here, Drange. So, go on, get out. You go on and have your war."

Drange hesitated.

"They're going to kill everyone, Mahon. That was the deal that was made. Quan Zao wouldn't shake hands with Tenskatawa unless the idea was to level the place, so that they could rebuild it entirely from the ground up. Which is... odd. I've known the chief a long time and he hasn't seemed himself since Zao arrived. I'm actually starting to worry about him a little, Mahon. Zao has always had an extremeness to him I never thought the Chief would go along with."

"People change," I said, not really caring too much about what he said, "it happens to everyone eventually."

"Yea, well, anyway... I seem to remember you sayin' something about there bein' someone here you care about. You never did give me the full story. You really think that nothin's gonna happen to her? Or you? For all the Chiefs know, you've been here fraternizing with the enemy, they won't believe me if I tell them otherwise, not unless you come back with me."

"You're askin' the impossible of me," I said, "leave me be. Besides, this cell ain't so bad. I've sorta gotten to likin' how it secluded it is. And yea, maybe it keeps me locked up, but it also keeps people like you *out*."

"I'm sorry you feel that way," Drange said, stepping back from the cell. "you know I, uh, back when I was supposed to kill you... and I didn't."

"You was only shootin' the shit just to shoot the shit. You woulda tried to kill me one way or another even if that Mancino asshole hadn't intervened. And you woulda failed because I woulda killed you first, I promise you that much."

Drange took a deep breath, and he removed a revolver from a holster, checking the chamber.

"I believe I owe ya six bullets," he said, sliding the gun in though the bars and placing it on the concrete floor, "in that chamber you'll find said six bullets. I threw in the whole gun for interest. I know it ain't exactly one of your own revolvers, but the trigger works just fine."

That got Hoxford's attention pretty quickly.

"And what is six bullets supposed to be good for against an entire army," I asked.

"Six bullets means six less men to kill, no matter which way you look at it," he said. "That is, if you're a good enough shot, or fast enough, whichever one gives you the upper hand," Drange turned back towards the entranceway and sighed, "Ya know this, this battle that's comin' tomorrow, it may break us all, and it may just be a quick draw. But it's going to put into motion something that'll be good for everyone in the end. And here you are, not wantin' to fight for that."

"That's the trouble, see," I said, laughing, "every side of every war thinks with the same mindset, only neither side seems to know it. And that's why even if you win the war, you really haven't."

Drange left.

I heard the sound of the door closing and the cell corridor was quite again, except for the sound of Hoxford's new, heavy breathing. I didn't even have to look toward him to know what he was staring at.

"Makes me wonder though," Hoxford chimed in as I picked up the gun, "isn't it better to be on the winning side, no matter what?" I opened the chamber to the revolver and counted all six bullets. At least Drange was a man who paid his debts.

Hoxford was asleep when Ostrander's men came to retrieve me. It was dark outside, but there had begun to appear the tiny sliver of intrusive light that woke up the east before the rest of the world. Drange had said they'd come at dawn. And dawn on its way.

They marched me along the path leading up to Ostrander's factory, the same way I'd been drug to the cells almost a month ago. There were hundreds of men sleeping in their tents all about the encampment. Hundreds more had arrived since my return, and so now where I stood it was impossible to even guess just how many men the old boss had at his disposal. Ostrander was of course readying himself. He was smart, one of the smartest men I knew. It was how he'd managed to stay alive as long as he had.

I walked through the many corridors and through the chambers of the factory until we reached the top-most floors where the man's office was situated. I was tired. I hadn't actually slept in a couple of days, and my stomach still hurt from that ground-up slop they passed off as food. One of the guards opened the dark double doors to Ostrander's office, and in we walked. The doors shut behind us and the guards remained.

Ostrander was, of course, surveying the land from his favorite spot out on the balcony, the sky ahead of him just beginning to light up. He turned around and we looked at each other. He appeared as the same man I knew and loathed, and worked for. He had no challenging demeanor to his stance, and stood strong and tall. What he saw in me this very moment, was a near-broken man beaten by the mine, but really, it hadn't been the mine that caused me the most pain. Maybe it was the steadily-increasing lull and vibe of an unsatisfactory death. Death had never scared me, I learned to shy away from that fear at a very early age. And I never much cared how or by whom I was to meet that death. But this morning, if I was meant to die, I wouldn't feel as though I'd led a satisfactory life. And I think Cassandra had something to do with that, in some way I wasn't quite too sure of yet.

"So two weeks really means a month, I guess," I muttered.

"I know I gave you a shorter sentence," Ostrander began, "but I figured you needed the extra time. It can take a while for a man to heal after he's witnessed first-hand his horse being shot."

"Startin' this out by openin' up old wounds is a surefire way to get yourself shot in the mouth, chief," I said.

"Speaking of chiefs," he smiled, walking into the office, "I'm well-aware of your friend's inclinations to attack. Their amassing has already been spotted, so rest assured, Mr. Mahoney, your *chief* is under close watch."

Interestingly enough, by the way he only mentioned one chief, it didn't seem as though he knew about Quan Zao and the Black Boars. I couldn't be sure of anything, really. I didn't know who or what to believe. I'd been digging in darkness for a month. Anything could be goin' on right now.

"Have you spent enough time in the darkness of the mine, Mr. Mahoney," Gunther asked, "have you thought over what we talked about before, your original task, and all of that? I have to say, when it comes to mountains, I have the patience of one. But I'm really starting to worry you may not actually tell me. I'm starting to think it doesn't matter what I do. You never seemed to me like a man who breaks easily, if at all. Even now, you still show a bit of strength left in ya."

"Then you'd be right about that," I said, "and I'm gonna tell ya now, Gunther. I'm gonna level with ya because there ain't no stoppin' what's comin' anymore. I did find the Mountain. I found it and the people there saved my life. The mineral is real and it really, really works. But it doesn't matter now because, as I've said before, their own mine was completely destroyed. Not even YOU could bring it back."

I felt the weight of the gun Drange had left me tucked under my belt in the small of my back. Was this his intention? Was he an advocate for Tuskatawa Law while simultaneously understanding the opposite matter of such nature? I noticed on Gunther's desk a new sign had been laid reading "O.R.E. OSTRANDER REFORMATION EXCAVATION".

"I take it that right there is the next step in completely removing old Boothe from anything historically significant about this place. New Canterton, and all."

Gunther's face told the whole story all on its own. He didn't even need to ask if I'd run into his old pal in the mine. I could only assume he might have expected me to, but that was just something out of his hands. He needed to get the truth outta me, and he couldn't do that with a bullet in my head.

"Been talking to questionable individuals, some

who may or may not have completely lost their minds."

"I'll talk to anyone who has an outlook on life dissimilar to yours," I said.

The office doors suddenly burst open, a heavy-faced guard crashing through with sweat pouring down both sides of his face.

"Sir," he gasped for his breath, for his lungs, "they're here. They're at the wall. They're-"

From a distance, equal to that of how far away the wall stood, there erupted a roar that could have cracked the sky wide open. Ostrander spun around and took to the balcony. I saw it from inside the office. The guard's eyes nearly fell from his face. And Ostrander's grip on the rail could have melted the iron. Fragments of the wall exploded high into the air. From here, it could have been a volcano giving birth to all of its flaming in-sides, casting its very soul into the sky. But it was not. The explosion was that of the only real security all of New Canterton depended upon. The wall had fallen with a single blow from the enemy.

"They've taken the wall, it seems," Ostrander said vacantly, "if they can break the wall, they can fill New Canterton with their filth," he turned his attention to the guard who'd crashed in, "see to it that every man is brought in near, muster every troop, get them into formation, and prepare for battle."

"You sound afraid," I said to him, smirking.

"You've never stood where I am now standing, Mr. Mahoney. Only someone who has completely lost their mind would not be afraid now. I'm not taking any chances. I can't. These are murderous tribesmen, god-dam savages, and they're here to murder us all."

The guard acknowledged his orders and fled. Os-trander had started to breathe heavy, but not in a way that would make him seem cowardly. Maybe he was right. Maybe he was smart to be afraid at a time like this. Though he was only mostly right about his enemy's intentions. They were here to kill *almost* everyone. Everyone except him.

Once again, I silently acknowledged the presence of the gun I had tucked away. I could pull it out now, fill Gunther full of every single one of the six bullets. I could kill the guards, there were only four of them, still two bullets left over for Gunther. I decided to wait. My thoughts fell on Cassandra. We hadn't exactly parted on what you might call *happy* terms, but her safety was still my first and foremost priority. As long as she lived, our child still had a chance.

Gunther suddenly looked to me. A part of him from the past shone through in those few moments, but he shrugged them away, as though they were a cancer he'd been trying to rid his body of for years. The comradery we'd once shared.... I was here, watching it die, and he was reluctant to do anything about it.

"How is it that you don't show anything that could be regarded as fear," he asked me, "you just stand there, accepting everything around you."

Even as he said those words, more sounds of war echoed from the world outside the window of his balcony. Another explosion let us know another part of the wall had been destroyed. Screams of horror and agony painted the early-morning sky, and as dawn took to the heavens, the smoke from the shattered, crumbled wall absconded the view, merging with the cold, winter clouds above. Drange and the Tuskatawa, united alongside the now notably innumerable Black Boars, were blasting through the troops at the gate, at the wall, running over them as if they were nothing. Next would be the great plains, I'm sure. But they didn't come, not yet anyway. Outside, Ostrander's troops awoke from their tents, colliding with one another in a scramble to ready themselves. They were tired, so they'd be fighting with less strength, but from here it was obvious there were still so many of them to contend with. In no time at all, their tents were cast down and as they formed up into a structure, their true numbers evolved into a monster of frightening proportions. Gunther watched them from above, and as they readied themselves for his orders, his confidence seemed to return.

"They have broken through the wall, but they will have some blood to spill before they can get to me here," he said as if there were someone here in this room besides the guards on his side. He nodded to himself, breathing through his nose, and I had to remind myself that the mass of tribesmen that was on its way, making sure I stayed alive during their attack was not part of their plan. They were not here to kill everyone, everyone except Gunther.... but in that idea of "everyone", that idea included me. And Cassandra.

The office door opened once more, but it was not a guard that came through, but Cassandra. She came in wearing a look of concern, and made eye contact with both me and Gunther, one after the other.

"Cassandra," Gunther said. "You shouldn't be here. You should be with the townspeople getting to the safehouses."

"I'm not going to be anywhere except by your side," she said, joining him, she positioned herself so that she could also make eye contact with me, "if we're going to die, it'll be together," she said it to Ostrander, but she'd been looking into my own eyes. The three of us stood on the balcony looking over New Canterton. Ahead, the dust of the battle at the wall began to settle, and slowly, little by little, the members of Chief Tenskatawa's and Quan Zao's men began to make their way across the plains, all of them riding on horseback. They galloped quickly, but stayed in formation, filling the entirety of our view. It occurred out of Gunther's line of sight, but Cassandra had reached down with one of her hands and felt for my own, giving my pinky and ring fingers a squeeze.

The tribesmen ahead formed and halted atop a hill leading down into the valley Gunther's factory settled in. And as the morning sun finally turned the sky all the way light, I could see almost everyone's faces. I could see the chief, Tenskatawa sitting atop his horse, and next to him sat his son, Owl Wing. On the other side of Tenskatawa sat a spiritually-ruined Til Drange, his face painted with the same colors as the hundreds of horseback-riding tribesmen behind him and all around to his left and right. There was... Quan Zao, I believe, of the Black Boars, and all of his men also on horseback. They all had their spears, some handled rifles, and some had their bows ready. But there was no attack just yet. Another tribesman handed off a long, heavy pike to Chief Tenskatawa, and when he took it, he rode forth about a dozen feet. It was then as he held the pike aloft, we all saw whose head had been stuck at the top.

"We are here for the justice of the free people of the land, to take back what was once our ancestors', now hundreds of years ago. Enough generations of injustice have been allowed to pass," the Chief called out, holding the pike with Mayor Henry Kenroy's bloodied head stuck at the top, his mouth hanging open in agonized shock. "On the end of this pike, you will witness a symbol that stands for the end of your reign! We are not here to negotiate! We are not here to meet terms! And before this day is through, we will have your master, Gunther

Ostrander! We will hold his life and take from it everything he knows it to be! But for the rest of you, before
this day is through... we will kill every last one of you!"
Behind the Chief, everyone cheered, raising their
weapon of choice into the air above their head. I saw
Drange, down below, sitting on his own horse, shooting
off two rounds into the air with a revolver.

Chief Tenskatawa turned around to face his men
and in the same motion he rode up and down the line,
keeping the pike with Kenroy's head stuck at the top
high into the air. As he rode up and down the line, the
men cheered. And suddenly, he turned to face the troops
who fought for Gunther Ostrander. He waved the pike
like a flag, and with it, he led the charge. He rode forth,
gathering speed quickly, and behind him the hundreds of
tribesmen on horseback followed. The Chief screamed
words of battle-rage in his own tongue, and behind him
those closest to his side returned the call. Charging at
full speed now, the men on horseback lowered their
spears to take on Gunther's men head-on. Down on the
ground, the soldiers listened to their orders from their
commanders, and held the line, while others began firing
into the charging Tuskatawa and Black Boars. Men fell
from their horses, but it wasn't enough to stop the
charge. They kept riding with full strength. I heard Ostrander say under his breath, "Oh my god". Just before
the collision, Chief Tenskatawa held his arm back and
launched from it the pike with Kenroy's head stuck to it,
and it flew threw the air, sticking through the chest and
out the back of one of the Gunther's soldiers, the force of
the pike going into his chest causing Kenroy's head to
split into two pieces. Not a moment later, the hundreds
of horseback tribesmen collided with his troops. There
was a sound like a crash of metal and human screaming,

and all at once, the Battle for New Canterton began.

I took my chance. I didn't even think about the guards. But I thought about Two Seas. I thought about what he'd said. I thought about Drange and the Tuskatawa Law. I thought about putting those bullets in Mancino Rolandraz, if I'd been right to do so.

I removed the gun from the small of my back and aimed it for Gunther's head, pulling back the hammer. The guards aimed their rifles for me, but I didn't flinch. Gunther froze, and Cassandra gasped in complete shock, backing away from the balcony.

"The Tuskatawa don't want you dead," I said to him, "and there are many who would very much like to see you at the nasty end of that law of theirs. I can't promise I won't kill you, but from up here, at least, you will command no army. You will not call out orders. From here you will do nothing, except watch as they make work of your filthy men. And when it's over, the Tuskatawa will have you the way their law demands."

Gunther began to permeate with sweat, but he kept the palms of his hands facing me.

"Your aiming hand is lookin' a little shaky there," he said, "the slave life isn't doin' ya any favors, old friend."

"The second I become too tired to hold this gun, the very next second is the second I pull the trigger," I said, "whether they've won the battle yet or not."

XIV.
THE FALL
of NEW CANTERTON

The guards at the door were trained riflemen, as proven by the directness their aim set for my head. But as men, their emotions had yet to be tested. The sounds of metal on flesh, and screams of agony and horror barraged their senses from every angle; the attack came at them without remorse for their inexperience. I knew this, because their legs had begun to shake, particularly around the knee area, as they waited for their master, Gunther P. Ostrander, to give them the next order. Ostrander remained on the balcony, both of his hands resting along the top of the railing. Having my gun aimed for his head didn't seem to bother him any, it was as if he expected long ago for this exact moment to transpire, and now that it was happening in real time, he had nothing more to worry about. Meanwhile, the destruction and chaos of the battle down below caused the walls and the floors and the ceiling to shake as though the earth itself were quaking.

"And suddenly," Gunther started, "you've adopted the ways of the Tuskatawa. How chameleon of you."

"I had a lot of time to think while I was with them. I had even more time to think about everything while in your prison. And I ain't gonna lie to ya, no use in that. But a big part of me had started to accept the idea of rottin' for the rest of my days down there. I don't care about your stupid war. I don't care about their beliefs. I just wanna get outta here. Folk like you will always eventually kill each other in the end. And anyone and everyone around ya will always be made to suffer for it."

"So why not end it now," he asked, stepping forward, "pull that trigger, blow my head off. Isn't that what you just *do* to people? That's your way, right? That's your way."

I looked to Cassandra, who'd already backed away from the balcony. She was standing by the far wall close to Ostrander's desk, the palms of both hands at her belly by involuntary default.

"Believe me, it's taking every goddamn fiber of my being to not pull this trigger. But you've done more wrong to others than you have to me alone. There's a selfish side of me that wants to see you put in your place, and between you and me, a mere bullet to the head just won't do," I said. The entire office shook, a sound erupted from outside like another explosion, dynamite maybe, followed by a victorious cheer. "I've been fighting against the thought, I have to admit. Because yes, it is in my nature to end what I believe should be ended. I could very much pull the trigger right now and watch all that brain matter splatter against the wall behind ya, and I wouldn't feel a damn bit bad about it. The more ya talk to me, though, the more accepting I am to the idea. So, keep talkin', Gunth'."

"I think you should pull that trigger," he said, still moving forward, "you look a little weaker than I remember. Life in the quarry will do that to a man, no matter how strong he is at the beginning. Pulling a trigger might be your only defense at a time like this, wouldn't ya think? And what about Cassandra over there. I know you two are friends. She's my wife and I love her, but I'd be a fool if I didn't recognize something between you two. Whatever that is, I'm sure you'd be willin' to die for. And those pseudonatives out there, they're comin' for everyone in this room, no way around it. Do you really think you alone can defend her against an entire army of bloodthirsty revolutionaries? Just you, and one gun?"

It was at this point I started to imagine whether or not Gunther actually did have a suspicion about us. The only thing that stopped me from believing he knew was because if he did, I'd never have seen the inside of that quarry cell, and more than likely, dear Maurice Hoxford would be eatin' my blended, spiced-up body parts for his supper.

Outside, there came another crash. It was Cassandra who took a look and nearly let out a scream at whatever it was that she saw.

"They have a battering ram! They're breaking down the main door!"

"They won't get through," Gunther jeered, "the main door is steel and iron reinforced."

There came another crash, shaking the entire factory building, and then a splitting of wood and the bending of metal. The office doors flung open and in charged a battered and worn soldier, his face bloodied and his sides gashed wide open. The man collapsed to the floor at the guards' feet, holding his sides and gasping for breath.

"They're...inside," he said, "they've broken down the main entrance, sir." He lay on the floor, the veins in his neck bulging under the weight of whatever pain he was enduring, and then... his breathing stopped, and he was gone.

With the office door still open, there began to emerge faint sounds of the battle outside. The Tuskatawa and their Black Boar brethren had entered the building and were making swift work of any and all they found inside on the lower levels.

"They're going to kill every one of us," one of the guards mumbled. He lowered his rifle's aim from my head, and looked out the office door.

"Pull yourself together," Ostrander growled, ignoring me and walking towards him, slapping him across the face. He slapped him twice more. "Give me the rifle of yours!"

"I'm sorry sir, I just, I never thought this sort of thing would ever happen," the guard nervously handed Gunther the rifle. Gunther took it, looked down the sights and then hit the guard square in the face with the stock. The guard's nose crunched and Gunther kicked out his legs. With the guard on the ground, Gunther aimed the rifle for the man's head, and pulled the trigger. The other three guards in the office froze.

"Anyone breakdown like that on me and I'll do ya all the same favor," Gunther grimaced. "Mahon, we're gonna need every hand available, you shootin' or not? Nah, I know you aren't a coward, but if you've got a gun in your hands you better be willin' to use it for the reason it was created."

Before I could decide which fate I wanted to play, an arrow whizzed in from down the hall and into the office, finding its mark right through the left temple of one of the guards. The man fell instantly. Next to him, two more arrows caught another guard through his neck. He stumbled backwards, choking on his own blood.

"First of all," I said, pushing my way passed the remaining guard. I shoved Gunther out of the way, slamming both office doors closed. "Grab the other end of your desk," I said. Gunther didn't ask why, he just did. Together we moved his massive desk and butted it up right against the office doors.

"That won't hold them for long," Gunther said.

"It's not supposed to," I said, "we'll move the couches to along the opposite wall. Nothing will stop them from breaking through those doors, but only a little at a time will be able to get through. It'll give us the time we need to pick them off one at a time. Better than taking them all at once."

I moved back and started sliding the office couches toward the opposite wall. Gunther had been right about one thing though, and this I took note on while moving the desk. The quarry had weakened me; my muscles, my bones, everything my strength depended on had been whittled down to a condition lower than I remembered ever having experienced. I ached already, just from moving the desk. And even while sliding the couches I felt like I needed a break. Gunther took note of this, and the sullenness in his brow began to take its own shape. He had kept me alive, sure, but in doing so... he'd only weakened me. He and I both knew that I was his best chance at surviving this attack. He was never very good at gunplay, at combat in general. He'd always bragged about and made a point at selling his talent for convincing or paying others to do the dirty work for him.

"Now I bet you wished you'd spent more time killin' out in the world than havin' others do it for ya, huh," I chuckled as myself, Gunther, Cassandra, and the last remaining guard began gathering the weapons from the fallen guards in the office and piling them up behind the couches.

"They aren't here to kill me," he said, "I at least have that on my side."

"That's just the thing, Gunth'," I said, taking a kneeling stance behind the couch. I motioned for the remaining guard to toss me a rifle. He handed me one and

I shoved the revolver Drange had given me back behind the waistband at the small of my back. "these people will kill ya without killin' ya. They know there's no Hell waitin' for the crooked and evil, so they make it their mission to create one for them. And believe me, they'll do just that."

"It sounds so awful out there," Cassandra said. We crouched behind the couch for a while longer, waiting for the Tuskatawa and the Black Boars to make their way further into the factory. With any luck, they'd go right by this door or press up against it and lose interest finding it to be barricaded. But out of everyone in the room, I was the only one who knew better. Outside, the sounds of battle filled the skies with gunshots, sharp weaponry piercing through flesh and gut and bone. It soon became hard to differentiate the bloodshed outside from the screaming horrors making their way through the factory... closer and closer they came, their footfalls growing louder and more furious, their motivation for victory amplifying with each kill. The Tuskatawa and the Black Boars together were an unstoppable flood, and they were filling every single room and corner and crevice the factory was made of.

We each held a rifle aimed for the door. Cassandra stayed as low as possible, placing her hands over her belly. She'd never fired a weapon before and neither myself or Gunther was going to allow her to show so much as her face within eyesight of the coming onslaught. She looked terrified, and she was right to be. But I knew it wasn't for herself.

"So Gunth'," I started, "you two figure out a name yet?"

"For what?"

"The baby," I said. He seemed to have forgotten

momentarily, given the turn of current events.

"Oh, right, yes, the baby," he looked back for a moment, taking in Cassandra, the woman he and I both in our own way loved and wanted. She looked back, holding her hands close to her belly as if to cradle the thing inside of her, "nothing has come to mind yet," he replied, "quite honestly we haven't put much faith in the survivability of its birth. There's a high likelihood it won't live, and so we decided we'd name it the exact second it's born."

"Yea but, sure ya two have some ideas," I prodded, and for a moment, the conversation made it seem as though we weren't about to be completely massacred.

"Mahon," Gunther sighed, taking a look down from his rifle's sights, he looked like a man now, a man who was ready to accept whatever fate had in store for him on the other side of whatever door he was about to open. I saw it in his face, it was unmistakable: the unspoken apology. It's the sincerest expression a man can wear, and one that doesn't need any words to back it up. He could have been apologizing for Eleanor. He could have been expressing his sorrow for how he'd treated me, nearly sending me to my death in the quarry, having Douglass Flood out to get me. It could have been anything. But right now, in this exact moment, he was sorry about some of it, or all of it.

"Never took ya for an apologetic sorta man, even this close to the end," I said. He might have been going to say something in response to that, but he never got the chance. The office doors exploded in flame and splintering wood. The desk remained sturdy but had been pushed back by the blast, allowing the doors to be cut down. The top half of the door were chopped away at by Tuskatawa and Black Boars with great axes and clubs. We fired our rifles whenever we had a mark. Blood spilled all over the carpet and over the wooden desk and splattered against the far wall of the outer hallway. The onslaught was relentless. A flung small axe found its way into the center of the last guard's skull, and had been thrown with such a force it pushed him backward, the blade killing him less than a second before his body crashed against the back wall. With my rifle out of ammunition moments later, I pulled the gun from the small of my back and began unloading round after round into the piling bodies before us. The warriors of the Tuskatawa and the Black Boar leapt over the mound of their dead compadres, swinging small axes and clubs and small blades. There was a brief moment in which Gunther and I simultaneously recognized we were completely out of ammunition. From the fallen bodies, we each grabbed what bladed weapon we could find and held one in each hand. Cassandra stayed behind us, and as the attackers began flooding into the office, Ostrander and myself took them on one and two at a time. We held them well for a time, but they were strong. It was strange, fighting against them rather than fighting alongside of them during the Crimson Collars' assault on Blackheart Mountain. The Tuskatawa brought a ferocity I hadn't yet seen, and each warrior I felled seemed at peace that he'd fulfilled his tribe's way of life. The Black Boar's, however, while fighting similarly, had their faces painted entirely black so that only their eyes and their teeth could be seen when they came at you. Whenever I sent my blade into the heart of a member of the Black Boars, I felt like I wasn't killing a man at all, but a beast with man-like features and attributes. Gunther held his own fairly well, for a man who'd claimed to have either rarely seen battle, or none at all. Time and time again though, I found myself saving him from being taken. The

Tuskatawa and the Black Boars seemed partial to killing me over him, as he was the main target. But still, we both dealt our deaths out strongly and just as fiercely as our enemy.

The initial attack felt like a blur, though it only lasted a few minutes, and shortly after the doors had exploded inward, I took down the last warrior and we were left to stand in a relative silence, minus the ongoing battle outside. Ostrander and myself were dripping with the blood of our attackers, and Cassandra stood up from behind the couch. We all breathed like giants. Ostrander looked down at his hands, his shaking, trembling hands and the tools of death he held tightly in either one. He stood like a man who's never actually seen war at all. I felt as though I were in the company of a child.

"You alright," I asked him.

"I thought I would be ready," he said, but he did not say it to me, nor to anyone in particular, "I thought I was ready. Look at these hands of mine, they're soaked. And they're shaking. Is this really what a man must do to cement his right to live?"

"For himself, maybe," I said, "if that is what he really wants."

"How is it that you're still alive," Gunther seemed to snap out of his momentary lapse of consciousness. "Your body is broken, no? It doesn't seem like it is, maybe you're also talented in deception."

I looked over to Cassandra, made eye contact with her, and let her know I loved her without saying a word.

"I am a product of my own choices," I said, showing her a small smile from the corner of my mouth, "but without the world I was born into, those choices would never need to have been made." I moved amongst the dead, kicking each one with the toe of my boot to make sure everyone who was down on the floor was actually dead and not just mostly dead. Outside, the battle sounds that had started so angrily had begun to die down. Gunther wandered over to the balcony after consoling with Cassandra, and took a view of the battlefield.

"I can't tell who's winning and who's not," he said. I joined his side and gazed far and wide. The field was covered in dead bodies and not a green blade of grass could be seen. The clumps of snow leftover from the last snowfall had all been dyed red and dark red, and where smoke rose into the air, down at the ground roaring flames ravaged the earth. There were still several hundred men down on the field. But I couldn't make out specifics. No Til Drange. No Owl Wing. No Chief Tenskatawa. No Chief Quan Zao. Either they were all dead, or they had been painted by so much blood they were simply all unrecognizable.

"Maybe we should go down," Gunther said.

"What?"

"Yea," he continued, "instead of hiding up here... instead of hiding behind a broken door and a couch, we should go down there."

"Gunth'," I laughed, "that's not how you win battles. And besides, there's Cass-"

"-they aren't here to kill me, Mahon. They've said it. You've said it. But they'll kill everyone that stands between them and myself, until they finally get to me. How many more men have to die... for me? That's not how you win battles, Mahon. Maybe winning isn't what the expectation reads it as." He turned towards Cassandra, who appeared just as bewildered as I'm sure I myself did.

"You can't be serious," she said to him as he took her into his arms.

"It's not death, my lady, but if this is what must be done to save you and all the other men who are still somehow alive fighting for me, for New Canterton," he looked away, going over it in his head, nodding in agreement. He took a long, depth of a breath and nodded once more. "I'm going down there."

Gunther left alone, and for a moment I stayed behind with Cassandra. We both looked at each other, not entirely sure what was about to take place.

"This doesn't make much sense for someone like him," I said to her.

"I don't like it," she said.

"Are you okay, otherwise," I felt her stomach gently with my hand, and she placed her own hand on my own.

Gunther made it to the ground level and reached the smashed-in entranceway long before we did. When Cassandra and I caught sight of him, he'd started making his way outside into the light. All around bodies lay dead and bleeding, mouths hung open in agony and defeat. Everywhere we stepped, we seemed to be sloshing through an ankle-deep sea of blood. We joined Gunther outside, as he stood atop a small hill just outside the entrance to his factory. Ahead, the remaining numbers of the Tuskatawa and the Black Boar stood. I couldn't count them all, some few hundred. But both chiefs were still alive, as well as Til Drange and Owl Wing, who stood out in front. Gunther's men, those who remained, retreated behind us, and it seemed there to be a mutual stalemate.

"Gunther P. Ostrander," Chief Tenskatawa began, his voice booming across the battlefield. He no longer sat atop his horse, in fact no one did. There were some lying dead on the ground amongst the countless human corpses, but it was probably that the men had sent the majority of them away sometime during the bloodshed. Drange removed a satchel from his side, and removed a small flask from it. He drank from it long and deep and raised it into the air when he saw that I was still alive.

"I'm here," Gunther replied, "and I see that, this day has been kinder to your people than it has to mine."

"That is because we fight with a truth that you cannot hope to fathom," the Chief replied, "your ilk has plagued this earth since the time of our own ancestors. And since that time there has never been an actualized, real, true, unwavering peace. That's why we've come to-day."

"All that, and you start with me?"

"You will not be the last, this is *just* the start. There are others we will see to after today, and we won't stop until you are all in your rightful place in Hell, or we are all dead. From the frozen oceans of the north down to the long, unending sands below the equator, the Tus-katawa, the Black Boars, and any other of those tribes in hiding who wish to take back the lands which were sto-len from them, will look back on today as the day it all began... in *your* filth-filled New Canterton. I see you as well, Rancid Mahoney. I see that you stand with the en-emy, and have slain many of my people today. It is not the fault of your master why this world ended, but those like him who came long before, they are the ones who are responsible for the devastation of the world. How you are blind to this is beyond my own sight and under-standing. Or perhaps it is that you do know this to be true, but simply... do not care. It is possible for a man not to care about so much, or anything at all. But the less a man cares, the less a man he is. Are you as empty as that, Mr. Mahoney? With whom do you stand and whom do you stand against?!"

Gunther stepped forward with intentions to speak, but I pressed him back with my forearm and stepped forward myself. I was surprised, of course, because I never saw myself having to ever be in this position. The ground was hard with rock and soot, but softened by the weight of the dead all around. The more blood that soaked into the earth, the softer the surface became, and I thought that maybe with just the right amount of weight, the land all around us would collapse into the depths of oblivion.

"I am not here to fight for either side," I said, "I... I have no interest in these things you call important. I never have and I can't ever. It's why I took up work with Ostrander. Because I didn't care. I just needed a way to live and to keep on livin'. What you've done here today is... well... it has its merits, I'm sure. But I'd like to make it through today knowin' that the people I care about are still alive. That's why I fight. Not for something that happened in the past no one on this whole goddamn earth can do anything about."

"I'm sorry to hear that," Chief Tenskatawa said, as though he hadn't heard a single word I said.

"Don't you worry about a thing," Gunther whispered to me from behind, "this is just the right place for them to be."

"What? What's the supposed to mean?"

Gunther trotted back toward the main entrance of his factory and opened a swinging metal panel. Inside there was a crank and a lever, the crank he cracked all the way around as quickly as he could until it clicked, and then he placed a hand on the lever.

"Good Chiefs who fight for the cause of their people's past," he called out, a grin spreading across his face, "I entreat ye to continue fighting the good fight. But how much more you will be willing to sacrifice is dependent on how you react to this. This land may have belonged to your people centuries ago, but at present, we men who are *at fault* have learned to cultivate it, grind into it, and from the depths of my peoples' souls who've worked tirelessly underground, this gift, I give to you!" And with that he pulled down hard on the lever. There came about a hollow quaking, and from all around the field starting from the quarry going around at random, various explosions erupted from the ground sending great plumes of brown dirt and hard rock boulders high into the sky. The ground began collapsing, and all those who remined on the Tuskatawa side wore faces of sheer shock and desperation.

Gunther returned to his hands the bladed weapons he'd used in his office not long ago. He seemed to forget entirely that Cassandra was standing next to him. As the grounds shook with each underground blast, suddenly Chief Tenskatawa and Chief Quan Zao surged forward on foot, seeing as there was no other way to go. The two Chiefs, Til Drange, Owl Wing, and the remaining few hundred of Tuskatawa and Black Boars collided with the soldiers of New Canterton and Vermouth, and the bloodshed was allowed to continue.

I remained as close to Cassandra as I could, using every part of my body to shield her against the attackers as they came. The warriors came in force, much stronger on an open battlefield than in the confined office. Behind the line of tribes, the ground had nearly collapsed in its entirety, and when the dust and smoke passed away, it was revealed all the various tunnels where the explosives had been planted. These must have been the same tunnels Cassandra used to find me, and some of them must have been the same ones Drange had used to escape. But everything was now out in the open. The last few hundred men fighting for either side were all out of ammunition, and were forced to defend themselves with tooth and nail and whatever they could find on the ground. I came face to face with Owl Wing, and he was poised for a killing strike, but he held back without saying a word. He seemed to get it, to understand me. Even though I was tearing through his own people, he knew I wasn't doing it on the offensive simply because they were who they were. He saw Cassandra, and saw her through me. But at the one moment of hesitation, he took a knife to the left side. He grunted against the steel, turning to face his attacker. I surged forward and took the man by his neck, tearing out his throat with my left hand. I took Owl Wing with me back towards the factory entrance and he knelt down, bleeding from his side.

"Do you really not care who you kill?" Was what he said, wincing against the pain in his side. Cassandra started to help with keeping the bleeding under control.

"I'm not particularly fond of that question," I jumbled my words together into something that was supposed to sound intelligent, but even now I can't recall what I was hoping to convey. Behind me, two more of Gunther's men saw the broken Tuskatawa and tried to finish him off. They lunged forward but I managed to shove a knife into one of their chests while slamming a fist into the face of the other. When he fell backwards, I wrapped an arm around his neck and snapped every bone I could with one movement.

"You," Owl Wing started, the blood loss seeming to get to him, "you can't win against everyone, but I don't see a reason to consider you... an enemy." He lay there against the wall, Cassandra held whatever she could against his wound to slow the blood from flowing out.

I turned around to face the many more who had caught sight of what I'd done. Some of them Black Boar, confused that I had killed Gunther's men, and some of them New Canterton soldiers, confused in their own right as to who's side exactly I was on.

"You all gonna keep lookin' at me," I growled, a bladed weapon in each hand, each one of them dripping with the blood of everyone on the battlefield, there wasn't a single spot of steel on these blades that weren't coated in crimson, "One at a time or all at once, I'll kill you all! So, come on!" They didn't hesitate further. But I was too fueled with rage to abide by my pains from the quarry. I could only see Cassandra, and it didn't matter who came forward, I ended every single one of them. I used their bodies against one another. I made their skulls crush into the ground and I watched them bleed and the ones who didn't die immediately bled out. And when more came, I stood back for a moment to reflect, "This might very well be the final chapter of my life," I said out loud, "and all I can be truly upset about is that I haven't had a drop of quality whiskey in over a month!"

And then he appeared.

Til Drange, just as covered in blood as I was. He stopped short of attacking me, and I of him. He looked all around at all the bodies I'd laid out. All of them belonging to each side. Drange lowered his defensive stance and his face fell with a rather disappointed, saddened glaze. I charged him, pressing him up against a pile of dead bodies high enough it could be a wall of its own. I pushed in further, the blood and the muck of human corpses dripping down all around us. But Drange didn't fight back.

"What," I grimaced, "you aren't gonna try to kill me? I'll let ya swing first this time." I stepped back, letting Drange stumble away from the pile of dead bodies. He caught his breath, coughing and holding whatever wounds he'd acquired during the battle.

"Look behind me, tell me what you see," Drange said, "look back there, passed my shoulders."

"I see smoke, what of it?!"

"Beyond the smoke, the fighting has stopped. Ostrander has given up."

It took a minute, but I realized he was right. The sounds of battle had ceased. There was still smoke, and fire, and blood, but there was also rest. Patches of smoke cleared, and I saw that very few on either side of the fight were still standing, but it was in fact Gunther P. Ostrander who was down on his knees being held in place by one warrior of the Tuskatawa and one of the Black Boar.

"What the hell happened?" I asked.

Drange slowly, with a trembling hand, placed it on my shoulder. It felt as though he were trying to calm me down for some reason.

"That battle's over, Mahon," he said.

"It's over?"

"Gunther, he, he just went crazy or somethin'. He crashed, collapsed and... just stopped. You okay?"

"Yea," I said between breaths, "just gimme a minute to let my heart catch up with the rest of me."

"Whose blood is that all over ya?"

I looked down and saw my hands. They were saturated in redness. My clothes were stained a dark crimson, sleek with soaked-in moisture. As my breathing slowed to a more normal pace, I began to feel the skin on my face, and that too was smeared with the blood of those I'd slain.

"Does it matter? I really don't think it matters, Drange."

XV.
SOVEREIGNTY

When a bird dies in midflight, its wings fail, its eyesight blanks, and its talons release from the gnarl of the life they once had. It falls from the sky without a sound, so silently you'd think it never once lived. It falls from the sky with a silence that betrays the very notion and truth of sound. As I stepped out onto the broken, collapsed field where they all gathered, the air was just as silent, a quiet reminder of all things and events that had transpired up to this very point.

The fires about the field gave off smoke trails in swirling tufts, mingling with a light snowfall from the sky above, where clouds had begun to gather themselves into clumpy groups to batten out the sunlight. Ahead, the two Chiefs stood bloodied and worn, surrounded by their own warriors in victory. And Gunther Ostrander knelt on the ground, a look of weary acceptance sweeping his face.

"Mr. Mahoney," Chief Tenskatawa addressed me as I neared in my approach, Til Drange not far from my side. "The man with many lives, I should say," he said. "as a matter of fact it should be your name."

"Or maybe I'm the man with few tolerances," I suggested. The Chief mulled it over in his head and lazily grouped his facial expressions in a sort of half-contorted agreement.

"My son, is he alive?" He nodded his head back from whence I strode, and I looked back. Owl Wing was still bleeding out, but he was alive and being tended to by Cassandra.

"He'll live, he may need some of that mineral of yours, but he'll live," I said.

"No doubt mostly in part to your efforts," the Chief said as I reached the assemblage of men. "By my understanding you've now saved both my life, and my son's."

I didn't respond.

"You make it very difficult to decide what to do with your fate," the Chief said. I looked at Ostrander, who'd lowered his head so that all he could see was the blood-stained dirt and mud his knees sank into.

"Well, you have your enemy, right here," I said to the Chief, "what comes next?"

"Punishment," the Chief declared.

"What about the people who aren't soldiers of his, what about them? What are your plans for New Canterton?"

"New Canterton will go on," I recognized the voice, and as I turned, I thought that maybe it couldn't be him, but it was. Two Seas... Christopher Carl Boothe. He strode up from the quarry like a cripple still with barely enough strength to keep his two legs moving. Behind him, the other slaves had slowly begun to emerge, as several of the Tuskatawa warriors had put into effect their release. Maurice Hoxford walked out amongst them, he winced his eyes looking up toward the sky, the last bits of sunlight being taken over by the gathering of snow clouds. Boothe wore a smile, wrapping a heavy cloak around his shoulders. "New Canterton will return to the people and will no longer exist as a fortress state controlled by a tyrant." Ostrander turned his head and for the first time in probably days innumerable, he made eye contact with his old companion.

"You won't live long enough to see the change in this place you speak of," Ostrander grumbled. Still, even in his accepting of defeat, upon seeing Boothe it brought up old feelings of resentment, hatred, and disdain, "you're old, and are only getting older."

Boothe stood in front of him, his hunch shoulders and crooked spine almost bringing him low enough to Ostrander's level. He grinned, smiling because in a way, Ostrander was right. "It's not important that I see that change, my old friend. The important thing is, that when the Tuskatawa are done with you, you won't be seeing much of anything at all."

"Til Drange," Chief Tenskatawa called out, "are you ready?"

"I am," Drange said. I turned toward him and we met eyes, but he didn't say a word. By then Cassandra had wandered up from the factory entrance to see what was to happen. She looked down at her husband, Ostrander, who looked back at her.

"What are they going to do?" she asked.

"He'll be kept alive," Boothe answered her, "he will live on here, but in darkness. And maybe, with a little hope, he'll begin to understand what it's like."

Drange stepped away from my side, forward and sturdy, even under the weariness of the battle, and Chief Tenskatawa handed him a metal, curved blade. The Tuskatawa and Black Boar warriors tightened their hold on Ostrander, as he had begun to shake in anticipation. Cassandra had grabbed a hold of my arm with one of her own hands, as even with the knowledge of all the horrible things Ostrander had done, there was still a part of her that loved him, I was sure. For a time, they had been together truly as lovers, and I think, in these moments in which Gunther had finally begun to show a little of his former self, a self that still emanated human fear, I think that was what helped Cassandra in finding her tears for the man.

Gunther looked up at Cassandra, and didn't say a

word. He didn't need to. The sweat dripping from his forehead, rolling down his cheeks and off the bottom edge of his chin...his expression of finality did all the talking it needed to. He looked down briefly at her belly, and for the first time, I felt a little sorry for him.

Drange had less sympathy. He gripped Gunther's face with one hand and turned it so that he was looking straight into his eyes. His knuckles turned white in his grip, and he rested the edge of the blade against the other side of Gunther's face.

"You don't recognize me, and that's okay. We've never been personally acquainted with one another," Drange said, "I was once a slave in your pit of death. And I was the one who you released in hopes of entrapping and killing Mancino Rolandraz. But you and I have never met. Not face to face, not until now. Tuskatawa Law requires me to take your eyes, but if it were in my hands, I would take everything, because to me you are not worth being kept alive simply to suffer. You are not deserving of such torment. But these are my people now. Their Law is my Law, because that is what true civilized men do. They respect order, and uphold it with their own hands. And with my own hands, I am here to take your eyes."

Drange hesitated no further. He stuck the curved blade into Gunther's eye sockets one at a time. Cassandra let out a horrible scream and turned her head into my shoulder. When Drange was finished, his Chief handed him a white-hot burning iron rod with a flat surface. With the iron rod, Drange pressed it up against each empty eye socket, sealing the wounds shut. When then incendiary work was done, the warriors let Gunther Ostrander go, and he crumpled to the ground from exhaustion and agony. He fell in such a way I did not think he would ever move again. But still he breathed, forever weakened, his remaining strength within him nothing more than an involuntary drive to stay alive.

Ostrander was dragged away back into the factory, where presumably his wounds were kept careful watch over so as not to fester with infection. Boothe and I never exchanged another word between one another. Not that day, not ever. Hoxford tried to take up conversation with me, after being released. But when he saw I was not in the mood for words, he said to me "alright then, we'll catch up later", and he departed for the factory.

Chief Tenskatawa approached me after the punishment of Ostrander and thanked me for saving his life and his sons, but he also said that I still was behind the deaths of many of his people. He said that still, something had to be done. He determined I was not fit for war, as I could not decide what side to fight on, and that alone made me a dangerous man to be allowed to live. He said normally, someone of my stature would be executed by the Black Boar Tribe. Instead, because of my other deeds, I was allowed to live, provided I agreed to leave this land and never come back. The Chief provided me with a horse and handed me my two revolvers, saying Ostrander had them on his person. I took them back, and found them to be completely empty of ammunition, of course. The Chief bowed his head, recognizing me for who I was, but also silently sorry that he could not continue on in peace knowing I was still out in the nearby world. "I must be completely honest with you, Mr.Mahoney, it will be very difficult for me to live knowing I let someone of your tenacity go, even if it is in exile. I cannot promise that if I see you again, I won't kill you. But for today only, I will look upon you as a conflicted man.

Perhaps, one day that will change. Say your goodbyes, it seems you have at least one in particular to be had."

"Chief," I called out to him and he slowly turned to listen, "we don't agree on much of anything, I know. We're two... pretty darn different fellas. I just hope ya know you don't have to... uh... you've got these laws, morals, whatever. I don't like em, but I understand why ya have em. It's my understandin' this Zao-person doesn't have any at all. And if he does... are you willin' to sacrifice your own?"

He sighed, but the Chief maintained his tall stance, his shoulders never lost their altitude. But on his face formed the beginnings of contortions illustrating an internal conflict the man may not yet be ready to fully realize.

"My father was more well-versed in the ways of compromise than either you or me. I'm not perfect, but I am learning. Before he died, he once said to me: 'how are we to forgive ourselves for the past, if we cannot make room for the future?' The last few months have shown much light on those words. You'll understand one day, or you won't."

As the two Chiefs and their remaining warriors, along with a barely-but-still-alive Owl Wing, began riding off toward the obliterated outer wall presumably to return to Blackheart Mountain, Cassandra remained standing and she approached me, touching my hands with her own. She knew without it having to be said that she could not go where I was headed. We'd had this conversation before and so there was no reason to have it again. But that didn't stop her from crying. There didn't seem to be anything either of us could say to make any of this better. So instead, she put her arms around me and I put my arms around her.

"I know I originally came here to... to get you out. But you'll be safe here, Cassie," I said, "you and the baby will be safe here."

"You don't know that."

"I know you'll be safer here than you will out there, with me. I don't know what I was thinkin', thinkin' we could make it out there. I can't protect you forever."

And then the silence took over again. I looked down to her stomach and I placed a hand there, feeling the slight curvature. A cold wind took hold of the falling snow, as if nudging me away.

"Goodbye, Cassie," I said, and turned to follow in the direction of the tribesmen. I didn't look back. I couldn't look back. But I knew she stood there watching me leave.

I passed through the crumbled and ruined gate of the outer wall, looking briefly at every single fallen New Canterton soldier and guard, their bodies hewn to pieces, the mouths in their heads permanently pried open from fear, anguish, and of the passing of their souls into nothingness. The gate burned on either side, the rocks smoldering even under the cold winter air. It was here, just on the other side of the broken wall, Drange met with me, passing me the reigns of a horse for my travels. I took hold of the reigns and gently pulled the black horse close to my face so that we may meet in the proper fashion.

"She's no Eleanor," Drange said, "but she's strong and will take you far. Her name is Scarlett."

"Scarlett," I said, touching her with an open palm and gently stroking her neck. Her muscle structure was strong and her eyes were dark, reflecting the eastward horizon with a pearl-like shine.

"And, uh," Drange reached into his pocket and

revealed to me a handful of bullets. "For your revolvers."

"You already paid me back."

"This isn't something given out of owing," he said, "it's more of a parting gift, between friends."

"Ah," I laughed, "and is that what we are?"

"We aren't enemies, if that's what you mean."

"We aren't enemies, but do you really think we're friends?" I started loading the bullets into each of the revolver chambers. One at a time until both were full. I holstered one and looked closely at the other, feeling its handle and pulling down on the hammer, listening to the *click*. Drange stood motionless, his hand having moved to the handle of his own sidearm, by default I'm sure. "So, you're really going to ride along with these folks into war."

"Gunther Ostrander was just the beginning. We'll rebuild the mine in Blackheart Mountain. We'll rebuild the village. After that, the crusade will begin. More tribes will come when they see what we're capable of. It's what has to be done, Mahon. It may take weeks. It may take years. But we're doing what's right."

"Well," I sighed, holstering my second sidearm, while Drange removed his hand from his own, "I'll try to stay outta your way then. Because if there's one thing I agree with it's what your chief said, that I'm not a man of war. It's not in my blood."

"But you're a killing machine, Mahon, you can kill without having to think about any of it!"

"It's not the same. It's not the same at all," I looked back toward the factory, to where Cassandra had stood watching me leave. She was gone, or I was now too far away to see if she was still there. I reached up to Scarlett's saddle and pulled myself up, adjusting my position and letting her get used to my weight. She neighed lightly, calmly, and I was reminded of Eleanor's voice.

"Where will ya go?" Drange asked.

"East, maybe. For now, anyway. As far away from your war as the road can take me."

"And what if the war brings itself to wherever you end up?"

I smirked.

"Like you said, Drange, I'm a killin' machine. And I'll kill everyone if I have to. And I'll kill without thinkin' about it, not one bit," I gave Scarlett a light kick with both heels and she started off away from the rubble, away from the burning gate. I rode east, and Drange and his people rode north and then west and then northwest. From a high and far away ridge, I took note of an odd shape not like the rest of the rock formations, and just before I turned to follow the road true east, I stopped to look. I had to narrow my sight, but could see him for his all that he was. The wolf on the ridge sat looking down over the land, perhaps pretending to be paying attention to everything else except me. But he stared dead ahead, watching me on my horse. And I think that we shared an understanding then. He and I both knew the truth of the land and perhaps the entire world.

The wolf let out a howl. The air wasn't terribly chilly, but pulling my long coat in tight, feeling the extra layers that'd been sewn in, gave me some unexpected reassurance. I turned away from New Canterton and started off into the east.

Two hours, two and a half maybe, as I was riding along a dirt road beside a gently-rolling stream, I stopped to listen to the sounds around me. The waters of the stream rolled over the rocks jutting up from beneath the silver surface, and from the west, there approached a rider on a horse at a heavy pace. I turned sideways, drawing both revolvers out and aiming both for the rider. But as he drew closer, I saw that it was not necessarily a stranger, but Maurice Hoxford. He rode up quickly and upon seeing the guns aimed for his head, he slowed to a stop.

"Whoa now," he said, letting out a light laugh. He raised his hands up, "take it easy, man. I'm not comin' to shoot ya."

"Prove it," I said.

"I'm not even armed," he said, motioning around so to give visual proof of his handicap.

"Expect me to believe that?"

"Well," he continued, "not really at first. But look. I've got nothin' on me!"

"So you rode out into the wastes without a way to defend yourself. You're real smart, ya know that?"

"I figured I had enough time to catch up to ya, maybe present ya with a uh... an opportunity, seein' as though you were just ridin' off to nowhere."

"Oh good lord," I muttered, holstering my sidearms, "an opportunity. Really?"

"I overheard you're headed east, true east, real far out there."

"Maybe I am."

"Well alright then. See, before all this work in the mine," he waved back from the way he came, "I uh... like I said, I was taken from the wild. I was on the run ya see. Had some problems... back east. Well, I was wonderin', hopin' rather, that I could accompany ya."

"Don't," I stopped him, "don't even ask. You don't have to say another word. I ain't gonna be your muscle. And before you try to insist, I know your type. You're just gonna fuck shit up for the both of us. Do you wanna know how many of your type I've had to put down in the past? TOO many. So it's gonna be a no from me. A heavy, hard, NO."

I started to ride away from him at a slow, steady pace, but he rode after me, reeling around in front of Scarlett and forcing me to stop.

"I could make it your worth. The business I need seein' to isn't quick by any measure... I mean, I've been gone years. But if things are as they are back east the way I left em, well... it'd probably take more than just you or I anyhow."

The air fell still, and all that made noise was that of the creek. To the left where the trees grew thick, I listened to the sounds of something creeping close. For a moment, Hoxford's voice explaining away the details of his endeavor faded away into nothingness as I listened intently.

"Mahon," he called out, probably seeing that I was distant, "hey Mahon, you listenin'?"

But before I could tell him to get lost, a grey blur launched out from the cover of trees, latching its jaws around his neck from behind. The wolf tore Hoxford from his saddle, dragging him to the ground while clamping down with his teeth deeper into Hoxford's throat. Hoxford gargled and struggled, punching the wolf in the side and in the face, but he was not a fighter. The wolf jerked its head this way and that, ripping into Hoxford's throat so brutally, I thought he might rip his head right off. Hoxford spit a geyser of blood, splashing it all over his face and into his eyes. I thought the struggle might go on forever, but almost as soon as the wolf attacked, Maurice lay motionless on the ground, a river of dark red blood streaming out from his open neck.

The wolf, still standing over its kill, looked to me with fury behind its eyes. I'd already drawn one of my revolvers, aiming straight out for its skull. The wolf arched its back, preparing to pounce. He didn't see my firearm as something to be worried about. He didn't understand weaponry. He only knew instinct. He only saw me. He only saw more food.

"Don't do this," I said under my breath, "you don't deserve this bullet." But the wolf crept forward, putting one paw over Maurice's dead body. It was the same wolf as before, it had to be. But why now... why now was it behaving this way? "I don't want to kill you," I said to him, "I thought we had somethin' good goin', buddy. I don't want to do this," I said with my finger steady on the trigger, the space between his eyes in my sights. The wolf stepped through the blood on the ground, staining his paws up to the first joint in the toes, and as he crept forward, drawing closer to Scarlett, Scarlett let out a worried whine. "This is it, wolf," I said, "this is it. I'm gonna have to kill ya."

But the wolf was only there for one purpose. He only had one thing on his mind. I couldn't hate him for that. I couldn't be angry at him, not for anything.

He arched his back, letting the fur stick up like spines. He showed his teeth, still stained with the blood of Maurice Hoxford. The wolf's eyes widened excitedly, hungrily, and he stiffened in preparation for the leap.

I swallowed.

And I pulled the trigger.

Epilogue

After they'd clamped the chains around my little wrists, they waited for my mother and father to leave. They'd allowed for a good-enough distance to make work of itself, but that only lasted for so long. There were two more gunshots that morning, and after the air fell silent, I was told I no longer had to worry about mom and dad.

We started off down the path with very little chatter among the men. I sat on the bed of an uncovered wagon alongside a dozen other chained individuals. An hour later we passed by the place where they fell, and already their bodies were being eaten by a small pack of wolves. One of the men riding a big brown horse saw that I was watching and he rode a little closer to me. On his head sat a wide-brimmed hat and under the shade of that hat, his eyes were dark but kind, in a sympathetic way. Back then, I didn't know what empathy meant, but he must have had a little empathy by how he looked at me.

"They have to eat too, ya know," the man said, "You're probably feelin' a lotta somethin' that you don't quite know how to put to words. It's probably a little bit of sadness, but also a lotta hate. And if you aren't feelin' that hate right now one day ya will, and that's understandable. But you can't hate *them*. Those beasts out there are the only innocent ones outta this whole mess."

Some years long since transpired, a long, long time ago before I was ever a person, the last man who'd been alive during civilization's great collapse, laid down and died. And along with his death, the truth of how the world fell to pieces... how it all happened, died. Not long after that, it became less imperative knowing the truth of how it all went down, and more pertinent deciding how you were going to survive with the times that were given to you, whether they were years, weeks, or minutes. I was born into a world already accustomed to this change, so from the beginnin', I was taught a very specific way on how to survive and make the most of whatever came to befall me. Some might say I was lucky that way. Bein' I was the one livin' with those so-called lucky experiences, I'd say luck is only somethin' given to the people who died first.

If you enjoyed this book, check out

www.TheTwoRevolvers.com

**to get an extensive look inside
the lore of Rancid Mahoney's
world, inside info on future books
of the saga, the story behind how
the saga came to be,
AND MORE...**

And if you REALLY enjoyed this book, please
consider leaving a review on Amazon.
I'd love to know what you thought of it!

-Dave Matthes

Dave Matthes was born and raised in Swedesboro, New Jersey. He has attended various colleges for computer engineering, automotive science and criminal justice-like degrees, though he is mostly self-educated in the subjects of World History, Philosophy, Political Science and Spirituality. During the day, he works as a service technician and system installer for the restaurant industry.

He is a writer of poetry and prose and is the author of autobiographical books "The Slut Always Rides Shotgun", its sequel "The Passive Aggressors", the novels "In This House, We Lived, and We Died", and "Sleepeth Not, the Bastard" and three volumes of poetry "The Kaleidoscope Syndrome: An Anthology", "WANDERLUST and the Whiskey Bottle Parallel", "Strange Rainfall on the Rooftops of People Watchers" and the books that make up "The Mire Man Trilogy".

Dave presently lives in Boothwyn, Pennsylvania with his wife Sarah, and their cat Hank.

To keep up to date with the current and future writings of Dave Matthes, find him online at:

Author Website:
https://DaveMatthes.org

Other Social Media:
www.Goodreads.com https://www.facebook.com/davematthesauthor
Twitter: @Boozie_Smoocher
SnapChat: boozie_smoocher
www.TheTwoRevolvers.com

Printed in Great Britain
by Amazon